A DIAMOND OF THE FIRST WATER

"What do you think, my lord?"

Desmond looked round, half annoyed at the interruption. Then he forgot to be annoyed, for the vision that stood before him was sufficient to drive every other consideration from his mind. He half rose to his feet, staring with all his might.

Susan stood before him—at least he supposed it was Susan, though so complete had been her metamorphosis that she looked not the same girl at all. The tumble of red curls was hidden beneath a mass of jetty ringlets that clustered about her ears and tumbled entrancingly down her back. Her brows had been skillfully darkened, and Desmond had the impression her eyes had been enhanced also, though he was not sufficiently acquainted with cosmetics to say exactly what had been done. He only knew the effect was extremely alluring. He gazed at her with his mouth open.

"You needn't answer, my lord," she said. "I never received a nicer compliment than the way you are looking at me just now. I do look nice, don't I?"

"Yes," said Desmond. "You look *beautiful.*"

Books by Joy Reed

AN INCONVENIENT ENGAGEMENT

TWELFTH NIGHT

THE SEDUCTION OF LADY CARROLL

MIDSUMMER MOON

LORD WYLAND TAKES A WIFE

THE DUKE AND MISS DENNY

A HOME FOR THE HOLIDAYS

LORD CALDWELL AND THE CAT

MISS CHAMBERS TAKES CHARGE

CATHERINE'S WISH

EMILY'S WISH

ANNE'S WISH

THE BARON AND THE BLUESTOCKING

LORD DESMOND'S DESTINY

Published by Zebra Books

LORD DESMOND'S DESTINY

Joy Reed

ZEBRA BOOKS
Kensington Publishing Corp.
http://www.kensingtonbooks.com

ZEBRA BOOKS are published by

Kensington Publishing Corp.
850 Third Avenue
New York, NY 10022

First Printing: July 2002
10 9 8 7 6 5 4 3 2 1

Printed in the United States of America

One

"Today," said Desmond, "I shall propose to Annabelle."

He surveyed himself in the glass. His reflection looked back at him steadily, but it seemed to Desmond there was apprehension in those mirrored eyes. He frowned. A man ought to look happy on the day he became engaged to the woman he loved. At the moment, his reflection looked more as though he were about to have a tooth drawn by the dentist. Desmond tried again. "Today," he said, addressing his reflection with emphasis, "I shall propose to Annabelle. And I have no doubt this time she will accept me."

He looked sharply at his reflection, as though daring it to make some protest. But the dark-haired young man in the mirror merely stared back at him with worried eyes. "Well, damn it all," said Desmond with disgust. "Anyone would think you didn't *want* to marry her. And you do want to marry her. You want it more than anything."

Again he looked at his reflection, as though daring it to protest. That was ridiculous, of course—as ridiculous as addressing a mirror in the first place. Still, as Desmond reflected, he was so used to having people protest the idea of his marrying Annabelle

Windibank that he might be pardoned for expecting his own reflection to do the same.

He had known Annabelle for six months now and had been madly in love with her for four of them. It was true when she had first appeared among the ranks of the Upper Ten Thousand, he had looked upon her askance. She had seemed to him a touch vulgar in spite of her undeniable beauty. But that was merely because he had been judging her by her associates. The aunt who was sponsoring her in society was the underbred second wife of an obscure baronet who moved on the fringes of the *ton* with others like herself. No wonder poor Annabelle had seemed at first to be at home in this company. But of course that was not the case. She transcended the vulgarity of her companions like a rose on a scrap heap, Desmond reflected poetically.

He had realized it the first time he had spoken with her. They had been together at a party, and she had dropped her handkerchief. When Desmond had politely returned it to her, she had looked him with eyes the color of summer skies and said, "Thank you, my lord," flashing a brilliant smile as she spoke.

The effect of that smile had been instantaneous. Desmond had realized then that Annabelle Windibank was not merely a pretty girl of dubious antecedents, but a Diamond of the First Water. Matched pearls weren't in it compared to her teeth, cherries could not compare to the luscious redness of her lips; and the gold of her hair put new-minted guineas to shame.

From that time on, he had begun to look at Annabelle in a new light. Indeed, he had begun not merely to look at her but look *for* her, seeking her out at parties and frequenting the places where he knew she was likely to be. He found her always surrounded by a crowd, and not only her aunt's crowd either. She had been long enough in London by this time for other gentlemen besides himself to discover her charms. There had been Fitzroy and Stevens and Foxborough, and even St. Armand had condescended to hang about and address half-sarcastic, half-complimentary speeches to her. This had reassured Desmond—not that he needed reassuring, but if the Earl of St. Armand found nothing wrong with Annabelle, then it was certainly not the place of Lord Desmond Ryder, a mere younger son, to do so. And indeed, after spending a few evenings in Annabelle's company, Desmond could find no fault with her at all. She was the loveliest and most enticing creature he had ever known, and within a matter of weeks he had made up his mind she was the woman of all others he wanted to marry.

Alas, there had been complications. His mother, the Dowager Marchioness of Merrivale, had been aghast when she learned of his intentions. "Marry Annabelle Windibank?" she had exclaimed in a failing voice. "Are you mad, Desmond?"

"Certainly not," replied Desmond with dignity. "I don't know why you should say so, Mama, merely because I want to marry Annabelle. She is a very lovely, unexceptionable girl, and I care for her most sincerely. Of course you would naturally prefer I married an heiress from a noble family, but really, I can see no necessity of my doing so. I'm not like Merrivale, with the succession to think of, and I have a perfectly adequate income of my own."

His mother protested that she had never expected him to marry an heiress, or a noblewoman either. "And I don't know why you bring your brother into it," she said with spirit. "You know perfectly well, Desmond, that I had nothing to do with his offering for Lady Louise. He did it of his own volition because he had fallen in love with her."

"Yes, of course," agreed Desmond impatiently.

"That's the point I'm trying to make, Mama. My brother was free to choose the woman he wanted to marry, and he chose Lady Louise. Now I am saying I wish to choose the woman I want to marry—and I choose Annabelle Windibank. And I take it very much amiss that you cannot welcome my choice with the same enthusiasm."

His mother looked troubled. "Oh, Desmond, it's only that I cannot see how you could ever be happy with Miss Windibank," she said. "She is certainly a very lovely girl, but"—she made a helpless gesture—"she is so very vulgar, Desmond!"

"I don't believe she's anything of the kind," said Desmond coldly. "Certainly her *aunt* is vulgar, but Annabelle herself is not. It's unfortunate you and so many other people insist on bracketing her with her relations!"

"Desmond, you cannot really believe that!" said his mother. "I cannot see how you can say there is nothing amiss in Miss Windibank's behavior, especially after the way she behaved at the Shaws' party last week. I never saw a girl romp so shockingly, and as for flirting, she quite broke poor little Miss Shaw's heart, the way she kept hanging on Tom Arkin all evening."

Desmond flushed. "I think Annabelle's behavior at the Shaws' was misunderstood," he said. "What you call vulgarity and flirtation, Mama, I should call rather playfulness and high spirits. As for Tom Arkin, you know he was not under any compulsion to sit with Annabelle all evening. He is a grown man and quite free to go where he chooses, and if he chose to sit with Annabelle rather than Miss Shaw, I cannot see it is Annabelle's fault."

His mother shook her head. "That might be so, dearest, if Annabelle were doing nothing to encourage him," she said. "But I know for a fact that she was encouraging him to the top of her bent. I was sitting right behind her and heard a good deal of what went on. I should be ashamed to see any daughter of mine comport herself in such a manner. There is no word other than vulgarity to describe it. She is the kind of girl who ties her garter in public—and in fact I saw her do that very thing, after romping through that Ecossaise with Captain Deleval."

Desmond was silent. He had not witnessed the garter incident, but he had heard it described by a few of his male acquaintances, and it had taken some ingenuity on his part to excuse it in Annabelle. He had managed to do so, however, by reminding himself that she was young and innocent: as innocent of her effect on men as of the minutiae of polite behavior, no doubt. In an access of high spirits, she had probably been betrayed into behavior she later regretted. "In any case, that is nothing to the point," he said, answering both his own and his mother's objections. "I intend to ask Annabelle to marry me, and I hope and trust she will accept me."

His mother said nothing, only looked at him wistfully.

Something in her gaze made Desmond uncomfortable. "I said that I intend to ask Annabelle to marry me," he repeated in a louder voice. "Have you nothing to say to that, Mama?"

"No, dearest," she said. "I believe I have already said all there is to say."

"Well, you might at least wish me happy," said Desmond resentfully.

"Oh, I do so, dearest. That goes without saying, of course. I wish all of my children happy." Drawing a deep breath, his mother said resolutely, "I hope you and Miss Windibank will be very happy indeed."

This was exactly what Desmond had wanted to hear, so he was at a loss to explain why he felt so ruffled in spirit. It was not his mother's allegation that Annabelle was a coquette. Of course she was a coquette—a maddening, adorable, exasperating creature whom no man could resist. That was part of her charm, and Desmond could not understand why his mother could not comprehend this self-evident fact. Of course once Annabelle was married, she would settle down and be a good wife. Desmond tried to think of other flirts he had known who had settled down to being good wives, but he couldn't name any offhand. Still, that proved nothing, he assured himself. Annabelle was not like other women. She was an Incomparable in a category of her own. As such, it was clearly unreasonable to judge her by other women's behavior.

So Desmond had assured himself, and for a time managed to solace himself with these reflections. But then he had sustained a visit from his brother, the Marquess of Merrivale, and his misgivings had sprung to life once more.

From the beginning, Desmond suspected his mother had been at the bottom of his brother's visit. He welcomed the marquess affably, however, and made him at home in an armchair before the fire with a glass of his best Madeira. "To what do I owe the favor of this visit, Merrivale?" he asked, pouring a glass for himself and holding the ruby liquid up to the light to admire its color.

"To the excellence of your cellar, of course," replied the marquess promptly. His lean, intelligent face wore a reflective look as he rolled a sip of wine about in his mouth. "By Jove, that's good," he said. "Very good indeed."

"Thank you," said Desmond. "But surely you did not come all the way to my humble abode merely to discuss my Madeira?"

The marquess smiled. "I might have done," he

said. "But it happens there is something else I was wanting to discuss with you."

"I'll wager I can guess what it is," said Desmond with bitterness. "I expect Mama's been talking to you about my matrimonial intentions."

The marquess nodded and took another sip of Madeira. "That's it," he said. "She came to me all in a pother about this business of your marrying the Windibank girl. Wanted me to talk to you about it."

"Talk me out of it, rather," said Desmond with a harsh laugh. "I know very well that Mama is prejudiced against Annabelle."

"Is she?" said the marquess.

Desmond stared. "Well, of course she is!" he said. "I should think that was obvious. She thinks Annabelle is low and common and vulgar, merely because her aunt happens to be so."

The marquess shook his head. "Do you know, that wasn't my impression at all," he said. "I don't know what Mama said to you, but when she was talking to me about Miss Windibank, it seemed to me rather that she was doing her best to make excuses for the girl. Very much as you are doing now, in fact."

Desmond flushed. "Nonsense," he said. "Neither I nor anyone else needs to make excuses for Annabelle. As if Mama would do so in any case! I know very well she is dead set against her."

"No, she isn't," contradicted the marquess. "I daresay she may have spoken against Miss Windibank when you first mentioned marrying the girl—as would anyone who cared a rap for you and wasn't blind or insane."

"Thank you," said Desmond ironically. "I suppose you mean to imply I suffer from both those agreeable disorders myself?"

The marquess smiled a little but chose not to address this home question. "Of course I don't know exactly what went on between you and Mama, but I gather you told her your mind was made up about marrying Miss Windibank. That being the case, Mama's doing her best to put a good face on the matter. But it's easy to see she's not happy about it, and so I thought I'd come and talk to you myself."

"How kind of you," said Desmond with heavy sarcasm.

"Yes, wasn't it?" agreed the marquess, ignoring the sarcasm. "Still, you mustn't be thinking I intend to play the heavy brother or anything of that sort. For one thing, it's not a role that suits me, and for another I know well enough I haven't any real authority over you."

"I am glad you recognize that fact," said Desmond with emphasis.

"So it wouldn't do any good for me to forbid you to marry the gel out of hand," continued the marquess tranquilly. "Obviously if you're set on marrying her, you will, and there's nothing any of your family or friends can do about it."

"No," said Desmond. He regarded his brother with curiosity. "Why did you come, then?" he said. "Seeing you knew it to be futile anyway."

"God knows," said the marquess frankly. "Just to relieve my conscience, I suppose. You really mean to marry the Windibank girl?"

"Yes, I do," said Desmond. "If I can persuade her to have me, that is." He hesitated, then went on, his voice rueful. "But as it happens, you and Mama may be worrying for nothing. I asked Annabelle to marry me a few weeks ago, and she turned me down."

"Did she?" said the marquess. "Turned you down flat, did she? Or did she give you reason to hope?"

"I presume there is still reason to hope. She just

said she had no thought of marrying at present and needed time to make up her mind."

The marquess nodded, rubbing his nose reflectively. "I daresay she's hoping to bring St. Armand up to scratch," he said. "I could tell her she'll catch cold at that. I went to school with St. Armand, and there's nobody I know with a stronger sense of self-preservation. It's ten to one he'll sheer off before he comes to the point. If he does, then you might have a chance, Desmond. Assuming nobody richer with a better handle to his name comes along, that is."

Desmond drew himself up. "Just what are you saying?" he said angrily. "Do you really believe Annabelle has wholly mercenary motives?"

The marquess, unimpressed by his manner, gave the question a serious consideration. "Since you ask me, I say frankly I don't know what to believe," he said. "If someone had told me six months ago that my own brother, whom I've always considered a sensible sort of fellow, could let himself be taken in by a vulgar adventuress, I'd have laughed in his face. On the other hand, I'm obliged to say the opinion generally current among my acquaintance is that Miss Windibank is out for whatever she can get."

"That's not true!" said Desmond hotly.

"Then there's nothing more to be said," said the marquess. "Presumably you know her a great deal better than I do."

He changed the subject then, going on to talk of politics and the chances of the coming election. The subject of Annabelle did not come up again, much to Desmond's relief. But later that evening, after he had bade the marquess good-bye, he found his brother's words recurring to him in spite of his efforts to banish them from mind.

Was it true Annabelle was mercenary? Desmond was obliged to admit she did seem to favor her suitors in exact proportion to their worldly wealth and title. The Earl of St. Armand undoubtedly had precedence at the moment, followed by Viscount Foxborough. And in Foxborough's case, at least, it was difficult to see any other qualities that might have attracted her. Foxborough was fifty if he was a day, all but toothless, and fat as a flawn. St. Armand was a different kettle of fish, being a distinguished-enough looking fellow in his way, but he had a disagreeable manner, and Desmond had never understood what Annabelle could see in him beyond his wealth and title.

Now he found himself wondering if these criteria were all that mattered to her. He found himself wondering, too, if Annabelle would have responded differently to his advances if he, rather than his brother, had been Marquess of Merrivale. Would he now be rejoicing in his position as her future bridegroom?

Annabelle may still accept my proposal, even though I'm not a marquess, Desmond argued to himself. *After all, she hasn't accepted St. Armand yet, or Foxborough either.* But he could not help wondering whether this was because Annabelle was not inclined to accept those gentlemen's suits, or whether neither of them had as yet proposed to her. Merrivale seemed to think it was the latter, and Merrivale was a man who usually knew the time of day.

Well, what of it? Desmond told himself. Annabelle was not to be blamed if she had an eye to the main chance. He had gathered from various things she had said that she hadn't been raised in affluent circumstances, and naturally she would want to better herself if she could. Everybody knew women couldn't take a profession or go into business like men. For a woman like Annabelle, there really wasn't any way for her to improve her personal circumstances apart from marrying well.

This was a plausible enough argument, and for a time Desmond was content with it, but before long his mind had detected various inconsistencies and brought them to his own unwilling attention. It might be necessary for Annabelle to marry well, but it was hardly the act of a nice-minded girl to encourage an elderly man like Foxborough or a disagreeable one like St. Armand merely because she aspired to the peerage. It might be permissible for her to promote her charms with fine clothing and fashionable hairdressing, but it wasn't necessary for her to tie her garter in public. And though it was well within her rights to decline Desmond's proposal for any of a hundred reasons, it wasn't necessary for her to torment him thereafter by flirting with other men in what appeared to be a calculated display of coquetry.

She had done this very thing at a party a few days before, making Desmond so miserable that he had ended up leaving early just to spare himself the sight of her coquetting with his rivals. For the next day and a half, he had suffered the pangs of jealousy and frustrated passion, feeling at times as though he would rather die than endure it a moment longer. But in the end, he managed to bring a kind of despairing philosophy to bear upon the situation. He had known Annabelle was a coquette from the time he had first taken up with her, and that was part of what he loved about her, wasn't it? "Yes, it is," Desmond told himself aloud.

It might be that his mother was right, and being married to Annabelle wouldn't make him happy—assuming she even agreed to marry him. Desmond, however, told himself this was nothing to the point. He *loved* Annabelle. He had loved her from the first moment he had laid eyes on her—or, at any rate, from the first moment she had smiled at him and addressed him in that breathy voice that seemed to promise so much. In fact, destiny had brought them together. And everyone knew it was impossible to thwart destiny. Desmond felt it would be shameful even to try.

Therefore, seeing it was his destiny to love Annabelle and to marry her if he could, Desmond had bided his time. He had scrutinized the true character of his beloved and seen she was unlikely to accept him as long as there was a prospect of her doing better. It would all depend on St. Armand and Foxborough. If one or the other of them proposed to her, all hope for him would be gone. But if they "sheered off," as his brother put it, or even if they dawdled overlong in popping the question, then Annabelle might decide a bird in the hand beat any number in the bush and accept his own proposal.

I'm not a peer, but I do have a title of sorts, and I can afford to keep her in reasonable comfort thanks to the money my grandmother left me, Desmond thought. There was the matter of personal appearance, too. Although he did not rate his own attractions high, he was at least more presentable than Foxborough. He found himself spending a great deal of time in front of the mirror, trying to reassure himself of this fact. His teeth were all his own, thank heaven, and his hair as yet showed no signs of thinning despite his having reached his thirtieth birthday. He had no actual warts or other disfigurements. He was, in fact, a perfectly ordinary-looking dark-haired man of medium build with gray eyes and a quiet manner. This did not satisfy Desmond, however. He wished with all his heart he had been a regular Adonis, a man worthy of Annabelle. If he had not had his title and fortune, he would have felt he had no chance with her at all.

But of late Desmond had begun to feel more hopeful about his chances. In the last few weeks, he had noticed a change in Annabelle's behavior. She had begun to treat him with the same favor she had used to show for Lords St. Armand and Foxborough. "Oh, Lord Desmond, there you are," she would cry gaily, and urge him to sit with her, dance with her, and bring her refreshments. At first Desmond could hardly believe his good fortune, but then he had heard rumors St. Armand had just made an offer for the daughter of Lord Loughmarsh, and he had also overheard one of Annabelle's friends twitting her about Foxborough having deserted her for Miss Pixley, the Pocket Venus. The beauty's reply had been snappish, but it seemed to show any chance of marriage between the two was definitely over.

The field was now clear for Desmond to make his move, if he wanted to. And of course he wanted to, he assured himself. He had arisen that morning with the firm intention of proposing to Annabelle before the day was over. Yet now, as he stood before the mirror, he found himself seized by a nameless apprehension.

"I love her," he told his reflection. "It's destiny. We were meant to be together." His reflection seemed unconvinced by his words, but Desmond repeated them several times, until there was a shade of conviction in his voice. Then he picked up his hat, turned away from the glass, and went forth to meet his destiny.

Two

It was a long drive to meet destiny that day. Annabelle was not staying in town at present but rather visiting the Byrnes, some friends of her aunt's who lived in a villa about thirty miles out of London. The Byrnes were fond of giving entertainments on a grand scale, and this time they had been holding a week-long house party that was to culminate that day in a grand fete to which a large portion of London society was invited.

Annabelle had coaxed Desmond into coming to the Byrnes' fete, though it was not the kind of entertainment he much cared for. Neither was it an ideal occasion for making a proposal of marriage. Still, he reasoned the fete would be held outdoors amid the villa's grounds and gardens, and there would likely be an opportunity to draw Annabelle apart from the crowd.

To propose to one's lady in a garden in springtime was a romantic enough business, Desmond told himself. Of course it was a nuisance to have to drive thirty miles when there were suitable gardens much closer to hand, but Desmond found he did not mind the prospect of the drive as much as he had thought he would. Eager as he was to propose to Annabelle, an unsettled feeling in his stomach made him welcome the soothing prospect of a long drive down quiet country lanes.

Only he found those lanes not so quiet as he had anticipated.

The first incident occurred when he was barely a mile out of London. Suddenly, over the sound of the horses' hoofs, he became aware of a strange noise. Desmond slowed the curricle to listen. The noise could be heard plainly, rising and falling in a steady cadence. It had an eerie, almost inhuman sound to it, and at first Desmond thought it must be some kind of bird or animal. Then he realized it was the sound of weeping. Someone at no great distance from the road was weeping as though his or her heart was breaking.

"Perhaps I'd better go see what it is," said Desmond aloud.

He glanced at his groom, who said, "Just as you please, my lord." His tone implied Desmond would much better leave well enough alone.

Still, Desmond felt he ought to investigate. It was a nuisance to be delayed in reaching Annabelle, but he could hardly ignore such evident and overwhelming distress. And perhaps, in the back of his mind, he was not altogether sorry to be delayed. It was not that he was reluctant to propose to Annabelle, as he assured himself. He merely preferred to let destiny unfold in its own fashion. There was no need to rush recklessly to meet it. Besides, if he ignored this claim on his humanity, he would always wonder and feel guilty about having left the unknown person in his or her distress.

Having justified his inclinations in this matter, Desmond drew his horses to a halt. "Take the reins, Dirk," he instructed the groom. "I'm going to see what's happening."

Stepping down from the curricle, Desmond paused and stood listening. The weeping was, if anything, louder than before and seemed to be coming from a nearby grove of trees. Desmond advanced toward it, feeling a trifle apprehensive. He half expected to encounter a scene of violence and bloodshed, so it was rather an anticlimax when he entered the grove and found a small girl of about six years of age wailing at the top of her lungs. To all appearances she was quite alone.

She was not in any way a prepossessing child. There were several visible tears in her dress, her feet were bare and dirty, and her fair hair was decorated with bits of leaf litter. What her face was like Desmond could not tell. Its features were so contorted that little could be seen apart from the wide-open mouth, from which issued those ear-splitting wails.

"Here, what's all this?" said Desmond kindly. He had a fondness for children quite apart from their decorative value, and in any case it was impossible not to pity this one in her distress. "Are you lost?" he asked.

The small girl stopped in mid-roar to regard him with teary eyes. "No," she said, "it's Bruce who's lost. At least, he's not lost, precisely. He's up in a tree, and I can't get him down."

"Bruce?" repeated Desmond. A pathetic *mew* overhead made him look up. There, on a branch far above his head, crouched a tabby kitten with wide, frightened green eyes.

"Bruce is my kitten," explained the girl. "He ran up the tree and now he can't get down. I've tried and tried to go up and get him, but I'm not big enough." Her eyes flooded with fresh tears. "And he'll starve to death up there. He won't be able to get anything to eat or drink."

It was clear she was on the verge of breaking into wails again. "To be sure he will," said Desmond, hoping to avert another display of the girl's vocal powers. "He'll come down in his own good time. Just wait and see if he doesn't."

"He won't," said the girl positively. "He's been

up there for hours and hours now. He's too little to get down by himself."

"Nonsense," said Desmond. "If he got up there in the first place, he is quite capable of getting down." Seeing that the girl was not convinced by this argument, he went on with would-be cheer. "Why, I'm thirty years old, and I've never yet seen or heard of a cat climbing a tree and staying there to starve. Not once, in all my thirty years."

"Just because you haven't heard of it doesn't mean it couldn't happen," returned the girl with unanswerable logic. "If only I was bigger! If I was as big as you, I'd climb up there and rescue Bruce myself."

Desmond felt there was a reproachful quality to this speech. "Look here," he said. "Do you want *me* to climb up and get your kitten?"

The girl's tears at once gave way to a beatific smile. "*Would* you?" she asked.

"Yes," said Desmond ruefully. A happy thought struck him. "Or perhaps it would be better to have my groom do it. He's a smaller, lighter fellow than I and probably a much better hand at climbing trees."

The girl looked dubious, as though she suspected Desmond of trying to fob her off with an inferior savior. Desmond gave her no time to argue, however. "Wait here," he told her. "I'll be back in a moment."

When he explained to Dirk what needed done, however, he found his servitor less than cooperative. "You want *me* to climb a tree?" said Dirk, as incredulously as though Desmond had proposed he climb the Matterhorn.

"Yes, to be sure," said Desmond, a trifle impatiently. "There's a girl over there whose kitten has climbed a tree, and she needs it brought down."

The groom shook his head with great firmness.

"Not my line o' country, my lord," he said. "Never climbed a tree in my life."

"But surely you must have climbed trees before," argued Desmond. "When you were a boy you must have climbed trees—"

"Never," said the groom firmly. "I'm a Londoner born and bred, m'lord. There weren't no trees to climb where I grew up. Besides, I wouldn't have had time to climb 'em if there had been. Me dad put me to work in the stables when I was four, and I've been busy there ever since. I don't know nothing about trees."

Seeing he was set against enlarging his experience, Desmond had no choice but to undertake the kitten rescue mission himself. He, at least, had climbed a few trees in his life, although it had been a good many years since he had done so. He could not help having a few misgivings about his ability to do so now.

The small girl was still waiting where he had left her. She fastened him with an expectant gaze as soon as he came into sight. "It looks as though I'll have to make the climb after all," he told her. "My groom says he can't do it."

The small girl nodded as though this was just what she had expected to hear. "I'd rather you did it anyway," she said.

Feeling oddly gratified by her confidence, Desmond grasped one of the lower limbs of the tree and swung himself into its branches. Both the girl and the kitten watched with interest as he made his way up to the branch where the kitten sat. Fortunately, his previous experience in tree climbing stood him in good stead. The main difficulty he encountered in rescuing the kitten was the attitude of the kitten itself. Now that help was at hand, it seemed not at all eager to leave its perch, and in the process of bringing it down, Desmond collected several painful scratches. This, combined with the damage the tree bark wrought on his glossy boots and immaculate pantaloons, served to inspire him with some cynical reflections about the reward of the Good Samaritan. Still, he felt somewhat repaid for his injuries by the glowing smile on the small girl's face when he put her pet into her arms.

"Thank you!" she said, clutching the kitten to her chest. "Oh, thank you, thank you, thank you, sir!"

"You're welcome," said Desmond. He watched ruefully as she carried the kitten, now perfectly quiescent, toward a nearby cottage. Then he turned and made his way back to where his groom was waiting by the curricle.

Dirk looked him over, taking in his disheveled state with ill-concealed amusement. All he said, however, was, "You've scratched your face, my lord," in a respectful voice.

Desmond put his hand to his face. "Yes," he said bitterly. "That damned kitten scratched me. *And* bit me, too. And after I went to the trouble of rescuing it!"

The groom shook his head. "You didn't ought to have meddled with it, my lord," he said. "A cat up a tree can get itself down in its own good time. Everybody knows that."

Desmond said nothing, but whipped up his horses in a manner more eloquent than words.

As he continued down the road, he swore he would let nothing else delay him. He was already late, and his appearance had been materially injured by the stop to rescue the kitten. *I won't stop again, though Hell itself should stand in my way.*

It was not Hell, however, but an old woman who presently appeared in his path. She looked up at his approach, her face tear-stained and despairing. The cause of her despair was obvious, for a farm cart stood beside her at a crazy angle, one wheel on the roadway and the other in the ditch. Thanks to the recent spring rains, the ditch was full of water, and the wheel within it was mired to the axle. An elderly horse was hitched to the cart, his sides flecked with foam and his eyes still rolling as at a recent fright. The cart was piled high with cauliflowers, which appeared in imminent danger of tumbling into the ditch.

Desmond's first impulse on viewing this tableau was to whip up his horses and drive past with all speed. But something in the old woman's expression touched him even against his will. Slowing his curricle, he addressed her in a kindly tone. "It looks as though you're having difficulties, ma'am. May I be of assistance?"

"If you could, sir!" The woman's words were heartfelt. "But I misdoubt there's much you can do. It's only that my horse shied as he was coming down the hill—he's a tetchy creature, for all he is getting on in years, and a bird flew out of the hedge just as we were topping the hill and scared him most to death. He started running like the devil himself was at his heels, and the upshot is he's landed us in the ditch. And I don't see no way in the world we'll be getting out again without a stout team to aid us."

"Well, that should be easily arranged," said Desmond. "The next town I come to, I'll stop and let them know about your predicament. There's bound to be someone there with a team who can come to your aid."

The woman thanked Desmond, but did not look as pleased by his offer as he had expected. "It's very kind of you, sir, I'm sure," she said. "But oh, if you could tell them please to hurry? You see, I was on my way to the market in Barnhart with my cauliflowers—very early they are this year, sir, and remarkably fine, too, as you can see for yourself. And if I'm held up too long, I won't likely get there in time to sell them."

It was easy to see the sale of the cauliflowers was a matter of vast moment to the woman. Desmond looked at her and then at the load of cauliflowers tilting precariously over the ditch. He felt an awful conviction that he was about to be embroiled in another scrape. But he had been raised to believe it was a gentleman's duty to help a lady in distress, even if the lady was an elderly one of humble estate. He simply could not reconcile it with his conscience to leave the old woman to her fate.

"I see," he said. "I did not realize time was an issue. In that case, perhaps if we work together, we can get your cart back on the road. You take one trace, and I'll take the other. Dirk, you go down in the ditch and push from that end," he added maliciously. Seeing that Dirk had wriggled out of the tree-climbing episode, he thought it only right he should bear the brunt of the labor now.

With a sour expression, Dirk descended to the ditch and bent his shoulder to the rear of the cart. Desmond urged the horse forward as he and the old woman hauled on the traces, and together they were able to dislodge the cart from its muddy snare. The woman thanked Desmond over and over with a beaming smile, saying she was sure heaven would bless him for his help.

Desmond looked ruefully at his boots, now muddied as well as scratched. But he brushed aside the old woman's thanks and said she made too much of the little help he had been able to provide.

"Indeed, sir, it's a great deal you've done," insisted the woman. "I don't know where I'd have been without you. I can't help feeling badly, for you've got yourself all muddied helping me, and scratched your poor face, too."

"No, the scratches came earlier," said Desmond. "I was helping to get a cat out of a tree."

"Ah, you'd have done better not to meddle with it, sir," said the old woman, shaking her head. "Cats is at home in trees. When they're ready to come down, they'll come down by their own selves. Everybody knows that."

There appeared nothing to say in response to this, so Desmond said nothing. He did attempt to give the old woman a tip by way of parting gift, but she refused it violently, saying Desmond had done enough for her that day. She then retaliated by pressing upon him the finest and largest of her cauliflowers, a gift Desmond found himself quite unable to repudiate. He looked at it ruefully as he resumed his seat in the curricle. "Now what shall I do with this?" he said.

"Throw it in the ditch?" suggested the groom.

Desmond did not like to follow this advice. He feared the old woman might see the cauliflower in the ditch upon returning home and be hurt by his contempt for her gift. In the end, he laid the cauliflower down at his feet, inwardly resolving he would give it to the first hungry-looking person he saw.

He also resolved nothing further should stop him on his way. He had promised Annabelle he would be at the villa by noon, and his previous stops had delayed him by nearly an hour. *Of course she will understand if I am a little late,* he told himself, but inwardly he felt uneasy. Annabelle had many fine qualities, but understanding was not among them. She was prone to pout for days over any fancied slight, and once, when he had innocently complimented one of her friends on her hat, she had given him the cold shoulder for nearly a week until he had managed to plead his way back into her good graces.

Desmond hoped his current offense would not be subject to such a heavy penalty. It would be most unjust of Annabelle to take offense merely because he had stopped to render assistance to other members of her sex. But, he reflected gloomily, it would be just his luck if she did. Or was it indeed a matter of luck? By endeavoring to be a gentleman and do his duty as he had been taught it, was he perhaps making himself vulnerable to being taken advantage of by the fair sex in general and Annabelle in particular?

The idea was not a comfortable one. Desmond frowned and tried to put it out of his mind, but now it had entered, it resolutely refused to budge. He thought of the small girl with her kitten and the old woman with her cart. There was no reason on earth why he had needed to involve himself in their affairs. If he had not stopped to help, ten to one someone else would have done so, assuming help were even necessary—a thing Desmond was coming increasingly to doubt, in the case of the kitten at least.

The simple fact of the matter was that he, Desmond, was so weak or so foolish he could not seem to say no to any request a woman might make of him. As a result, here he was, running nearly an hour late, with a scratched face, scuffed and muddy boots, and an inamorata who might well refuse to speak to him when he did finally arrive.

Something in this scenario disturbed Desmond, even beyond its obvious injustice. He could not see that he could have behaved otherwise toward the little girl and old woman without sacrificing his own self-respect. Yet he had, nonetheless, a niggling sensation he had been played for a flat. Or was it Annabelle who was playing him for a flat? Was it possible he might have compromised his self-respect during his dealings with her not once, but a multitude of times?

So dangerous were these reflections that Desmond absolutely refused to entertain them for a moment. Instead he chose to focus on the more immediate and material problem of his boots and pantaloons. He supposed he could ask one of the servants at the villa to see to them when he arrived there, but he had never visited the house before and knew nothing of its layout.

The fete, too, was an unknown quantity. What if he was forced to run the gamut of the partygoers before he could find a servant to help him? What if the other guests should see him scratched, scuffed, and muddy? Worse yet, what if Annabelle herself should see him? It would not improve his chances with her to be seen looking like a Yahoo.

Thus, Desmond was greatly relieved to see the signpost of an inn looming ahead by the side of the road. Here was the perfect solution. He could have his boots and pantaloons attended to by the inn servants with only a brief loss of time, and the delay would be more than made up for by the improvement in his appearance. Besides, the day was a warm one for so early in the year, and the idea of a pint of home brew did not come amiss.

In the event, this plan worked out splendidly. Not only did the landlord of the inn insist on loaning Desmond his own dressing gown to wear while the servants saw to his boots and pantaloons, he insisted on sitting with Desmond in the private parlor while his garments were being attended to and standing him several pints of beer. Desmond tried to protest this generosity, but the man was so insistent he found it hard to refuse. And indeed, now that Annabelle and destiny were looming close at hand, he found his nerves were the better for a few pints of beer. He wasn't taking refuge in Dutch courage, or anything of that nature, Desmond assured himself. It was merely that his nerves wanted steadying.

His nerves may have been steadied by the beer, but he found he was just a trifle unsteady on his feet as he took leave of his host and went out to his curricle once more. Still, he felt in a splendid mood, full of confidence and resolution. He swore to himself he would lose no more time hurrying to Annabelle's side. Quite likely his family were right in saying she would make him miserable, but he was in a mood to embrace such a fate with resignation and even with joy. It was his destiny, after all, and no amount of females with ditched carts or obstreperous kittens could keep him from it.

A glance at his watch showed he was more than an hour behind his time. Under the exhilarating influence of the landlord's home brew, however, Desmond felt assured he could make up the time on the road. The horses were rested, the highway ahead of him was smooth and level, and there was no other traffic in sight. The grays seemed eager to try out their paces.

Desmond took them up to a trot, then urged them forward to a canter. Gradually he let out their reins until they were approaching their top speed of thirteen miles per hour.

Just at that moment, someone stepped suddenly out of the hedge into their path.

"Damn!" swore Desmond. By hauling on the reins with all his strength, he was able to bring the horses to a plunging standstill just in time to avoid striking the unwary pedestrian. Dirk leaped off the back of the curricle and ran to take the grays' heads, while Desmond slumped back in his seat, feeling sobered and not a little incensed. Up till now he had been so busy dealing with the horses he had not had time to spare even a glance toward the person who had caused the near accident. Now he looked to see what kind of ignorant, irresponsible idiot would step directly into the path of a pair of speeding horses.

The idiot proved to be a girl, or rather a young lady. She had shrunk back against the hedge to avoid being struck by the horses' hoofs, but now she came cautiously out again. She was of medium height with a slender figure and looked to be about twenty. Her eyes were brown and her face oval, with a sprinkling of freckles across the nose. The most noticeable thing about her, however, was undoubtedly her hair. This was of that flaming red that cannot fail to catch the onlooker's attention, and so it was some little time before Desmond noticed she was dressed rather oddly for a mid-morning stroll along a country lane. She wore no hat or bonnet atop her fiery curls, only a wreath of flowers set atop a flowing veil, and her dress of white gauze trimmed with lace would not have been amiss at a London Assembly.

In truth, Desmond was still rather befuddled by the beer he had drunk earlier. He could only stare at the girl, unable to reconcile her fantastical appearance with the homespun rustic he had expected to see. The girl stared back at him, her gaze critical and appraising. She seemed not at all discomposed by the experience of having been nearly run down by a speeding carriage.

For some minutes they contemplated each other in silence. The silence was broken at last by the sound of wheels in the distance. This seemed to discompose the girl as her near accident had not. She cast an apprehensive look down the lane, then turned to address Desmond in an urgent voice.

"Please, sir, will you take me up with you?" she asked.

Three

Desmond could only stare at the girl's unexpected request. "Please take me up with you," she repeated. "Please, sir!" She cast another worried glance down the lane. "If only you will take me to the nearest town, I will gladly repay you for your trouble. I have money with me and some jewelry, too. Look!" She produced a square wooden box from beneath her arm and began to fumble with the catch.

Desmond found his tongue at this. He spoke the question uppermost in his mind ever since the girl had made her appearance. "Are you mad?" he asked.

The girl looked annoyed. "Certainly not," she said coldly. "I am merely asking a favor of you and promising to pay you for your trouble. Why should you say I am mad?"

"Because you don't know me from Adam!" said Desmond. "I might be a thief or a murderer or any other species of blackguard. And for you to be advertising you are carrying money and jewelry—why, it's an invitation to robbery."

"You don't understand," said the girl. She cast another anxious look down the road. "I'm in a bit of a pickle, and I have no choice but to trust you won't rob me. But I'm sure you're not a robber." She gave Desmond an engaging smile. "You don't look like it, for one thing, and for another, if you had been, you wouldn't be standing here arguing about giving me a ride. You'd merely have done it and then taken my jewels as soon as you got the chance."

Desmond had to admit this reasoning seemed sound. The girl was quick to see the capitulation in his face. "Please, won't you take me up?" she begged. "You needn't even take me all the way to the next town if you don't like to. If you can just carry me a few miles along the way and then set me down, that would be enough." She looked frantically down the lane, where the sound of wheels was growing nearer. "Please!"

Desmond gave in. It was impossible not to feel the urgency of the girl's request, and he was not a little curious to find out more about her. "Very well," he said. "Let me help you—"

But before he could dismount from his seat, or even complete his offer of assistance, the girl had sprung into the curricle. In the process she gave Desmond a fine view of her ankles and a goodly amount of silk-stocking-clad leg as well. Naturally he could not help gaping a little, but the girl merely advised him to whip up his horses and be quick about it. Gathering his wits together, Desmond obeyed, and soon the curricle was rattling down the lane at a great pace.

Great as it was, his pace did not satisfy the girl. "Won't your horses go any faster than this?" she asked, casting an anxious look over her shoulder. "I'm sure they were going faster when I first saw you."

"When you nearly got run over by me, you mean!" retorted Desmond. "I prefer to keep to a more moderate pace, just on the chance some other reckless pedestrian should run out suddenly into the road."

The girl threw him a look half penitent and half amused. "Yes, that was very bad of me," she said. "But indeed, I had no choice, sir. Your happening along just when you did was the most fortunate thing. I knew if I did not stop you, I might miss the chance of a ride. And I needed a ride very badly just then."

"So I perceive," said Desmond. "Er—would it be impertinent to ask *why* you needed a ride so badly?"

The girl went on as though she had not heard his question, though a slight heightening of her color seemed to show she had. "Indeed, it was very good of you to take me up," she told Desmond. "You have been most kind to me, sir, and not least because you have refrained from scolding me for putting you to so much trouble."

Desmond politely denied she had been any trouble. He had not failed to notice the girl had ignored his question, but he had no intention of giving up so easily. He decided to try approaching the subject in a more roundabout manner. "You said you wish to be set down in the nearest town," he said. "I'm afraid I'm not very familiar with the towns hereabouts. What town would that be?"

"It doesn't matter," said the girl. "Any town will do. Any town that has a posting house, that is." She cast another hunted look over her shoulder.

"Oh, so you mean to hire a post chaise?" said Desmond, still very casually.

"Yes, if I cannot catch a stage or the Mail instead. I should prefer to go by Mail, because that would be fastest."

"And where are you going?" asked Desmond.

He expected the girl would evade this question as she had evaded his other, but she answered quite readily, "I am going to London."

"To London!" exclaimed Desmond. "But in that

case, you ought not to be riding with me. I am headed *away* from London, not toward it!"

"It doesn't matter," the girl assured him. "In fact, perhaps it is better this way. It will better serve to throw him—her—them off the track."

Desmond looked long and hard at the girl. She returned his look with seeming candor, but there was a flicker of unease in her eyes, as though she were aware she had said something indiscreet. " 'Throw them off the track,' " he repeated. "Throw *whom* off the track? And what track do you mean? I think you had better tell me a little more about this business that is taking you to London."

The girl raised her chin. "Indeed, it is my own business, sir. You are kind to take an interest, but I would prefer not to say any more about it at present."

"No doubt you would," said Desmond dryly. "But I am beginning to have the feeling that by helping you I am embroiling myself in a rather equivocal business. Unless you can assure me otherwise, I am afraid I cannot carry you any farther." To emphasize his point, he slowed the horses to a walk.

The girl threw a harried look behind her, but it was clear she was proof against this kind of extortion. "Very well," she said haughtily. "If you will not, then there is nothing more to be said. You may set me down here, and I will give you a good morning."

Desmond immediately whipped up the horses again. "On second thought, I believe I do not dare set you down," he said. "Not until I have made sure I am not assisting in some criminal enterprise. Those jewels you mentioned before—how do I know you came by them honestly? Perhaps you stole them from their rightful owner and are now trying to flee with them."

The girl gave an indignant cry. "Indeed I did no such thing!" she said, clutching the box to her chest. "They are *my* jewels. When my mother died, she left them to me with instructions that they should come to me when I was twenty-one, or—or on my wedding day."

There was a catch in the girl's voice as she spoke these last words, a hint of something halfway between laughter and tears. Desmond looked at her, taking in once again her veil and elaborate dress. Comprehension came flooding over him in a sudden wave. "Your twenty-first birthday or your wedding day!" he repeated. "And is today your wedding day, by any chance?"

The girl opened her mouth, then closed it again. There was really no need for her to answer, for the truth was written plainly on her face. She looked helplessly at Desmond. In spite of all his resolutions to refrain from being taken advantage of by members of the weaker sex, he found himself softening. "I believe you'd better tell me the whole story," he said. "It may be that I can help you, but before I do anything I must know exactly what I am involved in."

"Oh," said the girl with a smothered gasp. She looked at Desmond with troubled brown eyes. "I don't know. I simply don't know. If I could be sure I could trust you! But I think I can." She looked long and keenly into his face, then nodded with more assurance. "Yes, I am sure I can."

"Yes, you can trust me," said Desmond in a gloomy voice. Ruefully, he reflected that he could be trusted to behave like a flat any time a woman needed a favor from him.

The girl, however, seemed reassured by his words. "Very well, I will tell you the whole story, sir. But indeed, I hardly know how to begin."

"You could begin by telling me your name," suggested Desmond. "A proper introduction is usually the first step in any acquaintance."

Although the girl had claimed to trust him, it was easy to see her trust did not extend very far. After a pause, and with an air of noticeable defiance, she said, "My name is Miss Chloe de Havilland."

Desmond gave her a long look. She lifted her chin defiantly, but her eyes kept sliding away when they tried to meet his own. "That is a very pretty name," he said. "But somehow I don't think it is your own."

The girl tried to look indignant, but a hint of a smile was twitching at her lips. "I am the most lamentable liar," she said. "I never tell a falsehood but I get caught out directly. Still, I can't see why it matters to you what I call myself, sir. And Chloe de Havilland is really a much prettier name than my own."

"I'll be the judge of that, if you please," said Desmond, smiling back at her. "Indeed, I should much prefer to call you by your real name."

"Then tell me yours first," challenged the girl. "Fair is fair, after all."

Gravely Desmond took out his card case, removed one of his visiting cards, and handed it to her. The girl studied the card, her brows rising high on her forehead. "*Lord* Desmond Ryder," she said. "Good gracious, a member of the nobility!"

"Only a younger son, I fear," said Desmond. Sketching a bow, he added, "Lord Desmond Ryder, at your service, ma'am. And you are?"

"Susan Doyle," said the girl with a sigh. "A dreadfully commonplace name. But"—her face brightened—"at any rate, it is still Miss Doyle and not Mrs. Hawkins!"

"Now we come to the crux of the matter," said Desmond. "I take it Mr. Hawkins is your bridegroom-to-be?"

"Yes, he was," said Susan. "But I left him at the altar." She began to laugh rather hysterically. "Truly,

I did just that! The servants were there in their best clothes, the vicar had his prayer book in hand, and Mortimer was wearing his new blue coat. Aunt Sarah had them all waiting in the drawing room for me to come down and be married. I came down, peeped around the door, saw them all gathered there, and knew suddenly that I couldn't do it. I simply couldn't marry Mortimer Hawkins, not if I was to die for it."

She brought these words out defiantly, looking at Desmond as though she expected him to reproach her. All he said, however, was, "I see. What did you do then?"

"Once I realized I couldn't marry Mortimer, everything was easy. I just tiptoed back to my room, grabbed my reticule and Mama's jewels that Aunt had given me this morning, and ran out the side door."

"You don't think it was a trifle hard on Mortimer, to leave him standing at the altar waiting for a bride who never came?" suggested Desmond.

Susan shook her head so vigorously that the fiery curls stood out on either side. "No, for it was his own fault—his and Aunt Sarah's. They knew I did not want to marry him, and yet they kept at me, day in and day out, until I finally said I would." Her forehead wrinkled. "Indeed, that sounds as though I must be a very poor creature. I do not really think I am, but I cannot explain how I came to be weak enough to say I would marry Mortimer in the first place."

"You don't seem weak to me," said Desmond, with a sideways glance at Susan's firm chin and determined mouth. "As far as I am competent to judge, I should say you know your own mind remarkably well."

"Well, I do, in the ordinary way," agreed Susan. "But since Uncle Asa died, Aunt and Mortimer have given me no peace. It has been very uncomfortable, and I think I must have said yes just because I was so weary of being nagged and urged and scolded."

"Who *is* Mortimer?" said Desmond. "Besides your ex-bridegroom-to-be, that is?"

"He is my cousin. At least he's not exactly my cousin, for he is Aunt's son by her first marriage. Since Uncle Asa was my mother's brother, there is really no blood relation between us at all. But we have been raised as though we were cousins—or, indeed, more like brother and sister. I came to live with Uncle and Aunt after my mother and father died, when I was only thirteen."

"I see," said Desmond. "And has it always been an understood thing that you should marry your cousin?"

"No, indeed. There was never a word said about it while Uncle Asa was alive."

"I see," said Desmond again. He looked reflectively at Susan, who seemed quite oblivious to the deeper implications of her story. "So the idea of your marrying Mortimer came entirely from your aunt and cousin?"

"It certainly didn't come from me," said Susan. "Mortimer is well enough for a cousin, but for a husband—no!" She shuddered.

"Do you think Mortimer's desire to marry you was prompted by an unconquerable passion?" inquired Desmond, as delicately as he could. "Or do you think he and your aunt might have had an ulterior motive?"

Susan turned serious eyes upon him. "Do you know, I have been wondering that myself," she said. "I have never thought Mortimer seemed particularly in love with me, for all that he was so eager to marry me."

"Then could there be another reason?" said Desmond. "Did your parents leave you some money, for instance, that might provide a motive for his wishing to marry you?"

"I don't know," said Susan frankly. "I remember Uncle Asa saying once I was my parents' heir, but I never knew whether there was any money involved, or only personal property. Like my jewels," she added, looking down at her jewel box with satisfaction. "I have asked Aunt about it several times, but all she would say was that I did not need to trouble myself about money. She said I would always have a home with her and Mortimer."

"Indeed," said Desmond.

The tone of his voice was not lost on Susan. She flashed Desmond a smile. "Yes, it's not very satisfactory, is it? It didn't strike me as very satisfactory, either. In fact, I was so dissatisfied that I actually wrote to my other aunt, asking *her* about it. That is my Aunt Theodosia who lives in London. But Aunt Theo said the same thing as Aunt Sarah did, or almost. She said I did not need to trouble myself about money, for I would be told all about my personal circumstances as soon as I turned twenty-one, and until then there was no reason for me to worry my head about them."

"So you have another aunt besides your Aunt Sarah?" said Desmond. "What does she think about your marrying Mortimer?"

Susan knit her brows. "Do you know, I'm not certain she knows about it. She and Aunt Sarah are not at all close. Since I am related to Aunt Theo on Papa's side, and Aunt Sarah on Mama's, their only connection is through me. Besides, Aunt Theo is very fashionable and lives in London most of the year, whereas Aunt Sarah thinks London a dreadful place and prefers to live in the country."

"But if you were to be married, surely your Aunt Sarah would have sent your other aunt a wedding invitation," persisted Desmond. "And surely you would have at least received a letter from her wishing you well, even if she could not come herself."

"Aunt Sarah said she did write Aunt Theo about my wedding, but that Aunt Theo was abroad and so the letter could not reach her," said Susan. "I didn't think anything about it at the time, for Aunt Theo does travel a good deal. But I have wondered since if Aunt Sarah wrote to her at all. Because I don't think Aunt Theo would approve of my marrying Mortimer. She told me once, years ago, she would bring me out and give me a Season in London when I was old enough, because there was no hope of my ever marrying anyone eligible as long as I was living in Barnhart."

"But she never has carried out her promise?" said Desmond.

"No, she never has. I have thought about reminding her, but did not like to, because I thought perhaps she might have thought better of it. Because of my red hair, perhaps," said Susan, inspecting a fiery curl with a rueful air. "Probably she thought it would be a futile business to try to foist someone as plain as I am upon the *ton.*"

Desmond regarded her with amazement. "Plain!" he exclaimed. "I wouldn't call you plain at all."

Susan fastened him with a skeptical gaze. "Wouldn't you?" she asked.

Desmond looked down at the smooth oval face with its scattering of freckles, the long-lashed dark eyes and clear-cut features, the slim, graceful figure, and finally at the rich curls of flaming hair clustered distractingly about her face. "Certainly not," he said with decision. "I believe if you were presented in London, you would make a great sensation."

"But would you know?" said Susan, still looking skeptical. "Do you move in society yourself?"

Desmond assured her he did, amused and yet resentful at her skepticism. "In fact, I think I am acquainted your aunt," he said. "Is her name Doyle, too?"

"Yes, Mrs. Andrew Doyle is her name. She is a widow now, because my Uncle Andrew died some years ago. Do you really know her?"

"Not to speak to, but I know her by sight. She is a very handsome woman and is said to be as amiable as she is handsome."

"I hope she is," said Susan. "For I expect I will have to throw myself upon her mercy now I have jilted Mortimer."

"Is that why you are going to London?" said Desmond.

Susan nodded. "Yes, it seemed like the best thing to do in the circumstances. Certainly I could not go back and live with Aunt Sarah and Mortimer now, even if I wanted to."

"But what if your Aunt Theodosia really is abroad, as your other aunt told you?" questioned Desmond. "What will you do then?"

Susan shrugged. "I'll cross that bridge when I come to it. Perhaps her servants would let me stay in her house even if she is away. If they won't, I can probably sell enough of my jewelry to keep me until I am able to find some way to earn a living."

Desmond was aghast at her insouciance. "But look here," he said, "I don't believe you've thought this business through. Have you considered what it would be like for you, a young lady gently bred, to be all on your own in London? You wouldn't know a soul there; you wouldn't know your way about—why, you couldn't even gain admission to a decent hotel without a maid and baggage."

"Couldn't I?" said Susan with naive surprise.

"No, you couldn't," said Desmond positively. "And as for the chances of your earning a living—well, I don't know what your training and education have been, but I can tell you it isn't an easy thing for a young lady living alone in London to find a job. A *respectable* job, that is," he added with emphasis.

"But I have some money," argued Susan. "And I have Mama's jewels. It's not as though I would be completely without means."

"Having jewels is not the same as having a comfortable balance at the banker's. Indeed, it's almost worse than having nothing at all. You would be a magnet for thieves the minute it was known you had jewels in your possession."

"But no one would know I had them," said Susan. "No one but you, my lord, and I believe I can trust you." She gave him another engaging smile.

"Yes, you can trust me," said Desmond grimly. "But what you seem to forget is that you cannot keep their presence a secret forever. Not if you intend to sell them."

Susan bit her lip. "Yes, that's so," she admitted. "I had not thought of that."

"Besides, selling them will not be as easy as you make it sound," continued Desmond. He was pleased he was finally getting his point across. "You can't just take them into the nearest jeweler and expect to get a fair price for them. You'd be lucky to realize a tenth of their value, if you were able to sell them at all."

For a moment Susan looked daunted. Then she shrugged. "All you say may be true, my lord," she said. "But still I intend to try. My only other choice is to return to Aunt Sarah and Mortimer, and I would rather die than do that." A passionate note had crept into her voice as she went on. "You have told me what a dreadful risk I am taking if I go to London on my own. What you don't realize is that after what I have been through with Aunt and Mortimer, I am willing to take the risk. It is worth it to me just to be free for a while."

Desmond opened his mouth to argue, but Susan swept on, heedless of interruption. "Since Uncle died, it's been just Aunt and Mortimer and I, living in the country. Our house is very isolated, and Aunt Sarah has never been a social woman. Since Uncle died, she has become even less so. I've scarcely seen a soul besides her and Mortimer and the servants these past six months. I think that's at least part of the reason why I said I'd marry Mortimer. When you are thrown together with two people on such close terms, and they beg you continually to do a thing and act very disagreeably when you don't, and you know it will make everything pleasant if you only agree—well, it's hard not to give in and do what they ask." She looked unhappily at Desmond. "But yet I knew all along I did not want to marry Mortimer. I suppose I must be a coward after all, not to have stood on my principles. It's only that it was so miserable being scolded and nagged day in and day out. It seemed there simply wasn't any other way out."

"No-o-o," agreed Desmond, rather reluctantly. "I can see your position must have been difficult."

"Difficult!" repeated Susan. "I felt like an animal in a trap." She looked despairingly at Desmond. "I don't expect I can make you understand. You're a man, and men can do whatever they like."

"Hardly," protested Desmond, but Susan paid him no heed. She went on, her voice almost fierce in its intensity.

"When one is a woman—a young lady—one is continually hedged about with proprieties. One can't do this, and one mustn't do that, and if one is to keep one's reputation as a respectable girl, one must be obedient and self-sacrificing and never think of rebelling against anything one is told to do. That's how it's always been, and I tried—I really tried to be a respectable girl. But this morning as I went downstairs, it suddenly struck me that being respectable had gotten me nothing but the prospect of being married to Mortimer. And I decided I wanted nothing more to do with it."

Desmond made an understanding noise. Susan swept on, her voice fiercer than ever. "It's as though respectability were being held as a sword to my throat. I was living in mortal terror of it—and then I realized its power was all in my mind. If I refused to acknowledge it, then it simply wasn't there. I could do what *I* wanted and never be forced to do anything again. So that's what I did. I just turned my back on Mortimer and Aunt and all of them and walked out of the house. And I don't care if I *have* ruined my reputation. I don't care if both my aunts turn their backs on me. I am going to *live* for a change, and let the consequences be what they may. And I'll go on doing things my way as long as I have breath in my body and the means with which to do it."

Desmond could not doubt she was in earnest. A flush had risen in her cheeks, and her breast was heaving with emotion. "All that may be very well," he said, striving for a pacific tone, "but you are forgetting one thing, aren't you?"

"What's that?" demanded Susan.

"You aren't of age yet. I take it from what you said before that your twenty-first birthday is still to come."

"Yes, it's not till June," agreed Susan. "But June is only two months away, and in the meantime I am determined to be my own mistress."

"I don't doubt you are. But you may have no choice in the matter. Until you are twenty-one, your relations *do* have control over you, whether you like it or not."

Susan merely looked obstinate at this and said she was not likely to let herself be put back into harness again now she had kicked over the traces. Desmond could not help admiring her spirit, but at the same time he felt uneasy when he thought of the perils awaiting a pretty, high-spirited young lady who had, by her own admission, cast respectability to the four winds.

"I can see how you might wish to be free of restraint," he said, as gently as he could. "I remember feeling so myself when I was your age. But really it won't do, my dear. You don't have an idea of what you'd be up against, living alone in London. I couldn't reconcile it with my conscience to let you even attempt it."

Susan's eyes flashed dangerously. "I'd like to see you stop me, my lord!"

Desmond gave her a meditative look. "I expect I ought to at least try," he said. "What I really ought to do is turn around and take you back to your Aunt Sarah. That would probably be the best and safest course, all things considered."

Susan stared at him aghast for a moment. Then suddenly her face broke into smiles. "But you won't," she said. "You haven't any intention of taking me back to my Aunt Sarah."

"How do you know?" countered Desmond.

"Because you are just as lamentable a liar as I am," said Susan triumphantly.

Desmond could not help laughing at this. "Since you say it, I must admit it sticks in my craw to return you to that woman," he said. "She stands in loco parentis to you, and yet she seems to have had no scruples about sacrificing your own welfare for the benefit of her son's. As such, I cannot think it right that you should return to her care. However," he went on, fixing Susan with a stern eye, "I cannot think it right, either, to let you go alone to London, where you might well fall into the hands of thieves or worse. I think, on the whole, the best solution would be for me to drive you to London and make sure you are safely in your other aunt's hands before taking leave of you."

"Oh," said Susan doubtfully. She turned this plan over in her mind. "That would be very kind of you, my lord, if you do not mind driving me to London. I confess I have been a little nervous at the prospect of taking the stagecoach, for I have never done so before and I don't know just how it is managed. But I don't wish to be a bother to you."

Desmond thought to himself that she *was* a bother. He could hardly take her to the villa with him, for she was not an invited guest, and Annabelle was likely to misunderstand his arriving in company with a strange and attractive young woman. Neither did he trust Susan to wait for him docilely in a nearby inn while he disported himself at the Byrnes'. He would simply have to abandon all thought of the party and return to London immediately.

So much for proposing to Annabelle today, he told himself ruefully. *Why must these things always happen to me?*

Still, he could not abandon Susan. He would feel guilty all his life if he went off to the fete and left her to her own devices. He manifestly had a duty here, and being the gentleman he was, he could not shirk it. His plans in regard to Annabelle would simply have to wait until another day.

"It's no bother," he said, as cheerfully as he could. "I was on my way to a party, but I don't mind changing my plans. The more I have been considering it, the more I feel I'd really rather return to London anyway."

"If you're sure," said Susan, still looking doubtful.

"I'm sure," said Desmond firmly. "Just let me get my horses turned around, and we'll be back in London before the cat can lick her ear."

Four

Desmond had exaggerated a little in saying he and Susan would be back in London before the cat could lick her ear. It took rather longer than that to reach the metropolis, owing to various matters that had to be attended to on the way.

First, he had to stop at an inn and send messages to Annabelle and his hosts that he had been unavoidably detained on the road and would be unable to attend the fete as planned. Watching the messenger gallop off, he wondered how Annabelle would react to his note. He felt a little uneasy about it, but his detention really had been unavoidable, he assured himself. Still, he was in a pensive mood as he returned to his curricle and resumed his seat beside Susan.

Pensive or not, he noticed immediately that Susan's expression was tight-lipped and angry. When he asked her if something were troubling her, she seemed at first disinclined to speak, but finally was brought to explain the cause of her displeasure. "There were some people—men—in the innyard just now," she said. "They stared at me in a most disagreeable manner and made *remarks.*"

Desmond looked at her and saw as though for the first time her showy bridal attire and lack of proper headgear. "What a bungler I am," he said penitently. "Of course we ought to have done something about your clothes before ever I left you by yourself."

"But what can we do about them?" said Susan practically. "I don't have any other clothing with me. I suppose I ought to have stopped and changed before I left Aunt's, but I was too eager to get away to stop for anything."

"Something must be done," decreed Desmond. "I wonder if there is a milliner in this village?"

There proved to be no milliner, although a local dry goods store had a few men's hats for sale of a quality Desmond pronounced execrable. "You can't wear a men's hat in any case," he told Susan.

Susan laughed. "Can't I just?" she said. Turning back to the clerk, who had been gaping at the entry into his store of two fashionably dressed persons of evident Quality, she instructed him to sell her a man's high-crowned black beaver. Having purchased the hat, she took it outside to the curricle, and while Desmond watched in bemusement, she removed her veil and wreath, tied the veil around the brim of the hat, ruthlessly wrenched the wreath apart to supply her with trimming material, and presently emerged with a very creditable-looking ladies' hat. "If I was trimming it at home, I should want a bit of color rather than just black and white," she told Desmond seriously. "But the style's all right. I've seen very similar hats in *Ackerman's* and *The Ladies' Monthly Museum.*"

Desmond thought the hat was marvelous and said so. He also thought it became Susan remarkably well in spite of its lack of color, but this he did not say. "If only I had a pelisse or spencer to wear over my dress," lamented Susan, looking down at her white gown. "Then I should not look so conspicuous."

Desmond could see what she meant. He looked up and down the village street, as though expecting to see a ladies' dressmaking establishment had suddenly sprung up during the last ten minutes. None had been obliging enough to do so, but his eye fell on his groom, who was standing stolidly at the horses' heads. Desmond was seized by a sudden inspiration. "Dirk, take off your coat," he said.

"My lord?" said Dirk, gaping at him.

"Take off your coat," repeated Desmond. "This lady came away from home so suddenly that she forgot to bring her coat with her. You are going to loan her yours."

Susan protested that she could not think of depriving Dirk of his coat, but Desmond assured her he would not need it. "Will you, Dirk?" he said, fixing the groom with a steely eye.

"No, my lord," said Dirk in an expressionless voice. He removed his coat and offered it to Susan, who thanked him with a smile. As Dirk was small and slightly built, the coat proved a decent fit, and it was amazing what a difference it made in Susan's appearance. It was not that she looked prettier, for Desmond had thought she looked very lovely in her bridal gown and veil. But the dark color and mannish cut of the hat and coat in combination with her feminine figure and flaming curls gave her an air at once dashing and sophisticated.

"Do I look all right?" she inquired, seeing Desmond's eyes upon her.

"Perfectly all right," he said with a smile. "If I happened to meet you in Hyde Park, I should think only that you were dressed very stylishly."

As he whipped up his horses, he observed Dirk also eyeing Susan. It occurred to him that perhaps he ought to make some explanation for her presence. Dirk had said nothing about her thus far, nor had he commented when Desmond had told him he had changed his mind about attending the fete and was returning to London. But Desmond knew he must be wondering at his change of plans. It would do no good to lie to him, for much as Desmond might wish to shelter Susan, he could see making up a story about her being an old acquaintance whom he had run across by accident was not likely to deceive the groom. Dirk had witnessed their initial meeting, after all, and could hardly have helped overhearing a good bit of the conversation that had ensued. It would be much better if he stuck to the truth or some modified form of it in explaining the situation. Beside, as Desmond reminded himself with an inward smile, Susan had told him he was a lamentable liar.

So turning to the groom, he said, "Dirk, you ought perhaps to understand how the lady comes to be here. She has—er—been forced to leave home rather suddenly and wishes to travel to her aunt, who lives in London. I am slightly acquainted with her aunt and thought it would be better if I took her there myself rather than leaving her to the mercies of the stagecoach."

"Yes, m'lord," said Dirk stolidly.

"Of course the circumstances are somewhat peculiar, as perhaps you may have gathered. We both rely upon your discretion, in helping to safeguard Miss—the young lady's reputation."

"Just as you say, m'lord," replied Dirk woodenly, folding his arms across his striped waistcoat.

Susan immediately inquired whether he was cold, in a voice of anxious solicitude. Dirk said he was not, but his voice was a shade warmer than it had been before. Desmond noted this with approval, but he would have been surprised if he could have known the thoughts in his servitor's head.

Accustomed to guard his master's consequence even more jealously than his own, Dirk had privately deplored Desmond's connection with Annabelle Windibank. In his mind, she was a low-born baggage who was no better than she ought to be. But the general opinion among Desmond's servants was that the master had made up his mind to marry Miss Windibank. Since this was an event Dirk could not regard with anything but trepidation, it followed that he was prepared to welcome anyone or anything that might forestall it. This red-haired young lady seemed likely to forestall it—for a time at least—and Dirk was grateful accordingly.

Dirk had not wholly made up his mind whether Susan was really the innocent she appeared, or an adventuress out for Number One. As he saw it, it didn't really matter. Any lady who took his master's mind off Annabelle Windibank was an ally in his book, and Dirk was willing to assist her to a much greater extent than merely loaning her his coat.

So he listened with satisfaction as Susan chattered away to Desmond, telling him all the sights she wished to see while she was in London. Presently, however, she fell silent. When Desmond asked if she were feeling unwell, she confessed she was feeling hungry. "I couldn't eat any breakfast this morning because I was worrying so about the wedding," she said apologetically. "But it's no great matter, my lord. I can easily wait to dine until I reach my aunt's."

"But there's no need for that," said Desmond. "I am getting rather hungry myself. I have been thinking for the last twenty minutes that I wouldn't mind stopping for a bite." He shot a sideways look at Susan. "Only—are you certain it is safe to stop? If your relatives are searching for you, perhaps it would be better not to spare the time."

In truth he was not troubled by this concern as much as by the impropriety of dining alone with Susan at an inn. Of course they might hire one of the inn's female servants to chaperone her while they were eating, but that would make Susan more memorable in the minds of the inn staff, and any of her relatives who might subsequently come around asking questions would find it that much easier to pick up her trail. And since his own identity could be easily ascertained from the coat of arms on his curricle, Desmond was anxious that her trail not be discovered until it had ceased to run alongside his own.

Fortunately, the idea her relatives might catch up to her was sufficient to dissuade Susan from the notion of dining at an inn. "Yes, perhaps it would be as well not to stop until we reach London," she said, glancing uneasily over her shoulder, as though expecting to see Mortimer and her aunt hot on her heels. "I don't mind not eating in the least. I only feel badly that you are obliged to forgo your own dinner, just because of me and my problems."

"Never fear, I won't forgo my dinner," said Desmond, smiling. "Judging by the sun, it can't be later than one or two o'clock. I should be back at my lodgings in plenty of time for dinner."

"But it will be hours yet before we reach London, won't it?" asked Susan, giving him a puzzled look.

"Perhaps an hour or two. Still, I shall certainly be home in time for dinner!"

"You must dine very late," said Susan. "Aunt Sarah always has dinner served at three o'clock."

Concealing a smile, Desmond explained that most people in London with social pretensions were hardly out of bed by three o'clock. "I think three o'clock is rather early to dine even in the country nowadays," he added gently.

Susan nodded with a gloomy air. "I daresay," she said. "Aunt Sarah is very old-fashioned. I know from books I have read that some people do dine as late as seven or eight, but I wasn't aware it was a general custom." She seemed strangely depressed to learn otherwise.

"Oh, I am sure there are plenty of people who

still keep the custom of an early dinner," said Desmond, hoping to cheer her up.

"I daresay there may be," said Susan, more gloomily still. "But it seems too ridiculous that I should suppose everybody did, simply because my aunt does."

"I think it was quite a natural assumption," said Desmond. "After all, you said you and your aunt and cousin lived very retired."

"Yes, but I ought at least to have some idea how other people go on. And I don't! I don't know anything except for what I have learned from books and the servants' gossip. And that's not enough. I want to *know,*" said Susan fiercely. "I want to see things for myself, not just read about them." She gazed ahead of her with a brooding expression.

Desmond, with a jarring sense of recollection, remembered fretting under similar restrictions when he had been a boy. It had been a relief to leave school for the comparative freedom of the university, and still more of a relief to reach manhood and the greater freedom he had found in London society. He tried to visualize what it would be like to be twenty years old and mewed up with an aunt and cousin in the country with no freedom, no money, and nothing except books to provide food for one's imagination. He did not quite succeed in this exercise, but the effort inspired him with a new sympathy for Susan's plight. "With any luck, we will find your Aunt Theodosia in London, and she will follow through on her promise to bring you out," he said soothingly. "That will give you some new experiences and the taste of life you are so eager to have."

Susan nodded, but her expression was dubious. "Perhaps," she said. "But I've always heard young ladies in London are subject to the most frightful restrictions. One can't stir a step outside without a chaperone, and there's a host of things one must refrain from doing lest one be considered quite outside the pale."

Something in her voice gave Desmond a vague sense of unease. "None of us are really free," he pointed out. "We're all subject to restriction more or less."

"That may be true," said Susan. "But it appears to me some people are more free than others."

"Yes, but it's all comparative," argued Desmond. "Imagine if you were a mill girl, living on your own in one of the cities up north. You might technically be quite independent, yet in practice you would probably have as little freedom as you did when living with your aunt and Mortimer."

"Yes, that is true, too," admitted Susan.

"It's as I said before: all independence is merely comparative," continued Desmond persuasively. "Even if you were subject to a certain amount of restriction in London, you'd be better off than you were at Barnhart, wouldn't you?"

"Undoubtedly I would be better off than I was at Barnhart," agreed Susan readily enough.

Relieved to see she was prepared to be reasonable, Desmond let the subject drop. Susan said nothing more about it, either, and it appeared her mind had reverted to its former preoccupation, for when she spoke next, it was to suggest that Desmond stop and get some sandwiches since he was prevented from taking a proper luncheon.

"Of course, and I'll get some for you, too, at the next inn we come to," said Desmond. "Is there anything you would like besides sandwiches?"

"No, thank you," said Susan with a determined shake of her head. "I want nothing at all."

Desmond looked at her in surprise. "But surely you must be hungry," he said. "You said you had had no breakfast, and if you are used to dining at three, it stands to reason you must be quite famished. I'll get you some sandwiches, and cakes, too, if they have any."

"But you must not, my lord," said Susan, looking flurried. "I can easily wait till I get to London."

"We're still some miles from London. If we were to suffer a breakdown or other delay, it might be hours before we reached your aunt's. You had much better have something now to stay your appetite."

Susan bit her lip. "You are very kind, my lord," she said after a moment. "But indeed, I think I must wait. I wasn't able to bring a great deal of money with me, and if it's as you say and I encounter trouble selling my jewels, then it would be as well if I kept as much cash on hand as possible. I think I had better not spend any more than I can help right now, for I have already bought this hat, and there's no saying what else I might find it necessary to buy before I am done."

"Is that the sticking point?" said Desmond with relief. "My dear girl, when I proposed getting you sandwiches, I did not mean you should pay for them yourself."

"But I can't let *you* pay for them," said Susan. "You have been so generous already, offering to drive me all the way to my aunt's. And I know very well I am putting you out. You were on your way to a party—"

"I don't think I was ever destined to go to that party," said Desmond. A whimsical smile curved his lips. "I'm a great believer in destiny, you see. And if I hadn't been before, today would have been enough to convert me!"

"You think it was destiny that you met me?" questioned Susan with a surprised expression.

Desmond was a little startled at this personal interpretation. He had been thinking in more general terms, without considering Susan to be more than one of a series of setbacks to his plans for the day.

But he smiled indulgently as he replied, "Who knows? When I tell you what my day has been, you will believe you are merely the final circumstance that convinced me I had better abandon all thought of going to that party."

He went on to recount his exploits with the kitten in the tree and the old woman's cart. Susan laughed delightedly at his account, but shook her head at the end of it. "Indeed, you make me feel quite badly, my lord," she said. "It appears I am only the last in a long line of people taking advantage of your good nature."

"Not at all," said Desmond, smiling. "It was destiny, I firmly believe. Though I could wish destiny had not possessed such sharp claws." Ruefully he rubbed his face where the kitten had scratched him.

"Yes, your poor face," said Susan, giving him a pitying look. "I was wondering what had happened to it, but did not like to ask."

"Well, I thank you for your reticence. I also thank you for refraining from saying I had much better not have meddled with a cat up a tree, and that it certainly would have come down on its own."

Susan gave him a surprised look. "But of course you had to meddle with it," she said. "I quite see how it was. I daresay I would have done the same in your case."

Desmond was pleased to have found at least one person who approved his actions. In a more cheerful voice, he added, "At any rate, my efforts did not go wholly unrewarded. In return for helping her with her cart, the old woman insisted on presenting me with the cauliflower that is currently knocking about your feet!"

Susan's face lit up with laughter. "Is that how it comes to be there? I was wondering about that, too, but did not like to ask." She threw Desmond a shy look. "Indeed, I am so ill acquainted with London fashions that I thought perhaps it was all the mode nowadays for gentlemen to drive about with their carriages full of garden produce!"

"No, that particular mode has as yet not come into being," said Desmond, laughing. "Though I have seen several yet more foolish come and go during the time I have lived in London."

Susan, inspecting the cauliflower, said it appeared to be a very fine one. "And it is remarkably early for them, too," she told Desmond seriously. "Aunt's are not half grown yet. You must have it for your dinner tonight, and I trust your cook will not spoil it with overcooking."

Desmond said gravely that he would caution his cook particularly against it. "But that reminds me," he said, with a glance at Susan. "We never settled the subject of your sandwiches. Here is an inn just ahead. You will let me stand you to a bite of something, won't you? I assure you, you need not regard such trifling expense as it will be."

Susan shook her head firmly. "I thank you, but I think I must decline your offer, my lord," she said. "You have done enough for me as it is."

"But I don't mind doing this at all," said Desmond. "In fact, I should feel badly if I did not."

"You need not feel badly," said Susan. "I can manage very well until we get to London." Turning serious eyes upon him, she added, "I simply cannot allow you to do anything more for me, my lord. You know I am quite determined to be independent from now on. It would be a strange kind of independence that accepted so much from a stranger."

Desmond was exasperated by her attitude, yet he could not help admiring it, too. She was obviously sincere about wishing to cause no further trouble or expense to him. He found himself thinking, a little ruefully, that that made her different from most of the other women of his acquaintance. Annabelle, for instance, was always sending him on little errands to fetch her shawl or fan or gloves, or to obtain some dainty she especially fancied from the supper room. She tended also to act as though his pocketbook was a limitless well from which she could draw at will. When they had attended a fair together the week before, she had insisted he buy her every fairing that caught her eye, regardless of what it cost him or the trouble it gave him to carry her prizes around for the rest of the day.

But of course Annabelle was special, Desmond reminded himself. She was the predestined love of his life, so he did not mind indulging her whims. It gave him pleasure to do so—at least it gave him pleasure when she thanked him with one of her dazzling smiles. When she took his efforts for granted and flirted instead with other men, that was not so pleasant. But what could he do? She was Annabelle, and it was irrational to expect her to be like—well, like Susan here, for instance.

Desmond stole a look at Susan beside him in the curricle. It seemed to him there could have been no two women more different than she and Annabelle. Of course they were both young and attractive, but there the resemblance ended. Annabelle had hair of the purest guinea gold, whereas Susan's more nearly resembled copper. Annabelle's eyes were blue, while Susan's were brown—a delightfully clear hazel brown, but by no means so attractive as Annabelle's cerulean orbs. Annabelle was tall and fashioned on a Junoesque scale, while Susan was small and so slim she almost might have been called skinny if her proportions had not been so fine and her carriage so graceful. No, there was no resemblance between them in appearance, and there seemed to be none in temperament, either. He could not, for example, imagine Annabelle declaring she wished to be independent. She was the sort of female who was forever begging or coaxing or cajoling one for something, and even he, who loved her to distraction, felt cynically sure she would trade independence and everything else for a large income and exalted title.

No sooner had this thought crossed Desmond's mind, however, than he caught himself with a feeling of reproach. He had no business to be thinking such thoughts of the woman he loved. It was one thing to have his eyes open to her true character—and since witnessing her change of attitude after St. Armand's decampment, Desmond trusted he did have his eyes open. But that did not make it right to subject her to disparaging comparisons with other women. He had decided long ago that Annabelle was unlike any other woman, and even if such comparisons had not been wrong on Annabelle's account, they would have been wrong on Susan's. Whether she chose to think herself independent or not, Susan was in his care at that moment, and it was inappropriate to think of her in such a personal way.

So Desmond pushed all these thoughts aside hastily and concentrated instead upon the subject that had inspired his mental diversion. "Independence is all very well," he said, "but I cannot allow you to starve yourself."

"I won't starve," said Susan. With a twinkling smile, she added, "Indeed, my lord, I promise you that before I would starve, I would eat this cauliflower just as it is! But I'm sure that won't be necessary. I will manage perfectly well until we get to London."

"But you can't expect me to stop and get sandwiches for myself and not get some for you," argued Desmond. "If you don't eat, then I won't be able to either."

He was unprepared for the look of disillusionment Susan turned upon him. "That is just the kind of thing my Aunt Sarah always says," she said. "I had not thought you would try to *manipulate* me, my lord."

There was such an *Et tu, Brute?* flavor about this speech that Desmond hurried to excuse himself. "Do forgive me, Miss Doyle. It did not occur to me that I was manipulating you. It merely seems selfish to order sandwiches for myself and none for you—"

"I understand," said Susan, her expression somewhat softened. "I suppose I would feel the same if I were in your place."

"And you will forgive me?"

"Yes, of course," said Susan. "I understand your intentions were good. It's only that I am so tired of people trying to make me feel badly, merely because I will not do what they want me to do."

She spoke so pathetically that Desmond resolved on the spot to say no more about sandwiches. Indeed, he no longer felt much like eating any himself, but fearing his abstinence would seem like a reproach to Susan, he made himself stop at the inn, buy a couple of sandwiches, and eat them. Susan, with a stoicism he could not help admiring, refrained from throwing so much as a glance in his direction as he ate, but instead conversed calmly about the progress of the barley crop and the probability of its being a good year for cattle.

Soon after this, they began to reach the outskirts of London. Susan sat up straighter on the curricle seat, looking about her with interest. "I have never been in London before," she told Desmond. "The biggest town I was ever in was Colchester, and that was when I was twelve. My, but London is big—and crowded—and *noisy.*"

Desmond laughed. "One soon becomes accustomed to that," he said. "And the part of town your aunt lives in will not be so noisy as this. With luck, we'll be there within the hour.

Their luck held to the extent that they reached Mrs. Andrew Doyle's town house within the space of an hour. But beyond that good fortune seemed to have deserted them, for the knocker was off the door, and there was an ominous air of vacancy about the house's shuttered windows.

"I'll go make inquiries," said Desmond. "Perhaps some of the staff is here, even if your aunt isn't."

He tried to speak cheerfully, but in his heart he feared the worst. Susan, too, looked as though she was fearing the worst as he got down from the curricle and mounted the steps to the door.

Five

Since there was no knocker on the door, Desmond was reduced to hammering on it with his fist. For a time he feared the house was completely unoccupied, but eventually he heard shuffling footsteps and the grating of a key in the lock. The door was opened by an elderly dame, who admitted under pressure to being Mrs. Doyle's housekeeper but utterly disclaimed any knowledge of Susan.

"I don't know nothing about any niece," she said, looking suspiciously toward Susan. "And Mrs. Doyle never said nothing about anyone coming to visit her. 'Twould be a funny thing if she had, for she's on the Continent this minute and the whole of the staff on holiday but me and the cook. No, sir, I wouldn't dare let anybody into the house without Mrs. Doyle's leave. Orders are orders, and I never had any orders about *her.*" She inclined her head in Susan's direction.

Desmond could see arguing would accomplish nothing. The woman was only fulfilling her duty as she saw it. He could hardly blame her for looking askance at Susan. The excuses he had given for her sudden, unheralded appearance on her aunt's doorstep seemed weak even to his own ears, and he was afraid if he urged her case too strongly the housekeeper might start questioning them anew. The last thing Susan needed was to be embroiled in a scandal immediately on her arrival in London. So Desmond merely asked the housekeeper for Mrs. Doyle's direction on the Continent, thanked her for her time, and returned to the curricle.

He had no need to speak, for Susan had gathered the true state of affairs from the housekeeper's gestures. "Is my aunt indeed not home?" she said, looking more apprehensive than ever. "What shall I do?"

Desmond had been asking himself this same question. He could hardly take Susan to a hotel and abandon her there, even if he could find a hotel willing to take her without baggage or maid. Of course both might be obtained here in the metropolis, but they would cost money, and Susan was by her own admission short of ready cash. Obtaining them would also take time, and he could not forget that Susan must be very hungry by now. There was a weary droop to her slim shoulders that filled him with compunction. Before he quite realized what he was doing, he spoke.

"I think the first thing to do is to get something to eat. After that, we can discuss what will be best for you to do."

This speech came out sounding more autocratic than he intended, and he feared it might provoke another assertion of independence, but Susan only said dully, "All right." It was clear her aunt's absence had been a heavy blow to her.

She did not even ask where they were going to eat. This, too, was a question exercising Desmond's wits. The quarter of town in which her aunt resided was a long way from any eating establishments. He hated to make Susan endure another long drive on top of everything else she had endured that day, and he feared also that if he took her to an inn or public hotel to dine, someone he knew might see her there with him. It wasn't exactly the thing for a gentleman to dine alone with a young lady, and if the gentleman in question was on the verge of becoming engaged to another lady, it was likely to provoke a full-fledged scandal.

This, however, was the least of Desmond's worries at the moment. He was too concerned about Susan's reputation to worry much about his own. If the thought of Annabelle did cross his mind, he dismissed it by telling himself that she ought to understand he could not abandon a woman in such extremity as Susan. Once again, he preferred not to dwell on the fact his beloved had never shown herself possessed of this particular kind of understanding.

So he devoted himself to a consideration of how best to get Susan fed. The more he thought about it, the more he felt that the thing to do was to take her back to his own house and give her dinner there. It seemed paradoxical that in order to avert a scandal he was obliged to resort to such a scandalous course, but his servants could be trusted not to talk, and he was confident he could get Susan in and out of his house with her reputation unscathed.

He was a good deal less confident of his ability to get Susan to accept this plan. When he tentatively proposed it, however, stressing that they would be in his home only long enough to dine and that his servants would be in attendance the whole time, Susan surprised him by accepting at once.

"Yes, certainly, my lord," she said. "I have no objection to dining at your home." Desmond must have looked as taken aback as he felt, for Susan gave him a quizzical look. "Did you think I would refuse?" she asked.

"Well, I thought you might," said Desmond. He was a good deal embarrassed, for though he knew his intentions toward Susan were pure, he had feared she might think they were not. And the fact that she had *not* thought they were not made him feel as though there must be something impure in his intentions after all. The idea embarrassed him so much that he hastened into speech again. "You were so reluctant to have me buy sandwiches, or to be under any financial obligation to me. I thought perhaps you would consider dining in my home to be in the same category."

Susan shook her head firmly. "No, that is quite a different thing," she said. "To accept an invitation to dine with someone does entail an obligation, but it is an obligation that is paid in kind. I do not at all mind being under that kind of obligation to you, my lord, for I am sure I will have an opportunity to pay it off someday."

"I am sure you can pay me back somehow," agreed Desmond. The words sounded horribly suggestive to him as soon as they were spoken, and he hurried on, anxious to erase any wrong impression he might have given. "Besides, dining here tonight will give you an opportunity to sample this cauliflower I acquired as a result of my day's labors."

Susan laughed at this, and Desmond joined in her laughter, reflecting with relief that they seemed to have gotten over the awkward moment. Yet to his annoyance, he found now that his thoughts regarding Susan had taken a suggestive trend, he was unable to reverse it. During the short drive to his lodgings he was intensely aware of her sitting on the seat beside him, and he ushered her into his house with as much haste and stealth as if he really had been bent on seducing her.

Seeking in some obscure way to make atonement for his thoughts, he apologized to Susan for having brought her to his house to dine. "It really is not the thing for young ladies to dine in gentlemen's homes," he said.

Susan gave him an amused look. "I know that,

my lord," she said. "But I assure you I do not regard it in the least."

"Well, I want you to know I never would have suggested such a thing if I thought it would compromise your reputation. But I believe we are quite safe. I took care none of the neighbors were about when we came in, and my servants are all old family retainers who can be relied on to hold their tongues."

"I'm sure you have taken every care for my reputation," said Susan. "But indeed, my lord, I don't care particularly even if it is compromised. I made up my mind when I ran away that I wasn't going to worry anymore about such things as reputations and conventions. I am quite eager to have some new experiences, and this seems a very good one to begin with."

Desmond looked at her and experienced a shock. He had supposed her readiness to dine with him was the result of innocence, and that she simply did not realize how improper it was to dine at a gentleman's bachelor residence. Now he realized she did know and had deliberately embraced the experience as an adventure. The realization gave him a sudden, startling insight into Susan's state of mind. It also filled him with consternation when he contemplated its long-term consequences. What might not be the result of a pretty, sheltered young woman deliberately casting aside convention to embrace adventure?

The thought nagged him as he gave orders to Reese, his manservant, for dinner to be served as soon as possible. His household staff was a small one, consisting only of Reese and the cook. Reese, however, was a whole retinue of servants in himself. His official position was ostensibly that of Desmond's valet, but over the years he had expanded his role to embrace that of butler, footman, and general factotum. Desmond had often protested at his taking so much work upon himself and on more than one occasion had tried to hire underlings to assist him, but it had been eventually borne in upon him that Reese preferred to run the household all but single-handedly. It was a matter of pride with him to fulfill his manifold roles to perfection, and since his pride worked so wholly to Desmond's advantage, Desmond had by and large allowed him to have his way.

Today, however, Desmond found himself a little nervous as he gave Reese the order to have dinner served immediately. "I know you and Mrs. Murphy did not expect me back until much later," he said apologetically. "I expect the preparations for dinner are hardly begun. But if you could hurry things along a little, I would greatly appreciate it."

"There will be no trouble in the world in having dinner served as soon as you please, my lord," said Reese, drawing himself up proudly. "I will speak to Mrs. Murphy and assist her in the preparations if necessary."

He sounded affronted that Desmond should think he might not be able to put dinner on the table at a moment's notice. Desmond was relieved by his words, but only in part, for the more difficult part of his task still lay ahead of him. In addition to requesting an early service of dinner, he had somehow to acquaint Reese with the fact that Susan would be sitting down with him. He would then have to make it clear that, though irregular, this situation was perfectly aboveboard. Of course Reese would hardly presume to question his actions even if he did not approve of them, but Desmond wished to present the case so that he might, if possible, gain Reese's sanction of all he meant to do for Susan. He reasoned that if Reese, a notorious high stickler, agreed he was doing rightly, then he could rid himself of the nagging sense he was participating in an illicit adventure.

So as Reese turned to go, Desmond cleared his throat and said, "Oh, and Reese, before you speak to Mrs. Murphy, I wanted to mention that I won't be dining alone tonight. There is a guest—a young lady guest—who will be sitting down with me."

Reese bowed and said, "Very good, my lord."

It was impossible to guess from his expression how he had interpreted this news. Desmond hurried on, anxious to waylay even a momentary suspicion that he might be playing a Lothario's role. "It is a very trying situation," he said. "I do not know if I did right to bring the young lady here, but under the circumstances I could think of nothing better to do." He went on to describe briefly Susan's dilemma, avoiding any mention of her abortive wedding but describing in full her journey to find her aunt and her consternation at finding her abroad. "Indeed, until I can get in touch with Mrs. Doyle, I am at a loss to know what to do with the poor girl. She came away so suddenly that she has neither baggage nor maid, and you know no respectable hotel would take her without them."

Reese shook his head emphatically. "No, indeed! It would appear the young lady had no choice but to put herself in your hands, my lord," he said.

He spoke sympathetically, yet there was an ironical note in his voice that made Desmond look at him sharply. Because of his own preoccupation with the subject, he imagined Reese must be thinking he had brought Susan there to seduce her—even perhaps that he had already seduced her and was preparing to install her as his mistress.

As displeased as Desmond was by this idea, he would have been still more displeased had he known Reese's real thoughts. Like Dirk, Reese had suffered agonies at the thought of his master's allying himself with a low-born baggage like Annabelle Windibank. Yet he had seen no way to avert the coming disaster. It was therefore a complete surprise to hear his master had brought an unknown young lady to dine privately with him in his home. Reese was not so sanguine as to assume this turn of events must necessarily be a favorable one, however. After all, the unknown girl might be as much an adventuress as Miss Windibank.

Ten to one she's a scheming baggage, too, he told himself cynically. Still, there was always a chance the unknown young lady might serve as a counterbalance to the specious charms of Miss Windibank. Reese resolved to have a look at her himself and see whether she was likely to prove a friend or foe.

His first glimpse at Susan reassured him greatly. His trained eye recognized her as a lady at a glance, and none of your shabby genteels either. Of course it was not precisely the thing for young ladies of gentle birth to dine alone in a bachelor's house, but Reese, watching Susan surreptitiously throughout the meal, soon acquitted her of any mercenary intentions. There was nothing of flirtation in her manner, and equally nothing of the clinging vine. True, she was rather silent until she had consumed a bowl of sorrel soup, a large serving of roast pike, and the best part of a roast pullet, but this appeared to be merely the effects of hunger, for she became quite animated as the meal wore on, arguing with Desmond over the best way to get in touch with her aunt on the Continent.

Desmond himself was a good deal concerned by this problem. He felt no time should be lost sending for Mrs. Doyle, even if it entailed the expense of a special messenger. Susan, however, could not be brought to agree to this course. Now that she had eaten, her spirits had rebounded with a vengeance, and the Bohemian tendencies that had so alarmed Desmond earlier came springing to life once more.

"I would rather not spend the money for a special messenger," she said firmly. "It's no matter to me if it does take several weeks to locate my aunt. In fact, I would rather it did take a little time, for it's ten to one she packs me off to the country again as soon as she gets home. If she really had been going to bring me out, she would have done so years ago."

"But my dear girl, don't you see that until your aunt comes home you will have nowhere to stay?" said Desmond, trying to hide his exasperation. "Not unless you go back to your other aunt in the country. And though I can't help thinking that's probably the best solution, I am sure you would rather not do so."

"Indeed I would not," said Susan vehemently. "I have no intention of returning to Aunt Sarah. I would very much rather stay in London."

"Well, then, we must get in touch with your other aunt as soon as possible. That's the only way you will be able to stay here, for I assure you it is quite ineligible for you to stay by yourself."

Susan raised clear brown eyes to his face. "I don't see that at all," she said. "I am twenty years old, my lord, almost twenty-one. And I have money—or will have, when I sell my jewels. I see no reason in the world why I cannot stay in London by myself."

"You can't stay here by yourself because it isn't the thing for young ladies to live alone with no chaperone or duenna," said Desmond, trying to speak evenly. "If it became known you had done so, you would have no chance of ever establishing yourself respectably again."

Instead of looking convinced by this argument, Susan merely looked amused. "But, you see, I really don't care tuppence about establishing myself respectably, my lord," she said. "It's as I told you before. I've been bound hand and foot all my life by respectability, and I'm tired, tired, *tired* of it." She accompanied each repetition of the word with a rap of her knife handle on the table. "Say I send a special messenger to call Aunt Theo home, and say she does decide to bring me out this Season. What then? I'll be back to being told what to do and what to wear, back to not being able to call my soul my own. I would much rather bring *myself* out. I've dreamed all my life of being able to do as I please, and now there's no one to stop me. Of course I will let Aunt Theo know I'm here, but there's no need to hurry about it. I intend to have a holiday first, and if I lose my reputation, so be it."

Desmond looked at her in despair. He felt sure she did not understand how disastrous such a loss would be. "But where do you intend to stay?" he asked. "You know it may take some time to sell your jewels, as I mentioned before. And as I also mentioned before, no decent hotel will take you without maid and baggage."

Susan gave him an indulgent look. "I know you keep saying that, my lord, but I think you are exaggerating. There must be plenty of young women in London who can't afford to keep a maid. It stands to reason they must stay *somewhere*. I am sure if I do a little searching, I can find someplace that will take me, even without a maid and baggage."

The thought of the kind of place she was likely to find on such a search filled Desmond with horror. Again he looked at Susan despairingly. She only smiled and went on eating her pullet with unimpaired relish, however. Reese was discreetly hovering at the sideboard, pretending not to hear this conversation, but Desmond, glancing his way, encountered such a look of sympathy that he was emboldened to appeal to him as an ally. "Reese, you know London even better than I do," he said. "Don't you agree it would be ill-advised for Miss Doyle to attempt to set up housekeeping on her own?"

"Indeed I do, my lord," said Reese with emphasis. "I would strongly advise against her attempting such a plan."

Susan's face assumed mulish look. "Well, what *would* you advise? I tell you plainly that I'm not going to return to Aunt Sarah."

"My advice would be to hire a special messenger, as I told you, and send word to your Aunt Theodosia that you are here. She will no doubt be able to suggest a course of action that will be mutually acceptable to you both," said Desmond, hoping desperately this was not overstating the case.

Susan, however, absolutely refused to take his advice. "I am sure you mean well, my lord, but I have had enough of relatives telling me what to do," she said. "I want to be independent for a while."

"But you don't know what risks you would be taking! Not merely with your reputation, either. There are some unsavory characters in London. Living by yourself, you would be vulnerable to all sorts of rascality, with theft being the very least of it."

It was easy to tell from Susan's face that these arguments were having no effect. Her mind was clearly made up to embrace freedom at any cost. Frantically Desmond racked his brain for a solution. The only solution that presented itself was so scandalous that he hesitated to suggest it, but at least it would preserve Susan's safety even if at the cost of her reputation. And her reputation would be sacrificed in any case if she set up housekeeping on her own. He glanced at Reese, standing at the sideboard. Reese's face was its usual polite mask, but his eyes met Desmond's, and Desmond had the oddest sense he knew and was silently approving the plan that was in his mind. Whether this was the case or not, Desmond was encouraged to take the plunge.

"Look here," he said, "how would it be if you stayed here with me?"

Six

To Desmond's relief, Susan seemed not at all shocked by his proposal. "Stay here?" she repeated. "Here in your home you mean, my lord?"

"Yes, here in my home," said Desmond. In a last effort to salvage respectability, he added, "I could vacate the house and let you stay here alone, while I removed to a hotel."

Knowing Susan pretty well by this time, however, he was not surprised when she put an immediate quietus on this idea. "That would be putting you out, my lord," she said decidedly. "I couldn't think of making you leave your house."

"Very well, then," said Desmond with resignation. "I will stay here, too, and you may have the guest chamber."

Susan, considering this idea, said she thought it might do. "But you must allow me to pay you for my board and keep," she told him. "That is the only way I could think of staying here."

Desmond had expected this caveat and consented to accept payment for Susan's board and keep, though he privately resolved to make the payment as nominal as possible. Even with this idea to comfort him, however, he felt not entirely happy about the arrangement. "You know that even if we make the matter a business arrangement, that will not make it any more proper for you to be staying here with me," he said. "I tell you frankly I would rather see you with your aunt in Barnhart. But since you are set against returning to her, it seems to me this is much the best course to follow until such time as your other aunt can take charge of you."

Susan lifted her chin. "You know I never asked you to appoint yourself my guardian, my lord," she said. "If my staying here will be a bother to you, then I would rather go somewhere else."

"I should be much more bothered worrying about your safety if you were living somewhere else," returned Desmond with asperity. "This way, I can at least see you come to no harm—or as little harm as is possible under the circumstances." Seeing that Susan looked affronted by these words, he hastened to qualify them. "It is harm to your reputation I mean. But I trust that by taking reasonable precautions, we may be able to keep your staying here a secret. Still, there's always a chance it may get out, and if so, God help us both!"

Instead of being sobered by these words, Susan gave a gurgle of laughter. "Yes, wouldn't there be a scandal?" she said. "But if I do indeed stay with you, my lord, then a scandal would suit me as little as it does you." In a serious voice, she continued, "I should not like to make trouble for you when you have been so kind to me."

Desmond was mollified by her words. "I am only glad if I can help," he said. "In truth, I can see why you wish to make the most of your freedom while you have it. I wouldn't mind taking you about a bit myself, only it would be so awkward if anyone I knew saw us together. They would be bound to ask who you are and how I became acquainted with you, and then the fat would be in the fire."

Susan, tilting her head, considered this. "Perhaps you could say I am a cousin of yours, up from the country," she suggested. "You could call me by a false name."

"Chloe de Havilland?" suggested Desmond with a smile.

Susan laughed but shook her head. "I'm afraid that wouldn't serve," she said. "I am forgetting about Aunt Theo. If she *should* decide to present me this Season, then everyone would learn Chloe de Havilland is not my name and that I am not related to you at all. And that would look rather suspicious."

Desmond, with a straight face, agreed this circumstance would look suspicious.

Susan, meanwhile, was thinking deeply. "I have it!" she announced at last. "I will get a wig and disguise myself whenever I go out in public. Then if I happen to be with you and someone you know sees us together, you can say I am your cousin Chloe de Havilland who is up from the country. And then if I should meet them later, after I'm presented, it would never occur to them that Chloe de Havilland and I are the same person."

Desmond agreed this would be a fine plan. He was privately amused at Susan's childish pleasure at the notion of disguising herself, but he had to admit her plan would avert many potential difficulties. "We'll need to get you a wig, then," he said. "I wonder where one goes to buy such a thing?"

As the question was merely a rhetorical one, Desmond did not expect any answer. He was thus considerably surprised when Reese gave a deprecating cough. "I believe I might be able to assist you in that, my lord," he said. "And I also have some small acquaintance with the—er—cosmetic arts. If you will allow me to lend a hand, I will undertake to see that the young lady's own mother would not recognize her."

Both Desmond and Susan looked at him in surprise. Reese continued, reddening slightly, "I beg your pardon if I am speaking out of turn, my lord, but I once served as a dresser to a gentleman in the theatrical profession, back when I was just starting out in service. A very long time ago it was, but I've never forgotten my time behind the footlights, and I don't believe I've lost my knack with a grease pencil, either."

"Reese, is there *anything* you can't do?" said Desmond, regarding his servitor with awe. "You never told me you had worked in the theater!"

"It was all a very long time ago, my lord. And of course the theater isn't what you might call a *respectable* profession. In general I prefer not to talk about my experience behind the footlights, for it's not the kind of thing to add to my consequence—or to yours, either. Indeed, I'm bound to say I saw some things in my time that were what you might call scandalous. Still, it was all rather exciting," finished Reese, in a voice of nostalgia.

Desmond was charmed by this unexpected light cast on the character of his servitor. But thinking it better not to pursue the subject in Susan's presence, he merely requested that Reese purchase a wig and such other supplies as might be needed to render Susan unrecognizable by any present or future acquaintances. Reese promised to do so as soon as the shops should open on the morrow. "What color wig would the young lady prefer?" he asked, turning to Susan.

It would never have occurred to Desmond to ask this question. Somehow, he had simply assumed any wig to be purchased would be a blonde one. Perhaps it was because he had always thought Annabelle's golden tresses the loveliest thing in nature. At any rate, if asked, he would have given it as his unhesitating opinion that any woman, given the choice, would prefer to be blonde. He was thus surprised when Susan answered promptly, "A dark wig, if you please! I've always wanted to have dark hair." She drew a sigh of pleasure. "It will be lovely to be a brunette. You can't think what a cross it is to have red hair."

Reese, smiling indulgently, said he thought she could be made into a very creditable brunette. Susan, looking pleased, told him she would give him the money to buy the wig and other things after dinner. "I should have enough for that, I trust," she said. "Then once I have the wig, I can set about selling my jewels to buy the other things I need."

Desmond said nothing to this, but in addition to the problem of Susan's lodging, he had also been doing a good deal of thinking about her jewels. He thought he had a plan, but he preferred to wait until Reese was out of the room before mentioning it to her. Accordingly, as soon as the dessert was on the table and Reese had left them to serve themselves, he spoke. "About your jewels, Miss Doyle," he said. "I have been thinking, and I don't believe there will be any necessity for you to sell them, at least not immediately."

"Oh?" said Susan. She looked at him doubtfully. "I must confess I would rather not sell them if I did not have to. They were Mother's and very precious to me on that account. But I can see no other way to get the money I need to live if I do not sell them."

"Yes, of course," said Desmond. "But it seems a shame to sell your jewels only because of that. I believe the best course might be for you to let me act as your banker while you are in town. Not to *give* you the money," he stressed, seeing Susan's frown. "Merely to lend it to you. I would take the jewels and hold them in security while advancing you money on their value."

Susan was looking doubtful again, but she made

no immediate objection. Encouraged, Desmond went on to explain the details of the transaction. "It's no different than if you took the jewels to a pawnbroker. If it somehow happened you could not pay me back the monies I advanced to you, then I would be able to sell the jewels and be nothing out. Conversely, if your aunt insists on repaying me as soon as she returns from the Continent, as I expect, then I will equally be nothing out. Either way you would not be in debt to me, and if we follow this plan you would be able to get your jewels back someday, which might not be the case if you sold them."

Susan was regarding him with awe. "What a wonderful plan," she said. "How clever you are, my lord! I never thought of pawning my jewels, only of selling them."

Desmond was pleased by her admiration. It crossed his mind that Annabelle seldom gave him much in the way of praise. She was a great deal more likely to call him stupid, though in such a pretty, playful way that the word carried no real sting. Still, it was pleasant to be thought clever by someone, even over such a trifle as this. He resolved Susan should find his terms lenient beyond those of any commercial pawnbroker, and if possible he would refuse to make a profit on the transaction at all. He counted upon her ignorance of the profession to lend credit to the pleasant fiction that pawnbrokers allowed the redemption of pawned objects for the same sum they had advanced for them.

With these altruistic thoughts, he sat watching indulgently as Susan polished off a second helping of strawberries and cream. At last she pushed away her plate with a sigh of repletion. "I was *so* hungry," she told Desmond. "I can't recall ever being so hungry before."

"No wonder, if you have not eaten all day," said Desmond. He hesitated, then went on in a tone he strove to make matter-of-fact. "I suppose I should show you to your room now. You must be very tired after all the excitement you have had today."

Susan owned that she was feeling tired. As Desmond helped her from her place at the table and led the way to the guest bedchamber, he had to fight down a rising embarrassment. He had been trying all during dinner to think of Susan in strictly impersonal terms and had succeeded tolerably well up to a point, but somehow the mention of bedchambers had reminded him again that she was an attractive young lady and he a man with the usual masculine urges. He stammered out something about hoping she would be very comfortable and for her to ring if she needed anything. This reminded him of another issue. "I suppose you—er—will need help in undressing," he said, his eyes on the flower-garlanded carpet. "I keep no maids, but Mrs. Murphy, my cook, sleeps on the premises. I am sure she would be happy to render any assistance you might need."

Susan thanked him, but said she did not require Mrs. Murphy's services. "I am used to dressing and undressing myself," she explained to Desmond. "I am sure I can manage quite well without any help. But thank you all the same, my lord."

Desmond wished her a good night and fled.

Going to his own room, he sat down on the end of his bed and mentally shook himself. It was ridiculous that he, a man of the world, should let himself be disturbed by a chit of a girl scarcely out of the schoolroom. After all, he felt no attraction to her, or at least none besides that which might be attributed to the obvious appeal of her pretty face and youthful figure. That was the poorest possible reason to let her presence unsettle him, especially since it was obvious she felt no personal attraction toward him at all. Clearly she looked upon him as a kind of brother or father figure. She had hesitated not at all to put herself in his power, even to the extent of sharing his home, and she never would have done that if she suspected for a moment he might cherish improper intentions toward her.

Desmond told himself he did not cherish improper intentions toward her. His intentions were nothing but good, which only made it all the more annoying that he could not get the image of Susan in the next bedchamber out of his head. He drew upon the image of Annabelle as a countermeasure against such thoughts, but somehow her image seemed no longer so tantalizing as it had only that morning. It was as though she were a waxen doll, lovely but inanimate, who might please the eye without in any way inflaming the senses.

But that's ridiculous, Desmond told himself. Whatever Annabelle was, she was definitely not inanimate. The way she walked, the way she talked, the witching way she smiled were half the charm of her. It was odd that he could not seem to summon a clearer picture of her to mind. Somehow Susan's freckled face and spritely figure seemed to be interfering with his imaginative powers. Desmond was appalled at himself. Could he possibly be so fickle that a single afternoon spent with a chance-met stranger could shake what he had thought to be eternal love?

Desmond assured himself he was not fickle. It was not as though he had fallen in love with Susan at first sight, or anything of that sort. He felt quite confident she was not the sort of girl to appeal to him at all. She was an attractive little thing, and he admired the way she had coped with the day's difficulties, but she possessed quite as many irritating qualities as endearing ones. What he felt now was merely the force of propinquity at work. There was, evidently, a good reason why society frowned on young ladies sharing the bachelor lodgings of gentlemen, however well intentioned those gentlemen might be.

Still, he was committed now, and his conscience assured him he had done right to take Susan under his wing. She was a pretty young girl with no real knowledge of the world who was currently rebelling against convention and society, and she was adrift in the city of London with no guardian near at hand whose authority she would accept. Taken altogether, these factors must render her vulnerable to forces far more dangerous than anything posed by his own primitive urges. It wasn't as though he couldn't resist such urges, Desmond assured himself. Still, before he went to bed that night, he resolved that the very next morning he would, at his own expense, send a special messenger to Theodosia Doyle on the Continent and summon her back to London with all speed.

Seven

Like Desmond, Susan was obliged to read herself a lecture as she prepared for bed that night.

It had been a day such as she had never lived through before and hoped never to live through again. Exhilarating as it was to know she had broken free of the tyranny of pleading, reproaches, and tears that had held her captive so long, she could not help feeling uneasy and even a little ashamed when she reflected on the course she had taken to achieve this end. One does not throw off the effects of a proper upbringing all in a day, no matter how strong the provocation.

Indeed, try as she might to justify herself, Susan could not help cringing when she recalled her offenses against propriety that day. She had jilted her cousin at the altar. She had flouted the advice of an aunt who had stood in the place of a parent to her since the age of thirteen. She had run away from home with not even a note to excuse or explain her conduct. She had then thrown in her lot with a man who, for all his kindness, was a perfect stranger to her. And now here she was, lying in his guest bedchamber, with he himself lying only a room away. It was enough to make any girl uneasy, even one who was resolved to cast convention to the four winds and embrace freedom with both arms.

Over and over Susan grappled with her conscience, telling herself she had done the only thing possible. *I had to run away,* she assured herself. *If I had stayed, Aunt and Mortimer would have bullied me into going through with the wedding somehow. Anything's better than being married to Mortimer.* This was undeniably true, so why should she feel so guilty about it? After careful examination, Susan decided it was because she was ashamed of her weakness in letting herself be bullied in the first place. If she had been a more resolute girl, she would have stood up to her relations from the beginning, and there never would have been any question of her marrying Mortimer.

Even when she had been describing her plight to Desmond that afternoon, she had found it hard to explain why she had been so weak. Now, in the present hour and from her present perspective, she felt she had been not merely weak but hopelessly poor-spirited. This was not the only reflection that troubled Susan's thoughts. In addition to worrying about her conduct in regard to Mortimer, she was also worrying about her conduct in regard to Desmond.

When she had first caught sight of him in his curricle, Desmond had appeared to her not so much a man as a means to an end. He had represented escape in capital letters, and she had not hesitated to fling herself into his path and beg him to take her up. It had seemed a case of necessity, one of those desperate situations that called for desperate measures. Now, however, as Susan contemplated her actions, she realized she had been dreadfully forward. The only balm for her conscience was that Desmond had not seemed to mind. If he *had* minded, he would hardly have lent his assistance so generously as he had done.

And there could be no doubt he *had* been generous. He had helped her every step of the way and would have done even more for her if she had allowed it. Indeed, the only way in which he had behaved at all ungenerously was when he had made those disparaging remarks about her youth and inexperience. At the time, Susan had not minded them so much, partly because she had been so grateful for the help he was rendering her, and partly because he was a good deal older than she was. Her experience had been that older persons did generally criticize the behavior of younger ones.

But it had been gradually dawning on her that Desmond wasn't so very much older than she was. She had been deceived at first by his stern manner when he had demanded to know her name and the circumstances of her running away, but later, when she had had an opportunity to look him over more closely, she had realized he could not be much more than thirty. He wasn't as stern as he had first appeared, either. When he had been telling her the story of his adventures with the kitten and the cauliflowers, for instance, he had shown flashes of a delightful sense of humor. Still, for a man, he seemed almost ridiculously prim and proper.

This had surprised Susan. From various works of literature, along with certain veiled comments made by her aunt, she had gathered that the male sex was more prone to encourage females in misbehavior than to discourage them. That had certainly not been the case with Desmond, however. It was easy to see he hadn't approved of the way she had jettisoned her unwanted bridegroom, though he had been sympathetic enough when it came to the point. Still, Susan found his disapproval rankled. It hadn't seemed to matter as long as she had thought him a staid middle-aged person, but now that she realized him to be a relatively young man and a personable one to boot, she found it did matter. No doubt her attitude was irrational, but there it was.

There were other points, too, connected with Desmond's being a relatively young and personable gentleman, that made Susan uncomfortable. When she had agreed to stay in his home, she had been glad to be spared the business of finding lodgings in London. It was all very well to talk of being independent, but once she had seen London and grasped something of its extent, she could not imagine how she would have gone about this business alone. Tired, bewildered, and still under a mental strain from the events of the day, she had closed eagerly with the idea of staying with someone she knew and trusted. Yet now, as she lay in Desmond's bed with Desmond's bedclothes covering her and Desmond himself lying in the next chamber, she realized how little real knowledge she had of his character. True, he had shown himself trustworthy so far, but perhaps that was merely a ploy to throw her off her guard.

When one considered the matter impartially, Susan told herself, one was bound to admit it was a highly questionable proceeding for a man to invite a young woman to stay with him in his home. Of course, Desmond had pointed this out himself, but Susan had been experiencing a reaction against convention and propriety at the time, and she had laughed his scruples to scorn.

Now that her reaction had passed, she no longer felt so much like laughing. Instead, she wondered how she could have consented to such a dubious scheme. It must be that she really *was* weak—weak and easily swayed. Susan looked uneasily around the handsomely furnished guest bedchamber. Had she exposed herself to disgrace by coming here? She knew pretty well in what form such disgrace might come, for though her aunt had tried to keep her in ignorance of the facts of life, her country upbringing had mitigated against such ignorance.

Susan found it hard to imagine the proper, well-bred gentleman she had ridden with that afternoon suddenly bursting into her bedchamber and attempting to ravish her by force, but neither could she quite dismiss the possibility from mind once it had occurred to her. She lay awake for the best part of an hour, straining her ears to catch a stealthy footfall that might herald Desmond's approach.

At last she could bear it no longer. Rising, Susan went to the door of the bedchamber and turned the key in the lock. She would have liked to push her chest of drawers across the door as an additional precaution, but on trial she discovered that useful piece of furniture was too heavy for her to move by herself; so she made do with a chair instead. She then returned to bed, lay down, and fell asleep almost instantly.

Since the previous day had been such a strenuous one, she might have expected to sleep late. But being used to country hours and a much quieter environment, she woke with the birds and for a moment lay gazing around the unfamiliar room, puzzled to know where she was and how she came to be there. Recollection of the previous day's events soon came flooding back, however, along with a memory of her fears concerning Desmond. In the clear light of morning, Susan was ashamed of having harbored such fears. They seemed not merely ridiculous but presumptuous.

Jumping out of bed, she went to the door, removed the chair in front of it, and turned the key in the lock. She was relieved to think there was now no clue to show her foolish fears of the night before. She would hate to appear mistrustful, after all Desmond had done to help her.

Somewhere far off she could hear a strident female voice raised above a clatter of pots and pans. This she concluded to be the cook in the midst of breakfast preparations. She could hear no sound of anyone stirring in the bedchamber next to hers, however. Probably Desmond was not yet awake. She remembered what he had said about people in London keeping much later hours than in the country. He had been visibly amused to find her so ignorant of the ways of the fashionable world. Susan flushed to think how ignorant she must have appeared to him. He had been very kind and excusing of her ignorance, but still she felt galled by the memory. She had no doubt she had appeared a veritable child to him. Somehow that idea rankled as much as the idea that he did not approve of her.

But I can't help being ignorant, she reminded herself. *There's no way I could be anything else, considering the way Aunt Sarah has kept me in cotton wool.* Once more, Susan registered a vow to see and experience as much as she could during her time in London. "London," she whispered aloud. The thought that she was really in the great metropolis sent a shiver of excitement down her spine. There could be no doubt London was a place where things happened. Even in the few hours she had been here, she had added greatly to her store of worldly knowledge. Perhaps there would be more new experiences for her before this day was over.

Still, it did not look as though the day had properly begun yet—from the worldly Londoner's point of view, at any rate. Susan stood hesitating with her hand on the door. She had no desire to go back to bed, but neither did she wish to call for service at an hour that would be inconvenient for Desmond's servants. She decided she would ready herself for the day as best she could without ringing for assistance. Accordingly, she made do with the cold water in her washstand to perform her morning ablutions, smoothed her hair as best she could with the tiny comb in her reticule, redressed herself in her bridal dress—how long ago it seemed since she had put it on the day before!—and looked about for something to fill the time until breakfast.

In the corner of her room was a case of books. Susan went over to inspect them more closely. Among a jumble of volumes of poetry, history, and biography were several novels. This struck her as a delightful opportunity to enlarge her worldly knowledge while simultaneously striking a blow against propriety and conventionality. Her aunt did not approve of novel reading at any time and would have regarded novel reading before breakfast as the height of dissipation. With a pleasant sense of flouting convention, Susan curled up in an armchair with the first volume of one of the novels and settled down to read.

Nearly an hour passed before the door opened and a stout woman came into the room carrying a can of hot water. "Why, you're already up, miss," said the woman, halting in surprise. "Reese asked me if I'd bring you your water, seeing as he was called out on an errand, but it looks as though I'm a bit late."

The woman sounded miffed by this circumstance. It developed that she was Mrs. Murphy, the cook for Desmond's household. She explained she had brought Susan her water to oblige Reese, despite its not properly being her place and despite being, as she told Susan, mortal busy with the breakfast. Susan suspected, however, that curiosity had played some role in her willingness to step outside the bounds of her own occupation. The whole time she was talking, she was surveying Susan with a critical gaze, and Susan was sure she suspected her of insinuating herself into the household for some nefarious purpose.

Susan found this more amusing than offensive, but for Desmond's sake as much as her own she thought it as well to allay the cook's suspicions.

"How kind of you to bring me my water, Mrs. Murphy," she said, giving the cook her sweetest smile. "I am afraid I am giving you and the rest of the staff a great deal of bother. I wish there was some way around it, but Lord Desmond thinks it best for me to stay here until other arrangements can be made." She went on to outline the circumstances of her coming to London and her aunt's unfortunate absence from home.

"Well, if that ain't a shame," said Mrs. Murphy, shaking her capped head with its festoons of multicolored ribbons. "I'm sure I hope you find this aunt of yours soon, miss. It's not the thing for a young lady like yourself to be staying in a gentleman's household, though it *is* my Lord Desmond. Still, we'll all take care that your reputation don't suffer for it, miss. If you'd like me to sleep o' nights in your room, or anything of that sort, just let me know."

Susan, reminded of her suspicions the night before, could not help blushing at Mrs. Murphy's words. "Thank you," she said. "But I don't think that will be necessary, Mrs. Murphy."

"Well, I'm glad to oblige if you should change your mind," said Mrs. Murphy. Over her shoulder, she added, "I've got breakfast just about dished up, so you can come along to the parlor whenever you've a mind to. There's nobody to call you, for Reese has stepped out, as I said before. I can't imagine what took him out so early, but he don't tell me his business, and I wouldn't lower myself to ask."

Susan was not much interested in Reese's business, so she merely nodded politely at these words. She was, on the other hand, very much interested in breakfast, so as soon as Mrs. Murphy had left, she found a marker for her book, gave a last touch to her hair before the glass, and proceeded to the parlor with all speed.

Desmond was already there, engaged in reading the *Morning Post.* "Good morning," he said, rising to his feet with a smile. "I hope you slept well?" Fortunately he was too busy seating Susan at the table to notice the blush these words elicited.

"Very well," said Susan, and went on quickly, "indeed, I slept very comfortably, my lord. But you must make allowances if I look a little disheveled. I found it hard to manage my toilette this morning without a brush or proper comb."

"You seem to have managed pretty well in spite of it," said Desmond. He had just been thinking to himself how fresh and pretty she looked, in spite of her somewhat rumpled dress. Her freckled cheeks held a delicate flush of color, her brown eyes were aglow with health and spirits, and a ray of light from the window illuminated her coppery curls with dramatic effect. Desmond, who had always thought red hair unattractive, found himself revising his opinion. Red might not compare to golden hair for sheer beauty, but it was as striking in its own way; perhaps even more striking, because more unusual.

But Desmond spent only a moment or two admiring Susan's hair before his thoughts returned to the all-absorbing problem of Annabelle.

The previous evening, he had been so taken up with Susan and her problems that he had more or less forgotten his capricious beloved. Desmond could not imagine now how this had come to pass. Of course Susan was his responsibility, but Annabelle was his life, his love, his very soul. Undoubtedly she would be displeased with him for not coming to the fete as he had promised.

Much as Desmond quailed at the thought of Annabelle's displeasure, he was an intelligent enough man to see that in the long run, it might work in his favor. It was clear from her behavior that she felt sure of him and his affections. By absenting himself from her side, she might become not so sure and—by extension—not so capricious in her behavior.

This idea had occurred to Desmond before now, but he had never had the strength to act on it. Much as he might wish to ignore the capricious orders Annabelle laid upon him, he invariably weakened at the last moment and ended up doing as she wished. He had rationalized that by doing so, he was merely following the behests of destiny. But on this occasion, destiny had clearly indicated he should not bow to Annabelle's demands. He had been thwarted on every hand in his attempts to attend the fete. Was it perhaps a sign that he should pursue a different policy in regard to her? Desmond thought it might be.

Such a policy ran directly counter to his inclinations, however. All morning he had been wondering what Annabelle had done when she received his note yesterday. She was due back in London today, for the fete had been the last of the festivities at the villa, and the house party was to break up this morning after breakfast. Desmond's normal impulse would have been to fly to her side as soon as she arrived in Town, throw himself at her feet, and reinforce his written apology with a verbal one.

Yet as he contemplated Susan's bright face across the breakfast table, he realized there were reasons why he ought to resist these inclinations even apart from personal pride. If he went to call on Annabelle today, she would undoubtedly demand to know why he had not appeared at the villa yesterday, and if he told her the truth, she would be furious. The alternative was to lie, and he disliked that idea even more than the thought of Annabelle's fury. Of course she was probably furious with him now over his nonappearance the previous day, but as matters stood now the offense could only be a general one.

If he told her about Susan, her displeasure would be given a particular and highly unpleasant focus. All in all, Desmond thought it might be better to keep away from Annabelle as long as Susan was staying with him. It could only be for a week or two, as he told himself, and this enforced absence might pay a dividend in making Annabelle value him more highly when he did finally come around. She would be less likely to take offense on the issue of Susan, too, if that young lady were already out of the picture.

Desmond did not delude himself that it would be easy to keep away from Annabelle for the space of one or more weeks. He thought he could do it, however, if the alternative was to lie. He reminded himself whimsically that Susan had told him he was a poor liar, and he was inclined to think she was probably right.

The thought made him look at Susan. To his embarrassment, he found she was studying him with an expression of lively interest. "You look as though you were pondering the fate of nations," she said. "Is it something in the newspaper that makes you frown so, or are your eggs not cooked to suit you?"

"Neither," said Desmond with an embarrassed laugh. "I was merely wool-gathering." He then, belatedly, recalled his duties as host and inquired of Susan whether she would take tea or coffee, and if she preferred cold beef to ham. Susan said she would like beef *and* ham, accepted a cup of tea, and settled down to eat her breakfast.

She was just finishing a second helping of beef, along with a couple of buttered eggs, when Reese came into the parlor. He was carrying several parcels, and he nodded significantly to Desmond, who beckoned him toward the table with a smile.

"Reese went out early to fetch the wig and other items for your disguise," he said. "Once you are finished with your breakfast, you can see how they suit you."

Susan was so delighted with this news she clapped her hands, regardless of the fork and knife she was holding. "Oh, so *that* was Reese's early errand! Mrs. Murphy told me he had gone out, but I did not guess why." Addressing Reese directly, she added, "You got a wig? May I see it? Oh, isn't it lovely! I can't wait to see how I look in it."

Reese, smiling indulgently, said he had no doubt the young lady would look charmingly. "It's a fortunate thing your hair is short, miss," he said, surveying Susan's cropped curls with a professional eye. "It makes it that much easier to hide the real hair beneath the false."

Desmond watched with amusement as Susan, having hastily dispensed with the rest of her breakfast, went off with Reese to be fitted for the wig. It was obvious she was scarcely more than a child: only witness her delight in fancy dress! Although conscious himself of a mild curiosity to see Susan in her disguise, Desmond was a good deal more concerned with the question of how long the disguise would be necessary. He had not mentioned it to Susan, but fetching the wig had not been Reese's only errand that morning. He had also engaged the services of a special messenger, who was even now speeding his way to the Continent with an urgent message for Theodosia Doyle.

With any luck at all, Desmond calculated Mrs. Doyle would be home within a week and he would be relieved of his unwelcome burden. Not that Susan was such a burden as all that, Desmond told himself with a stirring of guilt. She was a nice little thing, but still he would be obliged to take a lot of time and trouble with her even if she stayed only for a week. Today, for instance, he would probably have to spend most of the day helping her shop for necessities like a toothbrush and hairpins and a few clothes. This he expected would be a bore, but he saw no way around it. Unless he were able to delegate this duty to Reese as he had the matter of buying the wig? If Reese took her shopping, then he himself would be free—free to call on Annabelle if he liked.

The idea was a seductive one and quickly gained the ascendancy with Desmond, in spite of the fact he had just convinced himself he would do better to stay away from her for at least a week. He was just envisioning her face, her smile, and the possibility she might relent enough to kiss him when he had made his apology, when a voice jubilantly broke in on his reflections.

"What do you think, my lord?"

Desmond looked round, half annoyed at the interruption. Then he forgot to be annoyed, for the vision that stood before him was sufficient to drive every other consideration from his mind. He half rose to his feet, staring with all his might.

Susan stood before him—at least he supposed it was Susan, though so complete had been her metamorphosis that she looked not the same girl at all. The tumble of red curls was hidden beneath a mass of jetty ringlets that clustered about her ears and tumbled entrancingly down her back. Her brows had been skillfully darkened, and Desmond had the impression her eyes had been enhanced also, though he was not sufficiently acquainted with cosmetics to say exactly what had been done. He only knew the effect was extremely alluring.

He gazed at her with his mouth open.

Her lips parted in a smile every bit as entrancing as Annabelle's, though the comparison failed to occur to him at that moment. "You needn't answer, my lord," she said. "I never received a nicer compliment than the way you are looking at me just now. I do look nice, don't I?"

"Yes," said Desmond. "You look *beautiful.*" He spoke with reverence, for it truly seemed a matter for reverence. He felt as if a genuine miracle had been wrought in his presence. "I should never have known you if I met you on the street," he marveled. "Your hair—and your eyes!"

"And my complexion," said Susan happily. "You can't see my freckles at all. When I think what I have suffered all these years, thinking my freckles were a cross I simply had to bear! If only I had known before there were things to cover them up like this."

Truth to tell, Desmond had not even noticed the absence of Susan's freckles. He had, however, been marveling over the extreme fairness of her skin, a fairness which he supposed to be due as much to the contrast with her newly darkened hair as to any cosmetic. In the event, the effect was startling, although certainly not unattractive. Indeed, she looked remarkably lovely, so much so Desmond felt almost ill at ease with her. He laughed nervously as he said, "I don't know that a few freckles are any disfigurement. But you do look remarkably—er—handsome." Turning to Reese, he added in a more natural voice, "Reese, I've come to expect excellence from you, but I believe you've outdone yourself this time. Miss Doyle should be able to pass anywhere incognito, though certainly not unnoticed!"

"Thank you, my lord," said Reese, regarding Susan with proprietary pride. "I think the same myself."

Desmond turned again to Susan. "We can attend to your shopping now if you like," he said. "I have the whole day free ahead of me." He had forgotten there was ever any question of delegating the task of shopping to Reese. To spend his day assisting this lovely creature seemed the most natural thing in the world.

Susan said she would fetch her hat directly. "And Mrs. Murphy has loaned me her best shawl," she told Desmond. "So I need not trouble Dirk for the loan of his coat." She smiled as she spoke, but there was a little reserve in her voice that had not been there before. It was as though she had assumed a new character with her disguise and was no longer the artless young girl who had ridden beside him yesterday.

Desmond noticed the change without really analyzing it. Perhaps it was because he was having such a hard time keeping his own voice and manner on an even keel. He could not help feeling he was in the presence of a stranger. Of course, that was true to a certain extent, seeing that he had known Susan less than a day, but it was equally true that he had had no difficulty behaving as though he were Susan's uncle or elder brother during their drive from Barnhart. Now, in some indefinable way, their relations had changed. As he handed Susan into his town carriage, which he had chosen to take that day rather than his curricle, he found himself wishing, illogically, he had taken his curricle after all. He would not have minded being seen publicly with such a beauty. But that was ridiculous, he told himself sternly. He had never been the kind of man to seek prestige by parading with a series of beautiful women. In this instance, it would be definitely indiscreet for him to do so, for he loved Annabelle and hoped to induce her to become his wife. He would therefore have to be discreet in his dealings with Susan, and a closed carriage was much more discreet than a curricle, as well as more useful for hauling home any parcels they might acquire during their shopping trip.

So Desmond followed Susan into the carriage and pulled down all the shades very carefully. Susan promptly pulled them up again. "I want to *see,* my lord," she said reprovingly. "If the glare hurts your eyes, then we can leave the ones on your side down. But this is the first time I have ever been in London, and I want to see *everything.*"

Desmond could not help sympathizing with this attitude. He let the blinds go, therefore, and merely pulled his hat a little lower over his eyes, assuaging his conscience with the reflection that no one he knew was likely to be abroad this early. They proceeded first to a large emporium where brushes, combs, toothbrushes, tooth powder, and a variety of other useful and necessary articles were for sale. "Oh, my lord, they have *everything* here," said Susan, her eyes full of awe as she looked about the crowded counters. "Do you mind if I poke about a little? I never saw such a fascinating shop."

Desmond did not mind. He trailed after Susan as she went from counter to counter, deriving a good deal of amusement from the serious way she went about making her purchases. "Which of these do you think prettiest?" she asked Desmond, holding out several combs for his inspection.

"I think they all are pretty," he said with a smile.

"Yes, but I can only choose one. It will not do to be extravagant." Susan looked wistfully at the combs. "Indeed, it is very hard. I never saw so many pretty things in my life. There was never a choice like this in the shops at Barnhart."

"I think sometimes having so many choices merely makes the decision more difficult," said Desmond, smiling. "If there was only one kind to choose, you would have no trouble making up your mind."

Susan gave him a reproving look. "Yes, but that would not be making up my mind at all, my lord," she said. "That would only be accepting what I was compelled to take. It is better to have a choice even if it does make the decision more complicated. At least then one stands a better chance of being pleased—really pleased, I mean, and not merely satisfied." She looked at the combs again, then nodded with sudden resolution. "I like this one best, the one with the scrolls. The others are too fussy for my taste, or else a trifle plain."

Desmond obligingly paid for the scrolled comb, which the attendant did up in a neat parcel for Susan to take with her. They next visited a counter selling various beauty lotions and cosmetics, but Susan turned up her nose at these. "Reese says one should never wear Serkis rouge," she told Desmond. "It is very injurious to the complexion. And he said most of the powders contain lead and are very harmful, too."

"You don't need such things anyway," said Desmond, with an admiring glance at her complexion. But she shook her head with the utmost seriousness.

"On the contrary, my lord. I am wearing powder *and* rouge right now, and half a dozen other things as well. But the powder is only rice powder, which does not harm the complexion at all, and the rouge is after a receipt which Reese learned in the theater and which he made up himself over a spirit lamp."

"Indeed," said Desmond, accepting this correction with a becoming humility. Seeing he was prepared to be humble, Susan went on to deliver a very pretty little lecture about modern cosmetics, all of which information she had apparently gleaned from the infallible Reese. Desmond was amused but rather appalled, too, to learn to what lengths the female sex was prepared to go to appear attractive in masculine eyes. Self-poisoning with white lead, belladonna, and arsenic appeared to be the very least of it.

But of course none of the women I know would commit such follies, he told himself. *At least none who had any real beauty in the first place. Annabelle, for instance. She surely has no need for powder and paint.* Then he remembered an incident a few weeks before when he had been moved to catch Annabelle in an impulsive embrace. She had freed herself with a laughing rebuke, but later he had noticed that the lapel of his coat was discolored with a substance that looked very much like chalk.

Well, what of it? Desmond told himself. *Perhaps she does paint. But it sounds as though most other women do, too. It's the end result that counts, not the means to the end. Look at little Susan there. She certainly looks stunning, thanks to the rice powder and rouge and whatnot.*

He did look at Susan, and once again admitted to himself she was wholly lovely in her new guise. In some strange way, that seemed to settle the unease he had felt when it had first occurred to him that Annabelle might use cosmetics. So he accompanied Susan quite cheerfully as she went about her shopping, and when she was done, he suggested they stop and get an ice before going on to Bond Street.

Susan was amenable to this suggestion, but to Desmond's amusement she took almost as long to choose the flavor of ice she preferred as she had in the matter of the combs. "Pistachio, lemon, or strawberry?" she fretted. "Oh, dear, they all sound delightful."

"Another case of choice complicating one's decision," suggested Desmond, smiling.

Susan gave him a quick smile in return. "Yes, but I tell you I would *rather* have a choice, my lord," she said. "Even if it *does* make the decision more complicated."

"Well, in this case, I can make your decision perfectly simple," said Desmond, and ordered the waiter to bring Susan all three of the ices she desired. Susan protested at this extravagance, but Desmond told her it was his treat and he would help her eat any of the ices she could not manage. Susan agreed to this arrangement, but as it happened there was very little he was called upon to help with.

"That was *lovely,*" she said fervently as they left the pastry cook's together. "You are so very kind to me, my lord. I should be quite spoiled, I think, if I stayed with you very long."

"It's nothing," said Desmond. To himself, he reflected it was quite pleasant to spoil Susan. She was so grateful over a trifle like buying a few ices, and so unabashed in her enjoyment of them, too. Besides, he had to admit he had liked being seen in her company even among the relatively humble clientele of the pastry cook's shop. The elderly attendant had cast constant glances in her direction the whole time he was waiting on them; the youthful gentleman at the next table had been so busy staring at her that he had dripped strawberry ice on his neckcloth; and the stout gentleman with spectacles by the door had alternated between regarding Susan with admiration and Desmond with envy ever since they had come in. All this was very pleasant, and Desmond felt a distinct sense of pride as he ushered Susan out the door.

He had forgotten the old proverb about pride going before a fall. As he stepped onto the sidewalk he came face to face with Sir Stanford Kent, a gentleman of his own social set and one of his closest friends.

Eight

"Desmond, old man!" said Sir Stanford, coming to a halt on the sidewalk.

"Stan," said Desmond blankly. He cursed the ill chance that had led him to cross paths with his friend. But there was no help for it. He had to stop, and he had to introduce Sir Stanford to Susan, upon whom his friend's eyes were already resting with a mixture of astonishment and speculation.

"This is—er—my cousin," he said. "She is up from the country, and I am assisting her with some errands. Miss—er—Miss de Havilland, this is my friend Sir Stanford Kent. Stan, this is Miss de Havilland."

He had no real hope that Sir Stanford had been deceived by this speech. After stumbling so badly in giving Susan's name, the suspicion could hardly fail to arise that it was a false one. Desmond also felt his statement that she was his cousin had carried little conviction. In the event, however, Sir Stanford merely arched an incredulous eyebrow at him before turning to Susan. "I'm very pleased to meet you," he said. "You say your name is de Havilland?"

"Yes, Chloe de Havilland," said Susan, and gave him a dazzling smile.

Sir Stanford contemplated her a moment, then gave Desmond a look that said as plainly as words, *You lucky dog.* "A charming name," he said. "Are you related to the Devonshire de Havillands, by any chance?"

"No, that is quite a different branch of the family," said Susan.

She spoke with such composure that Desmond felt quite proud of her. Yet he feared Sir Stanford had been no more deceived by her words than by his own. Fortunately, Sir Stanford did not press the matter, but only said, "Well, I wish you success with your errands, Miss de Havilland. I wish you success, too, Desmond," he added with a wicked grin.

"Thank you," said Desmond, scowling at him. "Come along, Cousin." Putting an arm around Susan's waist, he began to shepherd her toward the carriage.

Sir Stanford, undeterred by Desmond's scowl, followed along behind, suggesting sights Desmond might like to show his cousin while she was in London. "You ought to go see Kean, at Drury Lane. Shakespeare, y'know, and a dashed fine show. I went last night with my aunt and uncle, or I'd suggest getting up a party and all going together. But no doubt you and your *cousin* would rather go alone in any case, eh, Desmond?"

"No doubt," said Desmond shortly, as he helped Susan into the carriage.

"Miss de Havilland, you really ought to make him take you to see Kean," said Sir Stanford, switching his attention back to Susan. "I advise you to tease him until he gives in. He would enjoy it, I know, and the outing would do him good. He really needs to take more recreation. I've told him time and again—"

But what Sir Stanford had told Desmond time and again was never known, for having got himself and Susan inside the carriage, Desmond slammed the door in Sir Stanford's face. That gentleman therefore contented himself with waving his hat after them, an unquenchable grin on his face.

Desmond sank back on the banquette with an exasperated oath. Glancing at Susan, he saw that her shoulders were shaking with laughter. After a minute, Desmond began to laugh, too. "What an idiot I am," he said. "Miss Doyle, I do apologize."

"For what?" said Susan.

Desmond hesitated. It occurred to him that perhaps Susan did not realize Sir Stanford's misapprehension. "I am afraid Stan did not believe you were my cousin," he said carefully. "I bungled the introduction so badly that he thought—he supposed—"

"That I was your *chère amie,*" finished Susan cheerfully. "Yes, I could see that's what he thought."

Desmond was relieved to find her so perceptive, but a little startled by her nonchalance. "I'm afraid so," he said. "I do apologize, Miss Doyle. If I had behaved with half as much sang froid as you did, we should have carried the scene off with perfect ease. You acted your part magnificently."

"Thank you," said Susan. "But I think that is because I was telling mostly the truth to Sir Stanford. You had mostly to tell him lies."

"That's so, I suppose," said Desmond. "And we've already agreed we are neither of us good liars!"

They smiled at each other. "Still, it won't do to bungle another introduction as I did that one," Desmond continued. "I will practice until I have 'Chloe de Havilland' on the tip of my tongue. That way, I can introduce you as my cousin without looking or even feeling that there is anything amiss."

Making good on his word, he spent the next fifteen minutes performing imaginary introductions between Susan and various other people. Susan giggled delightedly on being invited to make the acquaintance of Her Majesty, the Queen of the

Sandwich Islands, but rose and made a very credible curtsy in spite of the fact that the carriage was jolting along at a brisk pace. By the time they reached Bond Street, Desmond felt he could sustain with equanimity any introduction likely to arise.

Susan said she felt the same. "But I think it's easier for me than for you," she added. "You see, I don't feel like plain Susan Doyle when I look like this. People look at me differently—act toward me differently—and as a result I *feel* differently. It's rather odd, but quite exciting, too."

Looking at her face, Desmond could see she was enjoying herself. He found he was enjoying himself, too, even in spite of his annoyance over meeting Sir Stanford. After all, he reasoned, if he had to raise suspicions, it was as well to raise them in Stanford, who would never breathe a word about them to anyone else. This would not prevent him from teasing Desmond in private about Chloe de Havilland, of course, but if he did, it would allow Desmond to set the record straight about Susan and his relations with her. He was very anxious to set the record straight. He would not like Stan to think he was dallying with one woman while on the verge of becoming engaged to another.

But since there was no danger of Sir Stanford spreading such rumors, Desmond settled back and prepared to enjoy himself some more. They were approaching that quarter of Bond Street in which lay a number of ladies' dressmakers. Desmond ordered the coachman to stop, and he and Susan got out. "That looks a decent shop," he said, nodding to an establishment with the words LATREILLE,LTD. over the door. "Let us see if you can find what you are looking for here. What exactly *are* you looking for?"

"A new dress," said Susan promptly. "A *pink* dress." She regarded Desmond defiantly.

"Yes?" said Desmond, a trifle puzzled by her attitude. "Well, and why not a pink dress? I think pink a very pretty color."

"And I think it is pretty, too," said Susan. "But I've never been allowed to wear it. Because I have red hair, you know. When you have red hair, you aren't allowed to wear pink. It's dreadfully unfair."

"Indeed?" said Desmond, smiling. "I should call it unfair, too. Why should you not wear pink if you want to?"

"Why indeed?" said Susan. "But every time I have wanted to get a pink dress, everyone has assured me it would clash horridly with my hair."

Desmond could see the justice of this, but said kindly, "Well, there is no one to say you nay now if you choose to buy a pink dress. Let us go in and see what the dressmaker has to offer."

The dressmaker proved to have any number of pink dresses she was very glad to show the young lady. Susan was in transports as first one gown and then another was brought out and displayed for her inspection. "Oh! It's worse than the combs," she told Desmond. "However am I to make up my mind?"

Desmond laughed. "There's always the solution I used at the pastry cook's," he said.

"So there is. Perhaps I *could* get more than one." Susan looked hungrily from a rose-colored sprig muslin walking dress with matching velvet pelisse to a fashionable evening dress in apple-blossom gauze. "But I'm afraid these dresses are more expensive than ices. I don't believe I could afford to get them all, at least not until I have a better idea of how I am situated financially."

"Perhaps not all, but I am sure you could afford at least two or three," said Desmond, smiling. "I am your banker, you know, and at my last count you still had a very substantial balance with me."

"Indeed? Well—perhaps it would not hurt to get an evening dress as well as a walking dress. What your friend Sir Stanford was saying about the play at the theater sounded very interesting. I'd like to get a cheap seat and go one of these evenings."

"But you can't go to the theater by yourself," said Desmond.

"Why not?" said Susan, with a dangerous glint in her eye.

Desmond opened his mouth to explain it was improper for ladies to attend the theater unescorted. Fortunately, he remembered just in time that Susan was at war with propriety and likely to take any such caution as a challenge. "Because I would like to go see Kean, too," he said instead. "And I would take it very unkindly to be excluded from the expedition."

Susan relaxed and even smiled at these words. "Of course I would not exclude you if you wanted to come," she said. "But you didn't seem to like the idea when Sir Stanford proposed it."

Of course Desmond had not liked the idea. Strictly speaking, he did not like it even now, for he was certain he would see someone he knew at Drury Lane, and the chances were it wouldn't be someone as discreet as Sir Stanford. Still, there was nothing inherently improper about taking a lady to the theater, Desmond reflected. Even if the matter eventually reached Annabelle's ears, he thought he could explain himself. Better he should risk a little gossip than let Susan persevere in her plan to go to Drury Lane alone. He comforted himself with the thought that if they arrived early and took seats high in the gallery, they might well manage to watch the play without being seen by any of his acquaintances.

Susan, meanwhile, had turned back to the dresses and was trying to make up her mind. After a good deal of discussion with the dressmaker, she determined to take not only the walking and evening dresses, but an additional dress suitable, so the dressmaker said, for quiet evenings at home, or for the less formal sort of afternoon affair. The dressmaker had a model of this last in the final stages of completion, and she took Susan off to some inner sanctum to be fitted for it. Susan emerged a short time later, her head held high and her eyes shining as she approached the gilt sofa where Desmond was sitting. "Isn't it *lovely?*" she said.

Desmond agreed it was, though he had a little difficulty separating the dress from its wearer. The dress was of thin ivory silk with pink blossoms splashed across its breadths. There were several lace-trimmed flounces at its hem and a broad bertha of creamy lace at the shoulders. This dress did wonderful things for Susan's figure, highlighting its slenderness while also subtly emphasizing its curves, and its soft coloring made an alluring background for the cloud of dusky curls about her face. It was impossible to realize she was the same artless redheaded girl he had driven to London the day before.

Desmond was actually in danger of saying some such thing when he happened to catch the dressmaker's eye. This brought him to his senses with a jerk. He realized not only had he had been in danger of insulting Susan by comparing her previous appearance unfavorably with her present one, he was also in danger of being too warm in his praises altogether. He had told the dressmaker Susan was his cousin, and though he fancied he had done it glibly enough to carry conviction, somehow the expression on her face just now made him not so sure this was the case. "You look very handsome, Cousin," he said, drawing out his watch and pretending to consult it. "But I pray you will hurry in choosing your new finery. We must be on our way if we are to complete our day's errands."

Susan was immediately contrite. "I'm afraid I have taken more time than I ought to," she said. "But oh, I have enjoyed myself so much!" Smiling at the dressmaker, she asked, "And can you really have this lovely dress finished as early as tomorrow?"

"I can have it done *today*, miss," said the woman cheerfully. "And I daresay I can have the apple-blossom gauze finished this day also. The muslin and the velvet spencer will take a day longer, but I'll send them out as soon as they're finished." Taking up a small leather-bound book, she made a note, then looked inquiringly at Desmond. "To what address shall I send them, sir?"

Desmond gave her the address of his house, trying not to blush as he did so. Once more he fancied there was something knowing in her gaze. *But what the deuce does it matter if she thinks Susan is my mistress?* he demanded of himself. *She's got no call to be carrying tales to Annabelle, any more than Stan does.*

This reflection somewhat restored his equanimity, so he was able to meet the dressmaker's eye unwaveringly as he thanked her for assisting his cousin. She accepted his thanks with a discreet smile, wished him a good day, and bowed him and Susan out of the shop.

Out on the street once more, Susan put a rueful hand to her head. "Now I need a hat," she said. "I could tell that woman thought the one I am wearing not quite the thing, though she was too kind to say so."

Desmond started to say he saw nothing wrong with her hat, and that he thought it a very clever piece of work. Then he recalled he had already gotten in trouble through praising Susan too much and broke off in mid compliment. "There's a number of milliner's shops along here, I believe," he said. "Yes, here's one right here. Shall we go in?"

They entered the shop, and were immediately set upon by a chic Frenchwoman with a predatory gleam in her eye. "What may I do for you today?" she inquired.

"The young lady needs a hat," said Desmond.

He flattered himself that his tone was matter-of-fact, but still he felt uncomfortable. The Frenchwoman had given him a sharp look of appraisal as he spoke, obviously trying to sum up not only his financial position but the relationship between him and Susan. The conclusions she drew were obvious from her next speech. "But yes! I can sell you a hat. A lovely hat for a lovely lady." She smiled effusively at Susan, all the while regarding Desmond with a knowing air. "Is there any particular mode of hat the young lady fancies?"

"A bonnet, I think," said Susan. "A *pink* bonnet."

In an unctuous voice, Madame said nothing could look more ravishing upon Mademoiselle than a pink bonnet. She hastened away and returned a moment later with several specimens of ladies' headgear in various shades of pink. While Susan was exclaiming over these, she bustled off again, returning with another armload of millinery, and then another, until the counter around them looked like an apple orchard in spring.

Desmond was sure it would take Susan an eon to decide among so many hats. But to his surprise, she seized immediately on one bonnet she declared was just what she wanted. "Mademoiselle has good taste," said the milliner, regarding her with respect. "If I were choosing a bonnet for Mademoiselle, that is just the model I myself should select. Shall I wrap it up for you, or would you prefer to wear it?"

"Wear it, please," said Susan with delight. She set the bonnet on her head and tied the strings beneath her chin, while the milliner packed the makeshift beaver away in a bandbox.

Desmond surveyed Susan covertly as this process was going on. He decided she did indeed have good taste. The bonnet she had chosen was not so large or obtrusive as many of the others, but Desmond thought this nothing in its disfavor. It was trimmed with a spray of rosebuds at one side of the crown, and there was a frill of white lace and tulle about the brim that made an enchanting frame for Susan's face. She caught his eyes on her as she stood regarding herself in the glass and gave him a half-pleased, half-embarrassed little smile. Desmond smiled warmly in return.

"Indeed, Monsieur, she is *ravissante,*" said a voice in his ear. Desmond turned with a start, and found the Frenchwoman regarding him with an understanding smile. He opened his mouth to explain, recollected in time that he was under no compulsion to do so, and merely demanded the bill in a brusque tone.

The Frenchwoman presented it to him, an understanding smile still hovering about her lips. Having paid it, Desmond lost no time picking up the bandbox and hustling Susan out of the shop.

He looked anxiously about him as they came out on the sidewalk. There were a couple of young gentlemen lounging nearby who eyed Susan with interest, but neither of them was known to Desmond. "Where now?" he asked Susan. "Do you need anything else, or have you had enough of shopping?"

A faint flush rose to Susan's cheek. "Indeed, I need a *few* more things, my lord," she said, carefully avoiding his eye.

"What sort of things?" asked Desmond. He would have known better than to ask if he had been looking directly at Susan, but at the moment he was more concerned with making sure there was no one of his acquaintance about. Receiving no answer to his question, he repeated it a trifle louder. "What sort of things do you need?"

"*Personal* things," said Susan in an agonized whisper. This time Desmond did look at her and caught her meaning in a belated rush of comprehension.

"I beg your pardon," he said. "Of course. I understand completely." He had hard work not to blush himself as he helped Susan into the carriage and gave orders for the coachman to drive to the nearest dry goods store. Once there, he did his best to make up for his former obtuseness by putting his purse in Susan's hand and telling her he would wait outside while she made her purchases. She thanked him gratefully and vanished into the store, leaving Desmond to stand near the carriage and berate himself as an idiot. He knew she had come away from home with nothing but the clothes on her back, and it stood to reason she would have need of fresh underlinen and a nightdress, and perhaps other more personal items as well.

Without really meaning to, Desmond found himself dwelling on the various mysteries connected with the female sex. He had never been much of a ladies' man, and such amatory adventures as he had experienced during his life had all been brief and relatively impersonal. He had never dwelt on a day-to-day basis with any woman except his mother. It struck him now that he really knew very little about the female sex. This had been borne in upon him yesterday, when Susan had described the pressure that had been used to convince her to marry her cousin, and it was borne in upon him even more strongly now.

When Susan presently emerged from the store carrying a neat bundle beneath her arm, Desmond scrutinized her with a kind of awe. Young as she was, she was nonetheless conversant with the eternal mysteries of the feminine. He assisted her into the carriage, being careful not even to look at her bundle, and asked if there was anywhere else she wished to go. Susan shook her bonneted and bewigged head. "Nowhere at all, my lord," she said. "Unless—could we possibly see the Royal Menagerie? I have never seen a lion, and I have always wanted to, ever since I was a child."

"Of course," said Desmond. He smiled to himself as he gave the order to the coachman. One could, he reflected, always expect the unexpected from Susan. One moment a woman cognizant of all the mysteries of her sex; the next a child enthusiastic over lions. He looked forward to seeing in what incarnation she would appear next.

Nine

The trip to see the lions was a great success. It had been a good many years since Desmond had viewed these famous denizens of the Royal Menagerie, and he enjoyed looking at them almost as much as Susan did. They had such a good time that Desmond was moved to show her a few other interesting and picturesque spots around the city. It was late in the afternoon when they finally arrived back home.

"What a delightful afternoon it has been," said Susan as they disembarked from the carriage. "It was so good of you to show me about the city. I only hope I have not kept you from doing other things you had planned to do today."

"Not at all," Desmond assured her. The words were not a lie, for he had been having such a good time that he had actually forgotten about Annabelle and the reckoning awaiting him. When they entered the house, however, the sight of a note sealed with a profusion of blue wax lying on the hall table speedily reminded him.

"It was delivered earlier this afternoon, my lord," said Reese, seeing the direction of his gaze. His tone was strictly noncommittal, but there was a shade of anxiety in his manner.

"Yes?" said Desmond.

Susan looked from him to Reese, then at the note

on the table. "I believe I'll go put my things in my bedchamber, my lord," she said. "Perhaps I will rest a bit before dinner."

Desmond nodded absently. He had picked up the note and was studying its superscription as Susan left the room.

Once in her own bedchamber, Susan shut the door and laid her packages on the foot of her bed. She felt all at once tired and dispirited, though her spirits had been high enough a moment before. *But that is merely because I am fatigued from shopping and sight-seeing,* she told herself.

She began to untie her bonnet strings, glancing in the mirror to assist her. Because her mind was busy with other things, she had forgotten about the wig and cosmetics, and the sight of her own reflection came as a shock to her. Susan paused to regard herself searchingly. There could be no doubt that she looked very handsome as a brunette. It had been intoxicating to receive so many admiring looks from men, and so many envious and appraising ones from women. "If I looked like this naturally, I am afraid I would soon grow conceited," said Susan aloud.

As it was, she reflected she was unlikely to grow conceited. Such good looks as she had flaunted abroad that day were almost entirely artificial. Susan found something bitter in this reflection—a bitterness that tainted the sweetness of feeling herself admired. Perhaps it was the certainty that very little of that admiration would have come to her had she appeared in her natural state. It was directed toward the wig and powder and rouge, not the girl wearing them.

I don't care, Susan told herself stoutly. *It's something to be admired, no matter how it comes about.* But in truth she felt any admiration she had received that day had been undeserved. She could not believe she would have created such a sensation if she had appeared as prosaic Susan Doyle rather than Chloe de Havilland. Even Lord Desmond, who knew better than anyone else what a false face she was presenting to the world, had shown by many unmistakable signs he preferred it to her real one.

The idea made Susan very uncomfortable. She did not like to think such things of Lord Desmond, who had been so kind to her. But in her mind's eye she could still recall the expression on his face when he had first seen her in the guise of Chloe de Havilland. Neither could she forget all the compliments he had paid her, and all the times she had caught him looking at her when he thought she was unaware. It should have been gratifying to think she had had such an effect on him, and in a way it *was* gratifying. But on the whole, Susan felt more chagrined than gratified.

Analyzing these sensations, she decided it was because she had been thinking Desmond a man of uncommon taste and discernment. She would have supposed such a man would prefer the real to the artificial, no matter how much more superficially appealing the artificial might be. But sadly, he had seemed to prefer the artificial.

Well, you didn't seriously suppose he could admire freckles and red hair, did you? Susan demanded of herself. Her intellect assured her she had not supposed anything of the kind. Yet somehow, on a purely emotional level, the knowledge Desmond preferred the artificial her to the real one hurt. And there was another emotion there as well. Examining her feelings closely, Susan was astonished to recognize it as jealousy.

It's ridiculous that I should be jealous simply because a man paid more attention to me in a brunette wig than without one, she chided herself. *Utterly ridiculous!*

Ridiculous as such jealousy was, however, Susan

could not deny its reality. On further examination of her feelings, she found to her dismay her jealousy did not stop even at this folly. There was the matter of that note lying on the hall table when she and Desmond came in, for instance. It gave every appearance of being written by a woman. Susan told herself it was none of her business whether Desmond received notes from women or not. But try though she might to dismiss the matter from mind, her thoughts kept coming round to dwell on it with jealous curiosity.

She felt somehow certain the note had not been written by Desmond's mother or sister or any other feminine relative. There was a flaunting, flirtatious look about it that did not accord with a family correspondence. Then, too, there was the way Desmond had looked when he had seen it—stricken, yet excited, as though its contents were a matter of immense importance to him. Susan felt grimly certain no mother's note ever written could have put such an expression on a man's face.

It must be from a sweetheart, she told herself. *And why not? He is an attractive man, and he comes of a noble family. I daresay he could have any number of sweethearts if he wanted them.* Considering the matter, Susan felt she could sustain with equanimity the thought of Desmond having any number of sweethearts. What made her heart smoulder with jealous ire was the thought of his having *one*—and that one the author of the blue-sealed note.

But why should I be jealous of her? Susan demanded of herself in exasperation. *It's not as though I'm in love with Lord Desmond myself. After all, I've known him barely twenty-four hours.* Yet in spite of this undeniable fact, it seemed she must be harboring some kind of feelings for him beyond the merely friendly. Why else should she feel such jealousy at the thought of his loving another woman?

"Good heavens!" exclaimed Susan aloud. The thought she might be falling in love with Desmond smote her like a bolt out of the blue. Almost she laughed, it seemed so ridiculous. *If it were true, it would be a fine case of tumbling out of the frying pan and into the fire,* she told herself. *But I don't think it can really be true. It must just be a brainstorm on my part. Lord Desmond has been so kind to me, quite like a knight in a fairy tale. Somehow I have got gratitude and love confused. Really, it's not surprising I should be confused, given all that's happened to me in the last twenty-four hours.*

These reflections partly reassured Susan, but not entirely. If she could imagine she might be falling in love with Desmond, even as part of a brainstorm, then clearly she must have some tendencies in that direction. And under the circumstances, such tendencies could be nothing less than fatal. Lord Desmond was at least ten years older than she was and a member of a noble family. He had been good enough to assist her in getting away from her aunt and Mortimer, but he had also made it clear he disapproved of her conduct. For her to turn around and fall in love with him would be an act of folly, to put it no stronger. Susan felt she had already behaved like a fool by letting herself be bullied into marrying Mortimer. It would not do to commit two errors of such magnitude.

To that end, Susan determined to be on guard in her future dealings with Desmond. *It would be a fine repayment for his kindness to embarrass him by throwing myself at his head,* she told herself wryly. Fortunately, she had become aware of her weakness early on, making her hopeful that any such eventuality might be avoided. It was not as though she were really in love with him, she assured herself. She merely had a tendency that way. Now that she knew it, she could take steps to nip it in the bud.

* * *

While Susan was making these resolutions, Desmond was grappling with some troublesome issues of his own.

He had spent several minutes merely looking at the note from Annabelle before venturing to break the seal. It was odd how reluctant he felt to open it. Even more oddly, his reluctance did not seem to proceed from any fear concerning the note's contents. He had expected Annabelle would be angry with him for failing to meet her at the fete, and though the thought of Annabelle's anger was a legitimate reason for trepidation, his trepidation seemed to have nothing to do with this. It was more that the note seemed—somehow—an intrusion.

The plain fact was he had gotten along very nicely without Annabelle that day. He had certainly thought of her now and then, but on the whole he had been so taken up with shopping and sight-seeing with Susan that thoughts of her had been thrust into the background. And after being tormented so long with Annabelle-related doubts and fears, this respite had been a great relief.

Now, however, the respite appeared to be over. He felt certain Annabelle's note would plunge him right back into his former turmoil of doubt and fear. And Desmond found himself suddenly reluctant to return to that state of mind. It was as though his soul, having gotten a taste of freedom, was rebelling against returning to its former slavery.

But this was absurd, Desmond acknowledged to himself. If his soul were enslaved, then the slavery had been one of his own choosing. And it had seemed to him there was something glorious in such enslavement. Why now should he feel as though he resented it? Was not Annabelle the same divine creature she had been before? And was not the prospect of serving such a goddess worth any suffering and sacrifice it might entail? Desmond told himself firmly it was.

But though he told himself so, he could not *feel* it was so. Over the course of the past twenty-four hours, something had happened to shake his resolution—the resolution that had been so strong in him the previous morning when he had set off to propose to Annabelle.

Desmond was horrified to recognize this wavering in his affections. Certainly there was a part of him that had regretted surrendering to Annabelle's charm, but he had felt it was at least an honorable surrender. Any man might succumb to a grand passion without compromising his essential manhood. But having once succumbed, he ought to stay that way. If he did not, he would have to admit to himself his grand passion was not a grand passion at all, but rather a tawdry self-delusion that made him look a positive ass.

Since Desmond was not about to make any such admission, he assured himself he was as much in love with Annabelle as ever. Resolutely, he broke the seal on her letter. As he unfolded it, however, he found himself thinking that there was something not quite genteel about her sprawling handwriting, as well as something verging upon the vulgar in the perfume with which she had liberally scented her missive.

The letter read:

To my lord Desmond Ryder

Sir:

Miss Windibank begs his lordship will not think anything more *about not meeting her at the Byrnes' as was* arranged *between them because she managed* very well *without him and found plenty of* gentelmen *glad to fill his* place. *If his lordship wishes to see her he will find her at her aunts* as usual *but she must* respectfully ask *he will excuse her from attending the opera with him this coming Friday as she is feeling very* fatiged.

Desmond, as he read this note, was conscious of various conflicting emotions. The most prominent was resignation. It was clear Annabelle was miffed over his failure to appear yesterday, just as he had expected. As he had likewise expected, she was making him pay for his failure by canceling their engagement for the opera Friday evening and by deliberately tormenting him with the mention of the other "gentelmen" who had been glad to take his place.

Strangely enough, the thought of those other "gentelmen" did not torment him as had been the case in the past, perhaps because the word itself had been misspelled, or perhaps merely because the whole tone of the letter was so blatantly calculated to pique. In any case, Desmond found he was more amused than piqued. He read through the letter again, noting its errors in spelling and punctuation. How had he never noticed Annabelle was so near being illiterate? Thinking it over, he realized he had never had occasion to receive a note from her before. He had only heard her speak, and in speech her occasional error in grammar was cancelled out by the allure of her cherry lips and seductive voice. On paper, however, those errors were glaring. Desmond, as he read the note through a third time, had more than ever a sensation of shackles falling off. He refused to dwell on this aspect of the affair, however.

So Annabelle did not wish to see him? Very well, he would make no attempt to see her. He would wait until such time as her mood had softened and she was willing to welcome him back to her side. It would be soon enough then to go into the question of whether he really wanted a wife who could not spell "gentlemen" and "fatigued"—or one who took a malicious and petty revenge simply because he had failed to keep an appointment through no fault of his own.

In the meantime, Desmond found he was growing hungry. It occurred to him Susan, too, was probably hungry, being still accustomed to country hours. It would not do to keep her waiting. With a heart feeling oddly light, considering he had just been cruelly snubbed by his inamorata, he rose, rang for Reese, and gave the order that dinner be served as soon as possible.

Ten

When Susan came into the parlor that evening for dinner, she was still wearing her wig and rouge and powder.

She had had a struggle with herself over this. Although it might be necessary to disguise herself in public, her conscience assured her there could be no need to do so in private. Yet she found herself reluctant to remove her disguise all the same. She stoutly denied her desire to leave it on had anything to do with the admiration she had read in Desmond's eyes when he had first seen her wearing it, but the wig stayed on, and so did the powder and the rouge and all the other little artifices. And when Reese scratched on the door to inform her the package from the dressmaker had arrived, Susan decided she might as well be hung for a sheep as a lamb. Stripping off her ubiquitous white dress, she arrayed herself instead in her new apple-blossom gauze evening dress.

The dress was lower in the neck than any she had ever owned before. Susan felt a trifle shy when she contemplated her reflection in the glass. But she reminded herself she was no longer plain Susan Doyle, but rather Chloe de Havilland, a dashing creature who would certainly not scruple to show a moderate décolletage. Still, she felt a little uncomfortable as she entered the dining parlor, where Desmond was waiting. She could not bring herself to look directly at him, but merely cast a smile in his general direction as he came forward to meet her. "Good evening, my lord," she said.

"Good evening," he said. Susan fancied a quality in his voice spoke of surprise and something else besides. But she still did not dare look at him. She kept the smile on her lips and her eyes firmly fixed on the table as he helped her into her seat.

Not until Reese brought in the soup did she risk raising her eyes to Desmond's face. He was regarding her with childlike wonderment. So flattering was this regard that Susan forgot her embarrassment and smiled spontaneously. "Is something amiss?" she asked, knowing as she spoke that her words were deliberate coquetry.

"Not at all," said Desmond. "I was merely thinking to myself that you are very fine tonight. It seems a pity there is nobody but me here to admire you. That dress was never meant to 'blush unseen on the desert air'!"

The smile froze on Susan's lips at this. She knew it was true. The dress she was wearing was far too formal and elaborate for a quiet evening at home. The wish to be admired had simply been too much for her, she now acknowledged. She was embarrassed to have been caught out in such a childish fit of vanity, and in an effort to vindicate herself, she made the first excuse that came into her mind. "I thought perhaps we might go to theater this evening," she said. "You mentioned it earlier today when we were out shopping."

Desmond looked taken aback by her words. "Did I?" he said. "I remember we spoke of the theater, but I had not realized we had spoken of going tonight."

Susan, having accomplished her object, was willing to let the matter go. She told Desmond she must have misunderstood. "It's no great matter, my lord," she assured him. "We can go some other night instead."

"To be sure we can, but if you want to go tonight, there's no reason why we couldn't. No reason at all," he added, with an inscrutable look on his face.

To Susan, the day had been so full of shopping and sight-seeing and other delights that the idea of piling a theater visit on top of it seemed an embarrassment of riches. Like most of humanity, however, she had no objection to that sort of embarrassment. "If it could be arranged, I would like very much to see Kean," she said sincerely. "But only if it can be managed in an economical fashion. You know I cannot afford to pay a great deal for mere amusement."

Desmond said gravely that gallery seats cost very little. "Reese, would you be so good as to secure us a couple of seats in the gallery for tonight's performance at Drury Lane?" he said.

"Certainly, my lord," said Reese, bowing.

This matter settled, Desmond turned his attention back to the table. He helped Susan to Scotch broth, saddle of mutton, and asparagus, and urged her to take a portion of rhubarb tart by way of dessert. Having duly served her with the tart, he took a portion for himself, but ate it with a very absent mind.

It had certainly not been part of his plan to take Susan to the theater that night. Only a few hours ago he had been congratulating himself because, apart from the encounter with Sir Stanford, they had managed to get through the day without seeing anyone he knew.

Of course he had promised earlier that he would escort Susan to the theater, but that promise had been given only because it seemed to him a lesser evil than allowing her to go by herself. In truth, he had had hopes he might never need fulfill his promise. If Mrs. Doyle was prompt about responding to his message, she would be back in London within a day or two, and the theater scheme would be quenched without any effort on his part.

Such had been Desmond's thoughts before receiving the note from Annabelle. But now he had received and read that note, he found himself in a different frame of mind. Annabelle was being so unreasonable that it seemed to him he had nothing to lose by further misbehavior. And it was not as though he were *really* misbehaving by taking Susan to the theater, he assured himself. No rule of propriety forbade a gentleman to take a lady acquaintance to the theater.

Besides, he found pleasure in the idea of indulging Susan in her whim. How her face had lit up when he had agreed they might go to Drury Lane that evening. She had looked like a child anticipating some long-awaited treat, although he was obliged to admit there was nothing else particularly childlike about her. She had looked singularly womanly and alluring in the apple-blossom gauze, although he had been leery about paying her too many compliments. The incident at the milliner's that afternoon was still strong in his mind, and he wanted no further such embarrassments. The woman had clearly thought him smitten with Susan, merely because he had made bold to admire her.

Well, why should I not admire her? he demanded of himself. The more he saw Susan, the more he found himself admiring her—not merely her appearance, but her character, too. One moment shy, the next assured; one moment soaring on the wings of fancy, the next coming down to earth with a display of hardheaded common sense. Her concern about the theater tickets was typical. She longed to see Kean act, but "could not afford to pay too much for a mere amusement."

It had been on the tip of Desmond's tongue to offer to pay for the tickets himself. He knew enough about Susan's scruples by now to be sure she would have refused his offer, however. This, too, had its charms, for he was not any too used to women who were sparing of his purse. In fact, his past experience with women right up through Annabelle was that they were glad to let him spend as much money on them as he liked and even to urge him to further expenditure. By contrast, Susan's scruples struck him as both admirable and very refreshing.

Accordingly, Desmond made up his mind such unselfishness deserved a reward. Even if the worst happened and some other lady or gentleman of his acquaintance saw him with Susan, he was resolved to endure the embarrassment good-naturedly. He and Susan had created the cousin-up-from-the-country alibi for just such occasions, and he felt sure he could carry it off now he had practiced it. He would not again stammer and blush and make a fool of himself, as he had with Sir Stanford that morning.

As soon as dinner was over, Desmond retired to his room to change his clothes into raiment suitable for the theater. When he emerged, he found Susan still in her apple-blossom gauze but wearing an indecisive look on her face. "Is something amiss?" he asked.

"I was wondering if I ought to wear my bonnet," said Susan. "It seems very odd to be going abroad bareheaded. But *do* ladies wear bonnets to the theater?"

Desmond started to say that of course they did. He had seen hundreds of ladies in bonnets and hats at Drury Lane. Then he hesitated. Now he thought of it, he recalled that the ladies so attired had also been wearing ordinary street garb, not formal evening dress such as Susan was wearing. It occurred to him also that they had been among the humbler rather than more elevated classes. "Yes," he said slowly. "But I think it's more usual to wear just plumes or flowers or something of that nature."

"I thought so," said Susan with a sigh. "How foolish of me not to have bought some plumes while we were shopping today." A thought seemed to occur to her. "Would jewelry do? I have a very nice pearl tiara—and there is a diamond aigrette, too, among Mama's jewels. But oh, I am forgetting." Her face fell. "Of course the jewels are loaned to you. I cannot wear them until I have redeemed them."

Looking at her downcast face, Desmond was moved to contradict her. "Why not?" he said. "I can maintain titular ownership of them even if you happen to be wearing them. It would not diminish their value in any way."

"I suppose not," said Susan doubtfully. "But it doesn't seem quite *right,* my lord."

"Why not?" said Desmond. "As I say, I lose nothing by letting you wear the jewels. If I don't object to the arrangement, why should you?"

Susan's dimple peeped out. "No reason, I suppose," she said. "Except that you have already been so kind to me that it goes against the grain to let you do any more."

"Well, this is little enough for me to do," said Desmond. "Let me fetch the jewels, and we'll see what this tiara of yours looks like. I've seen scores of ladies wearing tiaras at Drury Lane, so that ought to be all right."

The box of jewelry was fetched from Desmond's safe, where it had been stored for safekeeping the night before. He watched with indulgent amusement as Susan took the box and opened it with a small key she produced from her reticule, but his expression changed when he saw the glittering bounty inside. "Good lord!" he said. "Is all that really yours?"

"No, it is *yours,*" said Susan firmly. She cast an experienced eye over the contents, then picked out a small velvet case and opened it to reveal a delicate pearl tiara. "Here is the tiara. And I could wear Mama's pearl necklet and earrings also, if you made no objection."

Desmond made no objection. He was still looking at the contents of the jewel box. Somehow he had not envisioned Susan's inheritance on quite this scale. Of course it might not consist of much besides jewelry, but then again it might. It certainly explained why her Aunt Sarah was so anxious to keep it all in the family.

He watched in silence as Susan set the tiara carefully atop her wig, clasped the necklace around her throat, and put the earrings in her ears. The pearls looked lovely against her dark hair, and Desmond wanted to say so, but he was suffering once more from the shyness that had afflicted him earlier that day when he had first seen Susan in her altered form. This time the difference went beyond mere looks. He was seeing her as an heiress as well as a beauty, a young woman with the world quite literally at her feet, and the realization left him curiously disturbed.

There was no time to analyze this sensation, however. The carriage was at the door, and Susan was saying anxiously that she did not want to be late for the performance.

"Ah, so you believe 'the play's the thing,' do you?" said Desmond, smiling. "I'm afraid it will come to a shock to you to see how little most Londoners esteem it. It's quite the custom among the more fashionable members of society to arrive halfway through the performance and make a great stir getting settled, in order to attract as much attention as possible."

Susan sniffed scornfully. "If one must behave like

that to be fashionable, I don't care if I am ever fashionable," she said. "I never heard of anything so silly. *I* would rather watch the play."

With a shake of his head, Desmond opined she was setting up to be a social revolutionary.

Susan surveyed him doubtfully for a moment, then smiled. "Perhaps I am," she said. "But at least I won't be the kind they have in France, who cuts people's heads off." She considered again for a moment, then gave Desmond a wicked smile. "Not unless someone disturbs me so I can't hear the play, at any rate!"

Desmond said gravely that such execution would be more just than many another committed in the name of social revolution. Susan laughed at this and, prompted by Desmond's sallies, began to outline the details of her revolutionary agenda. Redheads would be entitled by law to wear pink or any other color they chose, young men would be strictly chaperoned while young ladies were free to roam the countryside at will, and nobody would be obliged to eat rice pudding. "I *hate* rice pudding," said Susan. "Aunt Sarah was very fond of it, because she said it was such a nice, economical dessert. But I would rather have no dessert at all than eat rice pudding."

Desmond agreed that any dessert whose chief advantage was economy might well constitute a crime against humanity. He listened with enjoyment to Susan's revolutionary agenda, made a number of proposals himself, and altogether had such an enjoyable time that before he realized it, the carriage had arrived in Drury Lane and they were joining the throng of other people who were streaming up the steps and through the vestibule doors.

Their seats were in the gallery, as Desmond had promised, a good way above the stage but still commanding a decent view of it. Desmond was relieved to see they were also situated a good way above the boxes where most of his acquaintances were in the habit of sitting. As he helped Susan seat herself and took his own seat, he glanced around surreptitiously, but saw no one he knew. This, too, was a relief to his mind. Susan was also looking around, her eyes wide as she surveyed the crowded theater. "My goodness, I have never been in such a large building before," she whispered. "It's enormous! Is that the King's box down there?"

"Yes, although he's in no fit shape to use it by all accounts," whispered back Desmond. "However, we might see Prinny if we're lucky."

Susan wrinkled her nose. "The Prince Regent? I'd rather see the King, even if he is mad. I do not at all approve of the Regent and his behavior." She looked sternly at Desmond. "I suppose you are a Tory and support him?"

"No, I'm a revolutionary like yourself. I'd like to see Prinny and his ilk earning an honest living by following the plow," whispered Desmond. This made Susan giggle, causing the elderly lady in front of them to turn around and scowl.

"Be still, my lord, or I will be disgraced," whispered Susan, stifling another fit of giggles. "You know I have been speaking very harshly against people who disturb others while the play is going on. If I misbehave now, I will be forced to cut my own head off in order to remain in compliance with my agenda!"

These severe measures proved unnecessary, however, for as soon as the curtain rose, Susan ceased talking and settled back in her seat with a sigh of pleasurable anticipation. Desmond, too, felt pleasurable anticipation as he looked down at the lighted stage. It promised to be an enjoyable evening, despite his forebodings. Susan was proving to be quite delightful company, and he need not fear to be seen with her. There appeared to be no one else in the theater he knew or who was likely to know him in return.

He forgot that the fashionable world was in the habit of arriving late for theater performances.

Eleven

During the interval between the fourth and fifth acts, Desmond saw his brother.

He and Susan had decided against getting any refreshment during the interval. They had remained in their seats to discuss the performance. Susan was saying Kean's reading during the last act had made her feel shivers down her spine. Desmond, to tease her, told her it was merely because the theater was draughty. "You may wear my coat if you like," he told her. "It won't be so good a fit as Dirk's, but it might save you from discomfort during the rest of the performance."

Susan said reprovingly that it wasn't a draught that made her shiver, it was Kean's acting. "And a perfect figure of fun I should look wearing your coat, my lord!" she added with a laugh. "Indeed, I hope to eschew masculine apparel now I have gotten some of my own."

Desmond smiled back at her—and at that moment he happened to glance down and meet a familiar pair of gray eyes regarding him from across the theater.

"Merrivale!" he said, sitting up in his seat with a sharp intake of breath.

"I beg your pardon?" said Susan. She turned to follow the direction of his gaze.

"My brother," said Desmond faintly. He had had

no idea his brother was in town, let alone that he had planned to attend the theater that evening. Yet Merrivale it undoubtedly was. The marquess was sitting in a box some rows down, with an elderly couple whom Desmond recognized as Lord and Lady Cranbrook, Merrivale's mother- and father-in-law. He was looking at Desmond, however, and even at this distance, it was possible to see his expression was one of disquieting interest.

With an effort, Desmond pulled himself together. He reminded himself that however embarrassing it might be to be seen thus by his brother, it was really far better than if he had been seen by some distant and disinterested acquaintance. Merrivale, at least, could be counted on not to gossip, just as Sir Stanford could. So Desmond gave his brother a nod and a would-be friendly smile.

Merrivale nodded back politely, but remained in his seat. This was a relief to Desmond, who had feared he would immediately mount to the gallery to investigate what his younger brother was doing in that unfashionable quarter with an unknown and very lovely lady. Of course, it was inevitable Merrivale would question him about these proceedings eventually, but since the day of reckoning appeared to be postponed, Desmond was able to relax in some measure and turn his attention back to Susan, who was exclaiming with wonder over the coincidence of his brother being in the theater.

"So your brother is here? Is that he in the box next to the white-haired lady in emeralds? Yes, I noticed him looking our way several times earlier, but I never supposed it was because he was your brother. I ought to have guessed, for there is a great resemblance between the two of you. Lord Merrivale is a very distinguished-looking gentleman."

Desmond nodded absently, quite heedless that this speech contained a compliment to himself. He was still embarrassed over the idea of Merrivale seeing him with Susan. His last conversation with his brother had been a discussion of his intended engagement to Annabelle, which made his presence at the theater with another lady a questionable proceeding, to say the least. But Desmond assured himself that the matter could no doubt be explained satisfactorily to Merrivale, who was after all the most sensible of sensible men. If anybody could be counted on to understand his dilemma regarding Susan, Merrivale could. Merely the appearance of the thing was against him.

So Desmond reasoned to himself, but he was nonetheless relieved when the curtain rose on the play's final act. He was already planning how he could get Susan downstairs and out of the theater as soon as the performance was over. Of course there was really no need for hurry, for if his brother had intended to speak with him, it stood to reason he would have done it during one of the intervals.

According to Susan, Merrivale had been aware of their presence for some time, even if Desmond had not been aware of his. Nonetheless, Desmond thought it as well to quit the field as soon as possible. He told himself ruefully that Susan was simply too captivating for her own good. If she had been able to make him overlook his own brother's presence during the time they had been in the theater, there was no saying who else's he might have overlooked. For all he knew, there might be a dozen people of his acquaintance staring at him and Susan this very minute.

The thought made Desmond's skin crawl, but he reminded himself that he had been prepared for this eventuality. Being faced with Merrivale so unexpectedly had taken him off his guard, but he had nothing to fear from Merrivale except possibly a little teasing. As for any stray friends and acquaintances, they could easily be fobbed off with the excuse he and Susan had prepared that morning.

So Desmond was able to enjoy the last act of the play almost, if not quite, as much as the first four. At the curtain's fall, he joined in the applause that burst forth from the audience and smiled sympathetically at Susan, who was clapping with a fervor that seemed likely to split her new evening gloves.

"That was wonderful, my lord," she told him. "I am so glad that I was able to see it. I never enjoyed anything so much in my life."

"I enjoyed it, too," Desmond told her sincerely. He had relaxed from his earlier panic, and it no longer seemed so urgent to exit the theater without loss of time. The gallery was a sea of people milling about, talking, laughing, and gathering up gloves, shawls, and other possessions. It was clearly needless to worry about being seen. So Desmond and Susan remained in their places until the crowd had subsided a little, then made their way downstairs in a leisurely manner and out through the vestibule.

Dirk was waiting with the carriage near the curb. Desmond led Susan toward it and had just swung open the door of the carriage when he heard a voice that froze him in his tracks. "Lord Desmond! Oh, my Lord Desmond, is that you?"

Recovering from his paralysis, Desmond had just presence of mind enough to push Susan into the carriage and slam the door shut behind her. He then felt his arm seized in an iron grip. Turning reluctantly, he found himself face to face with Mrs. Percy Throgmorton, an inveterate gossip who also happened to be one of Annabelle's aunt's closest friends.

"It *is* you," cried Mrs. Throgmorton. "I made sure it was, my lord, though I certainly didn't expect to see you here. I had supposed you must be indisposed. Seeing you weren't at the Byrnes' delightful fete t'other day—dear Annabelle was *so* disappointed not to see you. But it appears you have been not ill, merely otherwise occupied." She looked slyly toward the carriage, lowering her voice as she spoke. "Who is she, my lord? I saw you trying to bundle her out of sight just now, but it won't do. You may as well tell me now as later, for I'm bound to find out regardless. And indeed, you can trust me with your secret. You must know I'm the soul of discretion."

Desmond, who knew very well that the opposite was true, mentally consigned Mrs. Throgmorton to the devil. Since the devil showed no immediate prospect of collecting her, however, he congratulated himself that at least he had a story prepared to satisfy her questions.

"Indeed, it is no secret, ma'am," he was beginning, when he was interrupted by a voice saying quietly, "Good evening, Desmond."

This voice was a pleasant, well-cultured one, the very reverse of Mrs. Throgmorton's, but it struck Desmond with even more dismay than hers had done. Spinning around, he beheld his brother, flanked on either side by Lord and Lady Cranbrook.

"Hi, there, Desmond, how d'ye do?" continued Lord Merrivale, as unconcernedly as though he had not noticed his brother's dismay. "You know the Cranbrooks, of course." The Cranbrooks smiled and nodded, while Lord Merrivale continued in the same easy, matter-of-fact voice. "They were coming up to Town for a few days, and Louise wanted me to come with them and show them a few of the sights. A decentish performance tonight, wasn't it?"

Mrs. Throgmorton, who had been fluttering impatiently while these civilities were being exchanged, could restrain herself no longer. "Indeed, the play was very well, my lord. But I found it not nearly so interesting as the identity of the lovely lady with whom Lord Desmond was sitting!" She smiled archly at Desmond.

"Her name is Miss de Havilland," said Desmond. "She is—" He paused in dismay, suddenly aware of the pit yawning before his feet.

If he claimed Susan as a relation, his brother would probably not be crass enough to deny the statement before company, but ten to one one of the Cranbrooks would innocently inquire exactly in what relation she stood to him. He remembered them as a gossipy and inquisitive old couple with a positive mania for the Peerage.

In dismay he glanced at his brother. He did not really anticipate that Merrivale would come to his rescue, for there was a glint of amusement in his brother's eyes that showed he fully appreciated Desmond's discomfiture. To his relief, however, Merrivale answered his unspoken appeal and took up his explanation smoothly where he had left off.

"Miss de Havilland is a friend of the family, ma'am," he told Mrs. Throgmorton. Turning to Desmond, he added, "Do give her my regards, Desmond, and those of Lady Louise."

Desmond realized he was being given an opportunity. He was not slow to take advantage of it. "Thank you, Merrivale, and my regards to Lady Louise in return, if you please. Lady Cranbrook, Lord Cranbrook, Mrs. Throgmorton, I give you a good evening." Bowing, he opened the carriage door, swung himself inside, and shut it again before Mrs. Throgmorton could ask the other questions obviously trembling on her tongue.

Looking through the glass, he saw his brother take Mrs. Throgmorton's arm and address some remark to her. The remark seemed to pacify her, for she smiled and rapped his arm with her fan before sailing off in the direction of her own carriage.

"Thank heaven," said Desmond aloud.

Susan, from the other banquette, was regarding him quizzically. "I am afraid I couldn't help overhearing most of what you were saying just now, my lord," she said. "When we decided I would be your cousin, we weren't thinking your brother might be around to contradict you, were we?"

"No, we weren't," agreed Desmond ruefully. "I never thought of Merrivale's being here tonight. He doesn't often come to London, and when he does I usually know about it in advance."

Susan nodded. "I could tell you were very surprised to see him." She cast a shy look at Desmond. "I must say, I was quite surprised when your brother said I was a friend of the family. Why would he do that, my lord?"

"Because he fancies himself a wit," said Desmond grimly. He knew well enough what Merrivale had been implying. He meant that any woman who distracted his younger brother from the pursuit of Annabelle Windibank must be a friend and benefactor to the Ryder family, even if that woman happened to be a demimondaine. Desmond was pretty sure Merrivale had supposed Susan a woman of this sort, and he had to admit the assumption was natural enough in the circumstances. Indeed, when he thought about it, he could see very well why his brother had been fighting a smile the whole time they had been talking. A reluctant grin curved his own lips. Susan, who had been watching him, smiled also. But there remained a quizzical look in her eyes as she regarded Desmond from the opposite banquette.

They reached home without further incident. Before going to her room, Susan thanked Desmond for accompanying her to the theater. "I had a delightful time, my lord," she told him. "I am only sorry if I caused any embarrassment for you."

"None to speak of," said Desmond, smiling. Now

that he was home, he could appreciate the humor of his meeting with Mrs. Throgmorton and the Cranbrooks. Of course Mrs. Throgmorton could be counted on to tell Annabelle she had seen him with another lady, but Desmond found he did not mind this idea so much as he would have supposed. Thanks to Merrivale, he now had a first-class excuse for squiring Susan about, an excuse even Annabelle must recognize.

Curiously enough, however, he felt rather indifferent as to Annabelle's feelings in the matter. The evening had been delightful in spite of its undoubted trials, and he found himself wishing to prolong it. "It's late and you have had no supper," he said. "Would you like to have a cup of tea and a bite of something before retiring?"

Susan hesitated a moment, then nodded. "Yes, I would quite like that, my lord. Just let me put my gloves and reticule in my room, and I will be with you directly."

In her room, however, Susan lingered a moment after depositing her gloves, shawl, and reticule on the bed. In the cheval glass beside the dressing table, she could see her reflection—dark-haired, dark-eyed, and enveloped in a mist of apple-blossom pink. Slowly, almost reluctantly, Susan drew nearer to examine it. The allure of that image smote her with a curious pain, even while she exulted in it. *But it's not me,* she told herself. *None of it is me.*

With a sudden gesture, she reached up and yanked the wig from her head. Her red curls looked more fiery than ever after their day-long eclipse. Absently, Susan ran her fingers through them, still staring at her reflection. Then she went to the washbasin, poured some water into it from the pitcher, and deliberately scrubbed every trace of cosmetic from her face. Having done this, she went to the glass again to reevaluate.

Her reflection, damp, pink cheeked, and devoid of artifice, looked back at her. The contrast between her former appearance and her present one was almost shocking. With dissatisfaction, Susan told herself she looked a plain-faced dowd. She threw a longing look at the dark wig flung carelessly onto her dressing table and at the battery of little pots and bottles with which Reese had transformed her face that morning. But when she thought of resuming her persona of Chloe de Havilland just to go have tea with Desmond, something within her rebelled.

She was aware Desmond admired her in her transformed state. She was aware also that she enjoyed his admiration. Yet this only made her more perversely determined not to take advantage of it. While she was wearing her wig and cosmetics, he might be able to forget for a time that she was plain red-haired Susan Doyle, but she could not. Therefore, it followed she had better give him a salutary reminder, even if it meant marring the end of a nearly perfect day.

So apart from fluffing her hair before the glass, Susan made no alteration in her appearance before going out to join Desmond in the parlor. She did not even change her dress. This, too, was motivated by an obscure conviction that Desmond ought to see her at her worst, after seeing her at her best. She never doubted that appearing in a pink dress with her own flaming hair was a sure way to appear at her worst.

To Desmond, however, there was nothing whatever amiss with the tousled, red-haired girl in the pink dress who presently joined him in the parlor. To be sure, he blinked rather at the change in her appearance, but on the whole he found it stimulating rather than off-putting. She looked just as attractive, only in an entirely different way. So Desmond reflected to himself as they drank tea and ate soup and cold veal pie. They chatted about the play and laughed over some of its incidents, and it was altogether a very pleasant and companionable interlude.

But though Desmond enjoyed it immensely, he could not help being aware there was something a little equivocal about dining tête-à-tête with a young lady at that hour. Perhaps it was the remembrance of the look in his brother's eyes or the crude hints of Mrs. Throgmorton. Or perhaps it was merely the presence of Susan herself across the table, sweet and fresh-faced as a garden rose. In any case, he kept remembering that he was a normal man with normal urges, and some of those urges were not in keeping with the role of brotherly protector he had adopted toward her.

So after finishing his second cup of tea, he pushed back his chair and said it was time they retired. "To be sure, it is very late," agreed Susan, looking at the clock. "Thank you very much for all you have done for me today, my lord. It has been a wonderful day."

"You are most welcome," said Desmond. The words sounded stilted and formal to his ears, and he felt as though he ought to say something else. Susan was looking at him inquiringly. It struck him once again that there was something very attractive about her fresh-scrubbed face, tousled hair, and wide dark eyes. She might have looked alluring in her guise of Chloe de Havilland, but in her present state she looked not only alluring but *approachable.* And since he was bound and determined not to approach her, there was nothing for him to do but bid her a hasty good night and quit the room as quickly as he could.

Susan felt the abruptness of his exit, but she put it down to her altered appearance. Of course he would behave differently toward her when she was not attired as Chloe de Havilland. Susan was quite convinced of this, for she had been conscious of a certain warmth in his looks and manner toward her several times that day—a warmth that had been absent when he wished her good night just now. Susan told herself this was exactly as it ought to be. She had done her duty, and now she could be easy. But as she went slowly to her room, she could not help regretting that doing one's duty should be such a uniformly depressing business.

Twelve

"I give you my word," said Mrs. Throgmorton, "I was never so shocked in my life!"

Annabelle, listening to this speech, reflected bitterly that there was more relish than shock in Mrs. Throgmorton's voice. This was hardly surprising, for everybody knew Mrs. T. delighted in being the bearer of bad news. But Annabelle was resolved not to let her see how very bad her news was. So she yawned, laying one hand against her cherry lips with pretty unconcern. "Indeed?" she said. "It sounds no great matter to *me.*"

"That's because you weren't there to see him, my dear. There was guilt written all over his face. He hemmed and hawed when I asked who she was, and if Merrivale hadn't spoke up and said she was a friend of the family, I don't believe he ever *would* have answered me."

"But perhaps she really was a friend of the family, ma'am. Now I think of it, I believe I have heard Desmond speak before of this Miss—Miss—"

"Miss de Havilland," supplied Mrs. Throgmorton. With an acid smile, she added, "It may be so, my dear. It may be so. But if he's spoke of her as much as that, it's odd you don't even remember her name."

Annabelle summoned up a laugh. "But I have

such a lamentable memory, ma'am! Why, I can hardly remember my own name from day to day!"

Mrs. Throgmorton brushed this aside with visible contempt. "You're not such a goose as that, my dear. Such airs may serve very well with the gentlemen—I don't say they don't. But between us women, we may as well be frank. I tell you I saw Lord Desmond with this girl. If you still have any notion of marrying him, you'd best be bringing him to the point without delay, and so I tell you."

"He already *has* come to the point," shot back Annabelle. "He asked me to marry him weeks ago!"

"Aye, and you refused him," said Mrs. Throgmorton, nodding sadly. "That was when you were still trying for St. Armand. I could have told you, you were flying too high there, my dear. You'd have much better taken Lord Desmond while you had the chance."

Annabelle summoned another light laugh. "Why, whatever do you mean, ma'am?" she said. "There's nothing to stop me from marrying Lord Desmond now if I choose. I could bring him to the point again, just like that." She snapped her fingers with a contemptuous smile.

Mrs. Throgmorton smiled back maddeningly. "You might not be so sure of yourself if you'd seen him last night," she said. "The truth is, you've let all this talk of being an Incomparable go to your head. You're a handsome girl, Annabelle, I don't deny, but there's other handsome girls in London besides you, and it looks to me very much as though Lord Desmond might have found one of 'em."

"A lightskirt," said Annabelle scornfully. "You can't tell me Lord Desmond Ryder means to marry a lightskirt!"

"Maybe not, maybe not. But at all events, he *was* with her at the theater last night. That shows his eye's starting to wander a bit. It wasn't so long ago that he had eyes for nobody but *you.*"

Annabelle was silent. Pursuing her advantage, Mrs. Throgmorton went on with a didactic air, "There's a time to be coy with men, and a time to be more forthcoming. I'd suggest from now on you be a little more forthcoming with Lord Desmond if you don't want him to slip through your fingers like St. Armand and Foxborough."

Annabelle tossed her head. "Foxborough! That disgusting old man? I wouldn't marry him even if he did ask me," she said hotly.

Mrs. Throgmorton laughed. "You're not likely to get a chance, my dear. I understand he's engaged to Miss Pixley." And with this home thrust she went away, leaving Annabelle to her own thoughts.

These were not of a comforting nature. Annabelle might have boasted to Mrs. Throgmorton that Lord Desmond was hers for the asking, but inwardly she was beginning to wonder.

In truth, it had been a disastrous month for Annabelle. When first Lord St. Armand and then Lord Foxborough had deserted her, she had comforted herself with the thought that she always had Desmond Ryder to fall back on. He might be only a younger son, but his family was an old and proud one, and she had taken pains to ascertain that his income was adequate to her purposes.

What was more, his brother the marquess was as yet childless, which made Desmond heir presumptive for the title. It wasn't a sure thing, of course, as marrying Lord St. Armand would have been, but it would give her a title of sorts to begin with and the possibility of a better one later on. All in all, Annabelle felt she could be content with Desmond Ryder as her husband.

Still, she was in no hurry to accept his proposal. She reasoned that some other, more eligible suitor might yet appear on the horizon. It would not do to be engaged to someone else if he did.

But three weeks had passed now, and no more eligible suitor had appeared on the horizon. Accordingly, Annabelle had made up her mind to accept Desmond. Her decision was strengthened by the decampment of two more of her suitors to the camp of a rival beauty. It was not that Annabelle would have considered marrying either of those suitors, for they were mere commoners with no particular fortune and thus beneath the serious notice of an Incomparable like herself. But though she was completely unacquainted with Shakespeare's famous quotation about there being a tide in the affairs of men, she was uneasily aware that there was a definite ebb and flow in the career of a fashionable beauty. Men were fickle creatures, Annabelle reflected bitterly, forgetting that she had a strong claim to be called fickle herself. It was beginning to look very much as though her star had reached its apogee and was now on its way down. That being the case, it behooved her to lose no time in seizing what matrimonial chances yet remained to her.

Although she was now eager to be engaged, she still had enough faith in her own attractions to wish to delay an actual marriage. Once Desmond was securely betrothed to her, she reckoned that she could take her time, look around, and see if some better prospect might yet appear. It might even be that being temporarily off the marriage market would revive some of her past swains' flagging interest. If so, there was nothing to prevent her from exchanging bridegrooms if the opportunity offered. And if it did not offer, she could always go ahead and marry Desmond.

Her position would be secure in either case, for though a lady was free to change her mind in these matters, a gentleman could not honorably withdraw from an engagement once he had entered into it. Annabelle felt confident that Desmond would behave honorably, no matter what provocation she might give him. Indeed, as she reflected complacently, even if she should find it necessary to break their engagement, she was quite sure she could convince him to take it up again if such a course ever seemed desirable to her.

So with her mind assured on these important points, Annabelle resolved to accept Desmond the next time he proposed to her. This she confidently expected to take place in the very near future.

At first it had seemed as though her confidence were justified. Desmond had jumped at the chance to meet her at the fete. She had gone off to the Byrnes' villa secure in the belief that she would be an engaged woman by the time the party ended.

But instead something had gone wrong: terribly, inexplicably wrong. Desmond had not come to the fete after all. He had only sent her a note saying he was unavoidably detained. And then had come Mrs. Throgmorton with her tale of seeing him at the theater with a beautiful brunette.

Even without Mrs. Throgmorton's tale, Annabelle would have been inclined to worry. She had a gambler's belief in luck, and it had appeared to her for some weeks that her luck was running out. She had hoped to turn its tide by becoming engaged to Desmond. Now he, too, had failed her.

It did not at first occur to her to suppose his failure had been a voluntary one. So secure was she in her belief of Desmond's devotion that she initially took his note at face value. However, it was annoying enough to have him fail her, even if his failure had been an involuntary one, and in a fit of pique, Annabelle decided to administer a little punishment. Of course this was harsh treatment considering the circumstances, but harsh treatment had only increased Desmond's ardor in the past, and Annabelle might have been pardoned for thinking it would achieve the same object now.

So she had dashed off a note to him, coldly acknowledging his own note and canceling an engagement made some weeks before. She had then settled back to wait, confident that the next twenty-four hours would bring Desmond to his knees both literally and figuratively.

But instead she had received the news that, far from groveling in her displeasure, he was off amusing himself with an unknown brunette. And though she made light of the matter to Mrs. Throgmorton, secretly she was much alarmed. Was it possible that she had miscalculated? Even if the girl was a lightskirt, it seemed to show that Desmond was not so securely bound to her as she had thought. Almost she regretted canceling their engagement for the opera. But after thinking it over, Annabelle decided Desmond's behavior was merely an attempt to pique her. He had deliberately gone out in public with this girl, knowing that news of his conduct was bound to come to her ears. Now she must decide what she was going to do about it.

Mrs. Throgmorton had advised her to be more forthcoming in her relations with Desmond. But this advice ran contrary to Annabelle's experience as well as to her inclinations. *Who is Mrs. Throgmorton to give me advice?* she demanded of herself scornfully. Mrs. Throgmorton had never been a beauty, and she knew nothing of the power beauty could wield. She, Annabelle, had that power. She would use it to make Desmond suffer.

And once she was securely established as his fiancée, she would make him suffer some more. It was the least she could do to punish him for making her endure the gloating condolences of Mrs. Throgmorton!

Accordingly, Annabelle began to lay her plans. These required the services of a rival gentleman who might be used to drive Desmond mad with jealousy. She considered the ranks of her admirers and decided Mr. Augustus Stevens was best suited for this role. He was not particularly wealthy, and his birth was no more than genteel, but he had the face and figure of an Apollo, and Annabelle judged these attributes more important for her purposes than wealth or lofty birth.

For the next week or two, she would encourage Mr. Stevens to the top of her bent. She would ride in the park with him, dance with him, and even let it be whispered that she was on the verge of becoming engaged to him. *And if that doesn't bring Lord Desmond back to heel in short order, I will be much mistaken,* she reflected with satisfaction.

Desmond, meanwhile, was finding life off Annabelle's leash surprisingly enjoyable.

The morning after the Drury Lane expedition, he had found himself with some small matters of business that required his attention. He explained the situation to Susan, who had just come into the dining parlor, looking very much as she had looked at supper the night before except that she was wearing her white dress rather than her pink one. "Should you mind if I left you for an hour or two this morning?" he asked.

"Certainly not," said Susan. Although disappointed, she spoke with composure, for she had already fought and won a battle that morning with her own worse nature. The battle had to do with her wig and cosmetics. As soon as she had risen that morning, she had been tempted to put on the trappings of Chloe de Havilland. But she had recognized this temptation as the same one that had beset her at supper the evening before and had succeeded in vanquishing it after a struggle.

There could be no justification to paint and bewig herself like an actress simply to eat her breakfast. It was all right to masquerade in front of the rest of the world, but not in front of Desmond. So much Susan had determined, and she had thus come to breakfast in her own red hair and her own white dress and kept her self-respect intact.

Yet even with self-respect intact, Susan found the news that Desmond had to leave her for a couple of hours disappointing. On thinking it over, however, she decided she had no reason to feel slighted. Of course a wealthy and important man like Lord Desmond could not dance attendance on her all the time. It was not as though she could not entertain herself perfectly well. There was that novel in her bedchamber that she had begun the previous morning, and perhaps she could write a letter to her Aunt Theodosia as well. *Indeed, it's high time I wrote to her,* Susan told herself guiltily. She had been thirty-six hours in London, and it was remiss of her not to have written her aunt before now. She knew it would not do to impose too long on Desmond's hospitality. Sooner or later she would have to leave his home. In the meantime, if he needed to excuse himself for a morning, or even for all of a day, the least she could do was accept his absence uncomplainingly.

So Susan did her best to accept his absence uncomplainingly. After he had gone, she dawdled over her breakfast, reading bits of the morning papers as she ate her toast and drank her tea. Her Uncle Asa had taken several of the London papers, and Susan had made a habit of reading them all, although Aunt Sarah tended to frown on this pastime, believing the content of newspapers largely unfit for the delicate sensibilities of young ladies.

Indeed, so strongly did she feel on this subject that when he had died, she had promptly canceled all his newspaper subscriptions. As a result, Susan had not had the chance to look at any newspapers for some months.

She read with interest an account of a debate in the House, smiled over a cartoon depicting the Prince Regent languishing in the arms of Lady Jersey, and folded away an advertisement for a masquerade at Vauxhall. She had never attended a masquerade in her life, and a masquerade at Vauxhall Gardens, of whose attractions she had heard even in Barnhart, sounded doubly intriguing.

Perhaps Lord Desmond will take me there, she told herself hopefully. Then she reminded herself that Desmond was a busy man and might have other things to do that particular evening. She must not get in the habit of expecting him to accompany her everywhere. But the idea of attending the masquerade without him felt oddly flat.

Having finished her breakfast and the newspapers, Susan went to her room and settled down with her novel. As she read, she kept telling herself she ought to put the book away long enough to write to her Aunt Theodosia, but when she finally heard Desmond's voice in the hall, the letter was still unwritten. Pushing aside her guilt and laying aside her book, Susan got up and hurried out to greet him.

Thirteen

Desmond was very glad to see Susan.

In point of fact, he was surprised by how glad he felt. Part of his sensation was relief, no doubt. Shortly after he had left the house, it had occurred to him Susan might take it into her head to go out while he was absent from home. If she only went shopping, this would be no great matter, but if she took the notion of doing some more sight-seeing, there was no saying where she might end up. There were quarters of London unsuited for a lady to enter, and still others in which no sane person ought to set foot.

Desmond fretted about this all morning while he went about his business. By the time he was ready to return home, he had made up his mind that the responsibility of Susan was too onerous by half. He found himself calculating how many hours it would be before he could reasonably expect a response from Theodosia Doyle in answer to his message.

And then Susan had come running out to greet him with a welcoming smile on her face.

And suddenly Desmond found himself revising his opinion. After all, there was something pleasant in having company around the house, even if it entailed an added responsibility. He had not been conscious of being lonely before Susan had come to stay with him, but now that she was here, he realized how nice it was to be greeted when he came in by someone other than Reese.

He found himself telling Susan about his activities that day, describing various little funny and interesting occurrences he had witnessed during the course of his errands. She seemed so genuinely interested that he felt guilty at having left her behind. "I suppose you must have been very dull here," he said penitently. "It was too bad of me to leave you to your own devices."

"Not at all," said Susan stoutly. "I had a delightful morning. And you know, my lord, if I had wished to go anywhere, I might easily have done so. Just because I am staying with you does not mean you must chaperone me wherever I go."

Desmond agreed this was true, although he privately resolved to instruct Reese to see Susan had an escort if she decided to go out. He still felt uncertain of her ability to stay out of trouble if left to her own devices. She was such an impulsive little thing, and so pretty that she was likely to attract attention of the wrong kind without even trying. Really, he found himself surprised by how pretty she was. It was as though he had just realized the fact, though he knew full well he had remarked on it almost the first moment he had seen her. But then, remarking and realizing were two different things.

He found himself studying her anew as they went into the dining parlor, where Reese had laid out a luncheon of fruit, cheese, and cold meat for them. Susan accepted a pear and a slice of ham, though she said she was not very hungry. "All I did was read all morning," she explained, as she peeled the pear and cut it into slices. "I am afraid I was abominably lazy. But it was delightful to be lazy for a change."

"What did you read?" asked Desmond, smiling.

"A novel I found in my room, and the newspapers. Oh, and that reminds me, my lord. There is to be a masquerade at Vauxhall this Saturday night, with a concert and extra lanterns. It sounds most delightful."

"And you want to go?" said Desmond.

Susan gave him a look that was half defiant, half apologetic. "I would like very much to go," she said.

"I see," said Desmond. He considered the matter as he helped himself to cold beef. Vauxhall was no longer much patronized by the *haut ton,* and masquerade nights in particular tended to attract the lower rather than upper classes of society, but he was sure this would not put Susan off the idea. And though he himself would not ordinarily look forward to an evening spent rubbing shoulders with Cits, shabby genteels, and demimondaines, he found that on this occasion he was quite willing to suspend his usual fastidious standards. Vauxhall on a masquerade night was a colorful spectacle to anyone willing to put up with a few inconveniences, and he thought he would derive enjoyment from viewing it all through Susan's unaccustomed eyes.

In the event, it never occurred to him to try to dissuade her from the idea. If Susan's mind was made up to go, then go she would, and he would accompany her as a matter of course. All this Desmond took for granted, so he was surprised when Susan said, with a kind of forced cheerfulness, "I can see you do not like the idea, my lord. Never mind, I will give it up."

Desmond looked at her in surprise. "I did not say I did not like the idea!" he said.

"But you don't, do you?" said Susan.

"I wouldn't say that," said Desmond. "Besides, what does it matter whether I like the idea or not?" He smiled at her. "I know perfectly well you have made up your mind to go to Vauxhall. That being the case, no mere male can hope to stand in your way!"

Susan did not return his smile. "That is not so, my lord," she said. "In this matter, I am willing to be guided by you. I wish you would tell me truly what you think. Would you find it a great bore to attend this masquerade?"

"Certainly not," said Desmond. "But—forgive me—you still haven't answered my question. Why does it matter whether I like the idea or not? I thought you were determined to do only what *you* liked while you were in London, without reference to anyone else's wishes."

Susan nodded, a faint flush in her cheeks. "I know I said that in the beginning. But that was before I realized you would feel obligated to go with me wherever I went. Don't think I don't appreciate it, my lord. I *do* appreciate it, very much. But I am not totally selfish, and for me to compel you to go someplace you don't want to, merely because I have a fancy to see it—well, that is a kind of manipulation. And I *detest* manipulation. It makes me feel I am almost on a level with Aunt Sarah and Mortimer."

"That you are not," said Desmond. "You haven't been manipulating me at all."

"But you wouldn't have gone to most of the places we've gone to these past two days if you'd been by yourself," said Susan. "It's only that you felt obliged to accompany me. And knowing you feel that way, how can I help thinking I am manipulating you when I propose going to Vauxhall?"

"You aren't," said Desmond again. "It's not like that at all." He hesitated, then went on, choosing his words carefully. "Look here. It's true I might not have chosen to go some of the places we've gone together, but I've enjoyed myself when we did go. Doesn't that mean you are not manipulating me?"

"No," said Susan. "It only means you are good-natured!"

Desmond laughed. "Well, I hope I am not *ill*-natured. But indeed, Susan—Miss Doyle—I assure you it's not just disinterested chivalry on my part. The fact that a plan didn't originate with me doesn't mean I may not like it and take pleasure in it. Does it?"

Susan did not answer the question. She only sighed and said, "I wish I knew if you were telling the truth, my lord."

"Now look here!" said Desmond. "You may question my motives, but I'm dashed if I'll let you question my integrity. I pride myself on being a man of my word. If you weren't a lady, it's ten to one I'd have to call you out for implying I'm not."

A dimple was peeping at the corner of Susan's mouth. "I'm sorry, my lord," she said. "I didn't mean to imply I doubted your word. Heaven knows I have ample reason to believe you are trustworthy."

"Then kindly trust me when I say I don't mind taking you to Vauxhall or anywhere else you like to go."

"Even if you don't want to go there, too?"

Desmond shook his head. "If I detested the idea, I should say so," he said. "But it's not a case of that. I'll admit I'm probably not as enthusiastic about the idea as you are, but I am quite willing to go along with it. We are friends, I hope, and any friendship must necessarily involve a certain amount of accommodation. It's a process of give and take, by which each person profits in the long run."

Susan still looked dubious. "But it seems all I do is take and never give, my lord," she said. "I'd feel better if I could do something in return for you."

Desmond, looking at her, was moved to an impulsive decision. "There is," he said. "You can put on your hat and come driving with me this afternoon.

My grays need exercise, and I'd like to have the company."

Susan's face bloomed forth in smiles. "I would love to come with you, my lord!" she said. "But indeed, what you propose is a treat rather than a sacrifice. To even the score properly, you ought to ask me to do something disagreeable."

Desmond laughed. "If I think of anything disagreeable, I'll let you know," he said. "Right now, just giving me your company will do."

"I'll go get my bonnet," said Susan, springing up. Then she stopped as though she had been shot. "I suppose since we are going out, I must put on my wig as well as my bonnet," she said.

"I suppose so," agreed Desmond. It struck him that Susan looked rather unhappy at the prospect, but if he thought anything about it, it was to assume she disliked the discomfort of wearing a wig. He therefore attached no importance to her expression, but went to his own room to get his whip and driving gloves.

He was waiting in the parlor when Susan presently emerged bewigged, bonneted, and gloved. Desmond shook his head wonderingly. "I can never get used to the transformation," he said. "It's wonderful what a wig and a little powder and paint will do. Why, I could imagine you are two entirely different women!"

Susan merely gave him an unsmiling look and said nothing. Desmond was conscious of a sudden chill in the atmosphere. It dismayed him, for he had looked forward to continuing their conversation during the drive. Now it seemed as though the easy camaraderie between them had been spoiled. But after they had been driving for ten minutes or so, Susan caught sight of a spectacle in the street that so intrigued her she begged Desmond to slow and let her get a better look at it. It was a Punch and

Judy show, and it developed that Susan had never seen one before. Her delight was so evident that Desmond turned the reins over to Dirk and helped her dismount to get a better look. They joined the crowd around the puppets, and in the process of laughing over the antics of Punch and his belligerent wife, all constraint between them was destroyed.

"That was delightful," said Susan, her eyes glowing as she took her place in the curricle once more. "I am so glad you gave the man a crown, my lord. Those puppets were almost human."

"Indeed they were," agreed Desmond. "Now where would you like to go? Is there anything else you would like to see while we are out?"

Susan gave him a smiling but reproachful look. "No, no, my lord! You have indulged me in my wishes, and now it's your turn to be indulged. I am content to go anywhere you like."

Desmond considered. He had meant originally to drive through the side streets without venturing near the more fashionable quarters, but now he was tempted to throw caution to the winds. What did it matter if someone saw him with Susan? He was *glad* to be seen with Susan. She wasn't just lovely, she was excellent company, and through her eyes he was able to appreciate the familiar sights of London as he never had before. "Then let us go to Hyde Park," he said.

It was nearly the hour of the fashionable promenade, as Desmond knew very well. The chances were good he would encounter someone he knew, but he reckoned Susan would enjoy seeing the *beau monde* as they paraded through the park on foot, horseback, and carriage. He made up his mind to endure whatever consequences might arise. Strangely, he hardly thought of Annabelle in this connection. He knew she held court in the park on an almost daily basis, but the idea of displeasing her did not weigh with him when compared to the idea of pleasing Susan. Annabelle had never thought twice about displeasing *him,* while Susan had always shown a most scrupulous concern for his feelings. Desmond wanted to repay her concern by showing her as good a time as she was showing him.

As he had expected, they had hardly entered the park before they encountered several gentlemen of his acquaintance, among them Sir Stanford Kent. Sir Stanford gave Desmond and Susan a knowing smile as they passed, but to Desmond's relief he made no attempt to speak to them beyond calling a genial, "Good afternoon, Des! 'Afternoon, Miss de Havilland."

Desmond might not have been so relieved if he had been privy to the conversation that ensued among Sir Stanford and his companions after they passed.

"Who's that with Desmond?" inquired one gentleman, looking curiously after the curricle. "A dashed handsome girl, by Jove!"

"Very handsome," agreed another. "A regular beauty."

"Her name," said Sir Stanford, with considerable solemnity, "is Miss Chloe de Havilland."

"De Havilland?" repeated another gentleman curiously. "Not one of the Devonshire de Havillands, surely."

"She says not," said Sir Stanford. He allowed his eyes to twinkle as he regarded the other gentlemen. "From the way Des attempted to sweep her out of sight when I went to introduce myself, I tend to think she is no known branch of the family, but rather a—er—offshoot of a different sort."

This speech caused a sensation among the gentlemen. "D'ye mean the gel's his particular?" demanded one incredulously. "Well, what d'you know!

I never heard of Desmond's taking a mistress before now."

"Aye, I heard he was as good as engaged to Annabelle Windibank," said another. "Do you suppose this means he's cried off from the match? I must say I'd be glad to hear it. Not that I'm an especial friend of Desmond's, but I'd hate to see any decent fellow leg-shackled to a gazetted flirt like Annabelle."

"She's a beauty, though," pointed out a third in a fair-minded way. "You must admit she's a beauty."

"So she is," agreed the other. "But beauty ain't so rare that one has to marry a vulgar flaunting creature like Annabelle Windibank to get it."

"No, thank heaven for that," said the first gentleman with a grin. "At any rate, it looks as though Desmond's found a source that don't come so steep. D'you suppose the fair Annabelle knows about his defection?"

"Let's follow along and find out," proposed Sir Stanford. "She was holding court by the Serpentine a few minutes ago."

"This ought to be good as a play," remarked one of the gentlemen as they spurred their horses after the curricle. "Does she know or doesn't she? If she doesn't, I'll wager her face is a study when she first sees Desmond with his dark beauty!"

Annabelle's face was indeed a study when she first caught sight of Desmond with Susan. She had arrived early in the park that day, accompanied by the handsome Mr. Stevens, whom she had chosen as her instrument of revenge. It was, she told herself, too much to hope Desmond would be there to see her flirting with Mr. Stevens, but undoubtedly he would hear of it in due time, and she meant the story should be colorful in its telling. So she teased and coaxed and flattered Mr. Stevens, laughed at all his jokes, and made it clear to all observers that she, the lovely Annabelle Windibank, was wholly smitten with Mr. Augustus Stevens. Of course her other suitors did not take this well, but their visible jealousy and resentment did not disturb Annabelle in the least. On the contrary, she judged Desmond's reaction ought to be much the same as theirs and was pleased accordingly. A few days of such treatment, she reckoned, ought to work Desmond into a frenzy of jealous love, at which point she would have him exactly where she wanted him.

And then she had seen Desmond in his curricle with that abominable dark-haired girl!

Annabelle was so taken aback by the sight that she was guilty of actually gaping. Desmond did not notice her expression, however. In fact, he did not notice her at all, being busy pointing out some of the sights of the park to Susan. But every symptom of Annabelle's shock and outrage was noted and appreciated by the little audience of gentlemen following along behind him.

"Well, it's plain to see the beauty didn't know she had any competition!" said one of the gentlemen with a gasp of laughter. "Did you ever see such a look?"

"No, I didn't," said his companion with relish. "And there's Desmond, cool as you please and not seeming to notice at all! I do believe he's going to give her the cut indirect. What d'you think, Stanford?"

Sir Stanford merely shook his head. He alone of the gentlemen had not given way to mirth at the sight of Annabelle's face. On the contrary, it had sobered him, for though he could appreciate the beauty's nose being put out of joint, he feared it boded ill for his friend. Desmond had been in Annabelle's toils so long it seemed to Sir Stanford his behavior today might be only a temporary show of defiance. Before long, he would probably give in to Annabelle's siren call once more. Sir Stanford knew as perhaps nobody else did how much Desmond had already suffered at Annabelle's hands, and judging from her face now, he felt she meant to make his friend suffer even more if she got the chance.

So Sir Stanford was quiet as he followed along behind the curricle with the rest of the gentlemen. Somehow he had lost his taste for baiting Annabelle. When one of his companions suggested going over to her and rallying her on Desmond's defection, he put a forceful veto on the idea. He even forced himself to bow politely to Annabelle—a salute neither appreciated nor returned, for Annabelle knew him as Desmond's closest friend. Supposing he was privy to, if not actually the instigator of, Desmond's affair with the handsome brunette, she resented him accordingly.

Meanwhile, Desmond remained quite unaware of Annabelle's fury. But another person had noticed it besides Sir Stanford and his friends, and that person was Susan.

She had been having a delightful time riding with Desmond, surveying the park in its spring glory and the illustrious company patronizing its walks and drives. Never in her life had she seen so many handsome equipages and beautiful horses. The people accompanying them were not so uniformly handsome and beautiful, but they were uniformly well-dressed, and Susan, regarding the display of spring millinery worn by the female portion of the population, was glad she had worn her new bonnet rather than the cobbled-together black beaver. There were hats as pretty as hers, she reckoned, but none actually prettier.

As she congratulated herself on this fact, her eye was caught by an upstanding poke bonnet with a sky-high cluster of sapphire blue plumes and enough ribbons to furnish forth a maypole. It was a rather vulgar hat, in Susan's opinion, but the lady wearing it was lovely enough to redeem its negative qualities. She had hair of a rich golden blond, a pink and white complexion like the best French dolls, and a truly spectacular figure.

As Susan surveyed her with respectful admiration, the lady looked up. Her china-blue eyes flickered briefly and contemptuously over Susan, then traveled to Desmond. At the sight of him, her expression underwent a startling change. Her eyes widened, her jaw dropped, and she stared as though she could not believe her eyes. It seemed to Susan there was not merely disbelief in her eyes but fury. And it also seemed to her a good deal of that fury was directed toward herself.

Not liking to be glared at more than most people, Susan stared back at the beauty an instant, then deliberately glanced away. But she was aware of the lady's furious regard as long as they remained in view. She was glad when the curricle finally rounded the bend of the carriageway and took them out of her line of vision.

As soon as she was relieved of that troublous glare, Susan glanced at Desmond. He did not appear to have noticed the blonde beauty's dagger looks. She was quite sure he had *not* noticed them, for she knew him well enough by now to be able to tell when something had annoyed or disturbed him. Nobody could have been glared at like that and not been annoyed or disturbed, Susan was sure. She wondered who the blonde lady was and why she had glared so.

It seemed to her in some strange way, however, that she already knew. There might be many reasons why a lovely young lady would display shock and anger at seeing a handsome and personable man, but the most likely reason was that at some time, in some way, there had been tender passages between them. Hell, as the playwright said, hath no fury like a woman scorned, and Susan felt instinctively that the blonde beauty's anger might be explained in this way.

Or perhaps not quite in this way. For when Susan remembered how very beautiful the blonde lady was, she could not believe any man would have scorned her. It seemed a great deal more likely her anger was based on some misunderstanding. Neither did Susan have far to look for the reason for such a misunderstanding. Undoubtedly she was responsible. The lady had seen her with Desmond, whom she supposed to be her own beau, and had been angered at his seeming faithlessness, not knowing he was only taking Susan driving as an act of kindness.

The idea she had come between Desmond and his ladylove made Susan feel dreadful. It did not help to tell herself it was merely an idea, and that she had not one iota of real proof to show it had foundations in truth. She simply *felt* it to be true, with a certainty both strong and fatalistic. Of course a man like Lord Desmond must love a woman like the blonde lady. She was a lady who really *was* beautiful and who needed no wig and paint to make her so. She might have a vulgar taste in hats, but apart from that she was peerless, a thousand times better suited to him than a woman like Susan Doyle.

Idiot, Susan castigated herself. That was the heart of the matter, as she very well knew. It was not so much that she felt badly because she had created a misunderstanding between Desmond and his ladylove, for though she might feel badly about that, she would not feel as though something precious to her had been stolen away. No, the fact was she was still cherishing romantic, inappropriate feelings toward Desmond, and as a result she felt jealous, or at least envious, of any other lady who enjoyed his regard.

Thinking of him together with the blonde beauty had made her feel the same way she had felt when she had seen the blue-sealed note lying on the hall table. And probably it had been the same lady who had written the note. It had looked like her somehow. Susan sighed. The day, which she had just been thinking delightfully warm for April, suddenly seemed a good deal chillier, as though a cloud had passed before the sun.

Desmond heard Susan's sigh, but attributed it to a different cause. "I'm sorry I can't go any faster," he apologized. "The traffic is so heavy now that I simply haven't any choice." He smiled at her. "We should be at the barrier soon, and we can go home from there, if you've had enough of the park."

"Yes, I've had enough of the park," said Susan drearily.

On the drive home, however, she took herself to task for her conduct. It was foolish that she should sulk like a spoiled child merely because she was jealous of the blonde lady. So she forced herself to sit up and make conversation with Desmond, who responded amiably, pointing out various sights along the way. Looking sideways now and then at his lean face and clear-cut features, Susan could not help feeling a pang, but she told herself she must be sensible. Whatever the blonde lady might or might not be to him, she herself was only a guest in his home, and it was beginning to look as though she might well have outworn her welcome there.

If her presence was going to make trouble for him with his friends, she had better be writing Aunt Theodosia and making plans to leave as soon as possible. Once she was out of the way, he could no doubt easily patch up matters with the blonde beauty, assuming it was her own presence the beauty objected to. Susan felt sure it was. *No one could quarrel with Lord Desmond on his own account*, she told herself. *He is the kindest, most considerate of men.* And she felt a bittersweet satisfaction it should be so.

Fourteen

In accordance with her resolution, Susan went to her room as soon as she reached home and sat down to write a letter to her Aunt Theodosia.

It proved an unexpectedly difficult task. It was not easy to put into words exactly why she had left her Aunt Sarah's house and still less easy to explain why she had taken refuge with a perfect stranger—and a bachelor gentleman at that. In the end, Susan abandoned any attempt to explain these things and merely wrote that she was in London staying with a friend and had urgent need of her aunt's advice on a number of matters. All other explanations, she reckoned, could much better wait until she saw her aunt in person.

She gave the finished note to Reese with instructions to have it sent as soon as possible, unaware a similar note had preceded her own by some days. Reese knew about that other note, but he said nothing of it to Susan, merely assuring her he would see her letter was promptly dispatched. "I'll see to it myself after dinner," he told her. "And speaking of dinner, I believe Mrs. Murphy is almost ready to dish up, miss. She's made mushroom fritters tonight, which is by way of being one of her specialties. I'm sure you'll like them."

"Thank you, Reese," said Susan. With sad cynicism, she reflected one could hardly enjoy mushroom fritters when one was suffering from heartbreak. But when the bell sounded for dinner, she found she herself feeling less heartbroken and more hungry than she would have supposed possible. Perhaps it was because the spirit of rebellion had risen in her once more, lifting her out of her momentary dejection.

Why should she fret about the blonde lady in the park? For all she knew, that lady might have no connection with Desmond at all. Even if she did have a connection, it might not be the one Susan imagined it was. Besides, as Susan told herself triumphantly, *she* was sitting down to dinner with Desmond that evening, not the blonde lady. That ought to be enough for her.

And it *was* enough, for the moment. Susan entered the dining parlor with her head held high. But she had taken care to array herself in her new flowered silk dress before she entered, and she did not remove her wig.

Meanwhile, in another part of London, Annabelle Windibank was throwing a tantrum in her bedchamber.

In still another quarter, Sir Stanford Kent was absently drinking sherry while pondering whether Desmond's conduct at the park that day meant he might after all be saved from the fatal error of marrying Annabelle Windibank.

And at White's Club in St. James's Street, a gentleman was telling several interested acquaintances about Lord Desmond Ryder's new Particular, who was so lovely she had bewitched him into forsaking the celebrated charms of Miss Annabelle Windibank.

Such news was not long in being circulated among the Upper Ten Thousand. Many of its denizens had bewailed Desmond's connection with Annabelle and were glad to think he might be saved from such a mésalliance. Desmond was generally popular among the members of the *ton,* while Annabelle most definitely was not.

It was not solely her birth that was against her. Persons of birth no higher than hers were welcome even in the most exclusive drawing rooms. But Annabelle had never possessed the knack of making friends. She had merely made conquests. This system had stood her in good stead as long as her conquests continued unabated, for even if some rival belle or straitlaced dowager saw fit to criticize her conduct, she could shrug it off as mere jealousy.

Now, however, she had met with a mortifying and public reverse of fortunes. And it seemed as though everyone she had injured in the course of her triumphal progress had now united to crow over her humiliation.

Little Miss Shaw, who had had the mortification of seeing her fiancé neglect her in favor of Annabelle, took care that everyone should know of Annabelle's own mortification. "They say he gave her the *cut direct,*" she told a group of wide-eyed young ladies at Almack's. "I wasn't there to see it, but Mr. Henry was. He said Lord Desmond looked straight at her without acknowledging her in the least. Miss Windibank just turned red as a peony and looked mad enough to spit."

"Serve her right, the vulgar thing," said a sharp-featured young lady vindictively.

"Indeed it does," agreed another of the young ladies. "I simply detest that girl. I've never been able to understand how she got the entrée to so many places. My only comfort is they don't allow her here at Almack's. The patronesses saw to that, thank heaven!"

"Yes, thank heaven," said another fervently. "But I want to hear more about this business of Lord Desmond snubbing Miss Windibank, Emily. You say he was with another young lady when he met her? Who was the young lady?"

Miss Shaw shrugged. "Nobody knows. Mr. Henry seems to think"—she waggled her eyebrows expressively—"that she wasn't a lady at all!"

"Then she's a deal like Annabelle Windibank," observed the sharp-featured young lady, eliciting a general laugh.

"I suppose she must be Lord Desmond's mistress," said another with a sigh. "It's a pity, isn't it, how many of the men prefer keeping mistresses to wives?"

"Well, I for one don't begrudge Lord Desmond his mistress if it means he won't be marrying Annabelle Windibank," opined the first young lady. "Of course, Miss Windibank is a handsome creature, one can't deny that. But imagine any man of decent family wishing to marry her! And the Ryders are so exclusive. I'm sure the Dowager Marchioness must be very relieved."

Desmond's mother was indeed relieved when she heard the news of her son's recent activities. She had lived too long in society to believe everything she heard, however, and the fact she wanted so much to hear Desmond had outgrown his infatuation for Annabelle made her hesitate all the more to believe it. "What do you think, Merrivale?" she asked, appealing to her eldest son, as was her habit in moments of stress. "Is there anything in these rumors I hear about Desmond?"

"Why, that depends what you hear," responded Lord Merrivale cautiously.

In a sharp voice, his mother adjured him not to be a chuckle-head. "You know what I am referring to," she said. "Is it true Desmond and Miss Windibank have had a falling out? Sophia Bloomsbury-Rush wrote to tell me he cut her dead in the park the other day and was actually seen driving out with another lady."

The marquess preserved a discreet silence.

"Merrivale, don't pretend you have heard nothing of this," said his mother with exasperation. "If even I have heard it, living at the Dower House, it stands to reason *you* must have. Besides, you were in Town only last week. Surely you must have seen or heard something of your brother?"

"Yes," said the marquess, after a scarcely perceptible hesitation. "I saw him at the theater one night, when I went there with the Cranbrooks."

"And was he with Miss Windibank?"

"No," admitted the marquess, after another barely perceptible pause. "He was not."

"Well, was he with some other lady? I do not see why you cannot simply tell me outright if he was, Merrivale. It seems to me you are being purposely provoking!"

"No, I am merely trying to spare your feelings," said the marquess evenly. "Desmond was there, but I very much fear his companion was . . . not a lady. Please don't make me say any more than that, Mama, or you will surely put me to the blush."

The dowager gave an amused snort. "I don't think I could do that, nor anyone else," she said. "But you needn't say any more, Merrivale. I am not such an innocent that I do not know what you mean. So Desmond has taken to consorting with the muslin company, has he?"

"It seems so," admitted the marquess.

The dowager raised her brows. "It *seems* so? But you saw this girl he was with, did you not?"

"Yes, I saw her."

"And is there any doubt that she is a member of the muslin company?"

The marquess wrinkled his brow. "I suppose not," he said. "And yet—"

"And yet what?" prompted the dowager, as he hesitated.

The marquess shrugged. "And yet she did not have quite the appearance one associates with a woman of that type. But doubtless she was one, all the same. I suppose the truth is any woman who could distract Desmond from Annabelle Windibank would appear like an angel of light to me, no matter what her character."

"I feel just the same," said the Dowager frankly.

The marquess laughed. "I am surprised at you, Mama," he teased. "I had not thought you would countenance vice, even to save Desmond from making a mésalliance."

"I'd countenance the devil himself if he'd save Desmond from marrying Annabelle Windibank," said the Dowager with a sigh. "You cannot know how unhappy I have been over this business, Merrivale."

"Yes, I can, Mama. As Desmond's brother, I may be supposed to have some feelings in the matter, too, you know."

"I suppose so," admitted the dowager. She looked wistfully at her elder son. "Tell me, Merrivale, don't you think this business of Desmond's going about with another girl seems hopeful? Even if she isn't a *respectable* girl? And you can't know for certain that she is not. You may suspect it, but you cannot *know.*"

Slowly the marquess shook his head. "No, I can't know it. But I'm quite sure I have never seen the girl before, and though I've made a few discreet inquiries in the last week or so, no one seems to know who she is or where she comes from. You must admit that doesn't sound very promising, ma'am."

The dowager refused to admit this at all. She pointed out that there might be many nice, respectable girls in London who were socially obscure. The marquess said nothing, for he saw no need to destroy his mother's hopes. But for himself, he had seen the hasty way his brother had bundled the unknown girl out of sight at the theater, and how embarrassed Desmond had looked when the Throgmorton harpy had questioned him about her. These circumstances struck Lord Merrivale as definitely suspicious, and so did the girl's claim of being a de Havilland.

Altogether, he was fairly well satisfied Desmond was embarked on some more or less disreputable love affair. Still, he trusted his brother's sense—up to a point—and on the whole, he felt encouraged by the turn events had taken. If Desmond was no longer dangling after Annabelle Windibank, that could only be counted a gain. The unknown dark-haired girl might be dealt with in due time should she prove a similar threat to his brother's happiness.

Fifteen

In the days that followed, Desmond found himself thinking less about Annabelle than he would have believed possible.

She simply did not monopolize his thoughts the same way as before. He could still think of her beauty with admiration, but the frenzied desire and longing that had once accompanied such thoughts had all drained away. Being a tolerably perspicacious man, Desmond could not help noticing this change had taken place more or less at the same time Susan had entered his life, but he felt satisfied it was not so simple a matter as cause and effect.

True, he had developed a warm admiration for Susan, and there were even times when he was conscious of being strongly attracted to her. But it wasn't a burning passion such as he had felt for Annabelle.

Annabelle had always seemed to him an exquisite, otherworldly creature, tantalizing in her femininity and maddening in her caprices. Susan's appeal was quite a different thing. Of course, she was feminine, too, and she certainly had her caprices, but her appeal was a more human one—the appeal of a friend and companion who just happened also to be a lovely woman. Hence, Desmond was reasonably sure he was not falling in love with Susan. Or at least he felt sure of it until the night of the opera.

After Annabelle had written saying she would not be able to attend the opera with him, Desmond had given up all intention of going. In the back of his mind he cherished a faint hope that she might relent, but though he had cherished this hope he had not done anything about it. This, in itself, was sufficiently indicative of a change in his feelings. A week before, he would have been in such an agony of suspense and longing that he would have been unable to resist the temptation to call on Annabelle and beg her to accompany him. On this occasion, he was able to await her verdict quite tranquilly.

By Friday afternoon, Desmond had still received no word from Annabelle, and he felt it reasonable to suppose she meant to persevere in her refusal. Running across the tickets as he sorted through the contents of his pockets that afternoon, he stood looking at them with sensations half rueful and half resigned.

When Annabelle had first consented to go with him to the opera, he had rejoiced exceedingly, feeling it augured well for his suit. When she had canceled the engagement, he had felt disappointed, but not as disappointed as he had expected to feel. And now, as he stood looking at the tickets, he realized he felt only indifferent. Let Annabelle stay away from the opera, or go with someone else if she liked. He simply did not care.

With a feeling of wonderment, Desmond explored his newfound indifference. He was almost afraid to, fearing his passion might spring up alive from the ashes when he examined it, but it really did seem to be extinguished. He wished Annabelle no ill, but neither did he wish any longer to make her his wife. The whole idea seemed ridiculous. He felt free as air now, free to do as he wished, and he found what he wished most was to go to the opera that night with Susan.

"Susan!" he said. With quick steps he went through the parlor to the sitting room. Susan had been sitting on the sofa with a book a little earlier, but he did not find her there now. Concluding that she had gone to her room to change for dinner, he tapped lightly at her door. "Susan?"

"Yes?" Susan sounded rather startled.

"It's I, Desmond," he said. "May I come in?"

There was a brief pause. Then Susan said, "If you like."

Desmond needed no further invitation. He opened the door and stepped into Susan's bedchamber.

She was seated at her dressing table with a hairbrush in her hand. It was evident she had just finished brushing her hair, for the short curls gleamed like molten copper. It struck Desmond that he had seen little of those curls in recent days. She had been wearing her wig almost every waking hour. Looking at her hair now, he thought it a pity that she had to hide it, but he was too intent on his errand to dwell on this side issue. "I wonder if you would like to go to the opera tonight?" he said in a rush.

"To the opera?" said Susan. She looked first pleased. Then her eyes shadowed. "I would like to go, but I think perhaps I had better not spend the money," she said hesitatingly. "After all, we go to Vauxhall tomorrow."

"Yes, but this will cost you nothing," broke in Desmond eagerly. "I already have the tickets—have had them for over a week. We may as well use them as not, for they will be wasted otherwise."

"I see," said Susan. A smile spread across her face. "The opera!" she said. "I have never been to the opera, my lord."

"I think you will enjoy it," said Desmond. "It's quite a spectacle, even apart from the performance itself. All the ladies wear their finest dresses and jewels, and the gentlemen do their best to outdo Brummel."

"I see," said Susan again, a trifle pensively. She glanced sideways at Desmond in the mirror. "Do you think the dress I wore to the theater is fine enough?"

"Oh, yes," Desmond assured her. He remained for a few minutes, telling her all about the opera and the singers they were going to hear, but then it occurred to him it was a rather equivocal proceeding for a gentleman to be chatting with a lady in her bedchamber. He had forgotten this fact in his eagerness, but something in Susan's manner now reminded him. He felt she must be wondering at his behavior. So he excused himself with a trifle of embarrassment in his own manner and took himself away to change into knee breeches and silk stockings.

Susan *was* wondering at his behavior, as it happened. It was the first time he had ever come into her bedchamber since the night she had arrived. His presence made her feel a little flustered, especially since she had just finished brushing out her hair.

Increasingly she shrank from being seen by Desmond in her natural state. All the while he was in her bedchamber she felt he must be mentally comparing her appearance in wig and cosmetics with the unadorned version he was looking at now. It made her very uncomfortable, so she was glad when he left.

Yet she found herself a little sorry, too. Feeling as she did about him, it had been a thrill to have him come to her like that, entering her room so casually and remaining to chat with her while she dressed her hair. But she knew it was wrong to feel this way. Desmond did not care for her more than as a friend, and if she felt more than that for him in return, it only showed she was a goose.

"I *am* a goose," said Susan aloud. Her reflection, red-haired and freckled, looked back at her from the mirror. Making a face at it, Susan picked up the dark wig and pulled it over her fiery locks. She then picked up a pot of paint, and with ruthless efficiency began to apply the elegant and polished complexion of Chloe de Havilland.

When Susan presently appeared, garbed once more in her wig and the apple-blossom gauze dress, Desmond surveyed her with an admiration that yet had in it a hint of dissatisfaction. Certainly she looked lovely, but he found himself wishing she had left off her wig and paint.

This was an irrational attitude, for if he had not known she was wearing them, he would never have thought of criticizing them, but since he did know, their falseness jarred on him somehow. He found himself wishing she had come as she had looked earlier, when he had found her at her dressing table.

But of course she could not do that, he reminded himself. The whole point of her masquerade was to render her unrecognizable to anyone who might see her later in her natural state. So he damped down his dissatisfaction and took comfort in the fact that, with or without wig and paint, she was a companion with whom any man might be proud to be seen.

"I suppose you will insist on being there when the curtain rises, as you did for the play the other night," he said, smiling at her. "That being the case, we had better be on our way. May I help you with your shawl?"

"Thank you, but I am not quite ready," said Susan, looking rather uncomfortable. "I do not have any jewelry, you see. And you said ladies wore their best jewelry to the opera—"

"Of course!" said Desmond. "You will be wanting to wear some of your jewelry. Just let me fetch your jewel case from the safe."

When he brought the box out to Susan, she stood hesitating for a moment, turning over the different pieces. The pearl set she had worn to the theater was, to her mind, the prettiest of her mother's jewelry, but Desmond had said ladies wore their best to the opera, and the pearls were not, strictly speaking, her best. That title must belong to the diamond necklace and aigrette that had come down to her from her grandmother. She never remembered seeing her mother wear them, for both pieces were a trifle heavy and old-fashioned, but the stones in them were of an excellent quality. On the whole, Susan felt quality mattered more on this occasion than superficial appearance. She wanted Desmond to admire her—desperately wanted it—but more than anything else she wanted to do him credit. So she picked up the velvet-lined case that contained the necklace and aigrette and said, "This, if you please."

It only took a moment to pin the aigrette in her hair. It looked dazzling against the dusky coils of her wig, and Susan regarded it for a moment with indefinable feelings before taking up the necklace. Here she experienced difficulty, for the clasp was an old-fashioned one and difficult to work.

Seeing her difficulty, Desmond came to her aid. "Let me," he said, and in a matter of seconds had clasped it efficiently about her neck.

There was nothing presumptuous about his touch, but Susan could feel it on the nape of her neck long after they were in the carriage and on their way to the opera house.

For his part, Desmond was experiencing another

revelation. Looking at Susan sitting across from him in the carriage in her flowing robes of gauze, he felt—something. He recalled the moment when he had clasped the necklace around her throat. There had been something very intimate and arousing about touching the soft skin at the nape of her neck, and Desmond admitted he had been aroused. But he had also felt something more—a kind of protective feeling, mingled with a sense almost of awe that he should have the privilege of performing such a service for her.

And yet he was still conscious of a sense of dissatisfaction, too. Watching Susan sit there, lovely and remote and seemingly unconscious of his regard, he felt as though he was viewing her from the wrong end of a telescope. When he thought back over the last week, he had the sense that in spite of their growing intimacy, she had been moving away from him somehow. Even now it seemed to him that she was, in some indefinable way, keeping him at a distance.

He found he did not want to be kept at a distance. He had the urge to get up and go sit beside her on the opposite banquette. But even if he closed the physical distance between them, he felt a distance would still remain. It was nothing he could put his finger on it, but he had a dim sense it had something to do with her wig and cosmetics, and he resented them accordingly.

Susan, meanwhile, was quite conscious of his regard, though she pretended not to be. She wondered why he was staring at her so. She hoped it was because he thought her attractive, but of this she felt a little unsure. He had not paid her a single compliment that evening—perhaps because she had been obliged to wear the same dress as on the night of the theater, and it did not have the same appeal a new one would have had. For a moment Susan found herself wishing she had thrown economy to the wind and gotten a new dress for the occasion. But that would have been almost impossible, considering the short notice Desmond had given her.

In any event, she had her diamonds, Susan reminded herself. Even if they were rather heavy and old-fashioned, it was something to be wearing diamonds. And it was something more to be going to the opera with Lord Desmond Ryder on a beautiful spring evening with the stars peeping through a sky of deepest blue. The thought made Susan's mercurial spirits rise once again.

There might be many things wrong with the universe, but there were also many that were right. For this one night, she would make the most of those things that were right. Soon her Aunt Theo would come, and probably she would be whisked away from London with no likelihood of ever seeing Desmond again. Probably he would not even miss her.

But he was with her tonight, and in the eyes of the world, at least, they would be a couple. Susan told herself she wanted no higher honor than that. Lifting her head, she looked Desmond in the eye and smiled a smile that held all the poignancy of imminent loss.

Desmond, receiving the full force of that smile, blinked. Then he smiled back, feeling his heart bound with relief. What difference did a wig and a trifle of paint make, after all? Susan was still Susan. And it seemed to Desmond that the distance he had felt between them had narrowed quite perceptibly.

Sixteen

When Desmond and Susan came forward to take their seats in the opera house, they immediately became the cynosure of all eyes.

The seats were very good ones, located in a box front and center above the stage. They had originally been obtained by Desmond at great cost and trouble because he knew Annabelle would be satisfied with nothing but the best and was hardly to be satisfied even with that. Now, as Desmond helped seat Susan in the chair beside him, it struck him with sudden force what a difference there was between the two women. Susan never would have insisted on the best seats in the house. She would have been happy sitting in the gallery, as she had proved the other night at Drury Lane. It was a measure of her unselfish spirit, her hardheaded prudence, and her happy ability to enjoy herself anywhere under almost any circumstances.

He had noticed these qualities of Susan's before, of course, on many occasions. But he felt he had never before appreciated how rare they were: how rare and how precious. She was like no other woman he had ever known, not merely lovely and charming, but intelligent, principled, and unselfish. And he knew suddenly, without any further reflection, that he loved her.

The revelation burst upon him like a skyrocket,

illuminating the landscape of his heart with sudden clarity. But though there seemed no doubt as to the authenticity of his emotions, Desmond urged himself to go slowly. *Why, only a week ago I was imagining myself in love with Annabelle!* he reminded himself. *It's early days yet to be falling in love again.*

What he had felt for Annabelle had been a completely different thing from what he was feeling now, however. Desmond could see, with the same sense of enlightenment, that his love for Annabelle had not been love at all, but rather a poor, superficial thing based on externals. The better he had come to know her, the less he had come to care for her.

With Susan, the exact reverse had been true. The better he had come to know her, the more he had learned to care for her, until now her visible qualities seemed the least important thing about her. Not that he did not think her lovely. He found her very lovely in any of her incarnations, but the beauty of the woman inside had won his heart in a way he had never thought possible.

This whole truth was revealed to Desmond in the few seconds it took him to help Susan into her seat. He sank down into his own seat quite overcome with the force of the revelation. As a result, he was utterly unconscious of the attention he and Susan were attracting from all over the house. Eyes were turned to them with curiosity, shock, and—in the case of one feminine observer, at least—furious disbelief.

That observer was Annabelle Windibank.

It had been a last-minute whim on her part to attend the opera that night. Still furious with Desmond over the incident in the park, she had decided it would be a fine revenge to attend with Mr. Stevens the same performance she had declined to attend with Desmond. He should see she had spurned his invitation in favor of a more worthy suitor. Of course, Mr. Stevens could not really be counted a more worthy suitor in any sense except looks, but she counted on Desmond's jealousy to make the fiction work. She still labored under the apprehension Desmond was hers at heart, no matter how much attention he might seem to pay to another lady. After all, he had been dangling after her for four months now and had never failed to jump through the highest hoops she could devise in order to prove his devotion. That such devotion could evaporate virtually overnight was a thing Annabelle simply could not imagine.

As a result, when she saw Desmond taking his seat in the box alongside the same pretty brunette who had been driving with him in the park, Annabelle drew a single outraged gasp, then schooled her features to immobility. She was resolved Desmond should not see he had succeeded in piquing her. Neither did she wish anyone else to see it. Quizzing glasses had turned toward his box from all over the house, and Annabelle was bitterly certain those same glasses would soon be turning toward her to see how she was reacting. She was determined they should find her gay and insensible. So she immediately fell to flirting with Mr. Stevens, laughing and coquetting and making great play with her fan, all the while keeping a jealous eye on the couple across the way.

It did not take her long to notice Susan's necklace and aigrette. *Surely he has not given her diamonds!* Annabelle thought incredulously. The question was a rhetorical one, however. Since she had already made up her mind Susan was an ill-bred hussy who was no better than she ought to be, there was no other way she could have obtained such a display of jewelry—a very vulgar and improper display, Annabelle told herself righteously.

Still, a cold chill of unease was creeping over her. It was one thing for Desmond to flirt with another girl and take her riding in the park. That was quite within the rules of flirtation as Annabelle understood them, and though she might not like such a maneuver, she could comprehend it. But it was another and far more serious thing for Desmond to buy another girl diamonds.

What could he mean by it? Annabelle supposed it might be simply a further attempt to pique her. But somehow she could not imagine Desmond carrying matters this far. He was not rich enough to be bestowing showy diamond necklaces on a lightskirt for no better purpose than piquing another lady. At the very least, such an expenditure must make a serious dent in his bank balance, and as the future Lady Desmond Ryder, Annabelle wanted the disposal of that bank balance for herself. It was enough to make her gnash her teeth with anger and frustration.

Chiefly, however, what she felt was not so much anger but fear. Was it possible this other girl had succeeded in winning Desmond's affections away from her? She had scoffed at the idea before, both to herself and Mrs. Throgmorton, but now she began to fear there was something in it.

Watching Desmond smiling into Susan's eyes, Annabelle had to admit he appeared smitten. Of course, that might merely be an act like the one she was putting on with Mr. Stevens, but somehow she could not believe this. Unlike herself, Desmond had never been much of an actor. He had always been perfectly straightforward in his emotions, so much so that Annabelle had often been amused at his transparency. Now she felt not amused at all, but very much afraid.

With barely suppressed hatred, she appraised Susan out of the corner of her eye. There could be no doubt this other girl was pretty—not so pretty as she herself, perhaps, but definitely pretty. She also appeared to be barely out of her teens. This was a further offense, for Annabelle had celebrated her twenty-fourth birthday a few weeks before, and perhaps this circumstance as much as any other had decided her to accept the proposal of a mere younger son.

But in Annabelle's eyes, the crowning offense Susan was committing that evening was to look happy. She was simply glowing with happiness in a way that struck Annabelle as almost indecent. *She is proud to be scandalizing us all, the unprincipled hussy,* she told herself with virtuous indignation.

Desmond, too, was looking happy, and this further exacerbated Annabelle's ire. He had no business to look happy when she was punishing him. In short, things were looking very serious indeed.

Much as she hated to admit it, it looked as though Mrs. Throgmorton had been right. She had held Desmond at a distance too long, so that this other girl had had the opportunity to slip in and cut her out. She, Annabelle Windibank, had been guilty of a miscalculation.

But though Annabelle was willing to admit she had made a miscalculation, she was not about to admit the situation was hopeless. Not much more than a week ago, Desmond had been frantically in love with her. Surely the embers of that passion must still be alive, even if the flames had subsided a trifle. She would just have to add a little fuel to the fire, that was all.

Annabelle had no doubts of her ability to do this. She only regretted she had let it go so long. If she had relented sooner, those diamonds might have been clasped about her own neck rather than the hussy's over yonder. But there were other diamonds in the world, Annabelle assured herself. Even if this set was lost to her, there was nothing to prevent

Desmond from buying her another just as good and perhaps even better.

So with this philosophical reflection to comfort her, Annabelle fell to planning her next move. She must lose no time in showing Desmond she was willing to welcome him back. Unfortunately, the first act of the opera was in progress, and both Desmond and that insufferable girl were watching the action onstage with rapt attention. Annabelle, who had little enough patience with opera at the best of times and none at all at the present moment, thought this a queer taste, but she settled herself to wait with such patience as she could muster until the first act should be over.

For Susan, that first act was sheer bliss. It was not merely that the music was divine, the costumes wonderful, and the singing superb. It was rather that she was so thoroughly in tune with her surroundings. There were many pretty dresses and impressive displays of jewelry to be seen on the ladies around her, but none she thought prettier or more impressive than her own. Likewise, there were many handsome gentlemen in the opera house, elegantly garbed in well-tailored dark coats and satin knee breeches. But there were none like Desmond.

Susan turned her head to look at Desmond sitting next to her. He looked back at her, smiled, then reached out and covered her hand with his own. Susan felt herself tremble at his touch. Her heart soared with delight and with other emotions that she could not bear to define. She only knew she was very, very happy. Even the thought that he was seeing her as Chloe de Havilland could not spoil her happiness. Her hair and complexion might be artificial, but something in Desmond's eyes was very real indeed.

When the first interval came, Desmond suggested they go get ices. Susan agreed, as she would have agreed to any suggestion he had made just then. She was floating on a wave of euphoria, and Desmond was evidently in high spirits, too. They laughed and bantered back and forth while they were eating their ices, and when at last Desmond gave Susan his arm to escort her back to her seat, she felt so supernally happy she had to take herself in hand.

Remember who he is, she reminded herself. *And remember it's only for tonight that you have him. Perhaps a few nights more as well—but I mustn't count on that. I mustn't count on anything beyond tonight.* Susan repeated this admonition to herself several times, but it had no effect on her euphoria. Even if she had nothing but tonight, tonight seemed enough—for the moment, at least—and she was determined to make the most of it.

Thinking these thoughts, she turned her head to smile at Desmond and became aware of someone staring at her from a box across the opera house.

Susan looked curiously toward the box. Seated there was the same beautiful blonde girl she had seen in the park a few days before.

There could be no doubt she was the same girl. Such beauty must be rare, Susan reckoned, even in a great city like London. The lady was looking at Susan very hard, but the next instant her gaze shifted to Desmond, and she smiled and bowed graciously toward him. Susan turned to look at Desmond. He did not appear to have seen the lady's greeting. Touching his arm, Susan nodded toward the lady. "There's someone bowing to you," she said. "That lady in the box across the way."

She indicated the box in question.

Desmond followed her gaze, and Susan saw him give a slight start. The lady, finding his eyes now on her, gave him another bow and a smile much warmer than the previous one.

Susan glanced at Desmond again to see how he was reacting. His face was grave, but she had the oddest impression he was amused.

"She does seem determined to recognize me, doesn't she?" he said. "Well, I suppose it won't do to cut her." He gave the lady a slight bow, then turned to smile at Susan. "Are you enjoying the opera?"

"Very much," said Susan. She burned to know more about the blonde lady, but it was clear from Desmond's manner that he considered the matter closed. That being the case, Susan did not like to ask any questions. Out of the corner of her eye, she studied the blonde lady. She could not help feeling jealous of her beauty, but it was beginning to look now as though her jealousy had no foundation. Certainly Desmond's reaction had not been one to inspire jealousy. He had showed no emotion at all on seeing the lady, except for his initial start of surprise.

On the whole, Susan felt she had been foolish to postulate a relationship between the lady and Desmond on such slim evidence as had been given her. Her spirits, momentarily depressed by the idea of a rival, went soaring up again. Desmond was still hers as much as anyone's, and there was no reason why she need fear any number of beautiful blondes, for this evening at least.

For Desmond, seeing Annabelle had been an undoubted shock. Yet he was pleased to find that after the first surprise was past he felt nothing but a sense of amusement. So Annabelle had decided to attend the opera after all, had she? And she had found someone else to accompany her.

Desmond told himself she was welcome to Augustus Stevens if she wanted him. He suspected, however, that it was more a case of Annabelle being up to her old tricks again. It was a regular policy of hers to play off one of her suitors against the others.

Likewise, it was one of her favorite maneuvers to blow hot on an admirer whom she had formerly frozen. He had seen her do it many times before and merely written it off as feminine caprice.

Now he saw it for what it was, a deliberate and cold-blooded strategy. Her greeting just now had been an attempt to manipulate him, just as he had been manipulated by her from the moment he had first picked up her handkerchief. As long as he had been warm, she had been cool; since he had become cool, she was going to be warm, as witness her bow and smile just now.

Desmond saw it all with sudden clarity. He wondered how he could ever have been taken in by anything so obvious. But at least he had come to his senses in time. He looked down at Susan beside him. Wig, rice powder, and all, she was still more real than Annabelle. What was more, she had a sense of integrity that never would have let her stoop to emulate Annabelle's crude strategies. He would have been willing to stake his life on it. In fact, he *was* willing to stake his life on it, as he realized in another flash of enlightenment. Was not marriage often called a gamble? Well, he, Desmond, was willing to take that gamble. He wanted nothing more than to marry this wonderful girl destiny had swept so curiously into his life.

My goodness, it has been an evening of revelation, Desmond told himself, feeling both amused and a trifle dazed. He reminded himself there was no need to rush his fences. If his love for Susan was real, as he felt sure it was, then it could certainly endure a few weeks' wait until he had made certain of it.

Besides, he must not take it for granted that Susan returned his feelings. She might have no feeling for him at all apart from friendship. Still, when he had reached out to touch her hand earlier in the performance, she had made no attempt to draw it away. That seemed a promising sign.

On an impulse, Desmond reached out and took her hand in his once more. She smiled at him, and Desmond felt a flood of warmth and happiness suffuse him. He settled back in his chair with her hand still secure in his and felt as happy a man as any in the four kingdoms.

When the opera ended, he had to let go of Susan's hand, but he had the compensatory privilege of helping her with her shawl and taking her arm to lead her through the crowd. He saw several acquaintances as he and Susan made their way out of the opera house, but the press of people around them made a good excuse to give them no more than a bow or smile in passing. He could tell by the looks of interest and speculation that were cast his way that wholly wrong conclusions were being drawn about him and Susan, but he was not inclined to worry too much about this. His reputation could stand the imputation that he was keeping a mistress, and Susan's was safe behind her wig and cosmetics.

And come what may, both Susan and I know the truth of the matter, he assured himself. *There's no danger it will cause a misunderstanding down the road.* Still, he thought he would be glad when the time for masquerade would be over. He longed for the day when Susan could appear at his side sans wig and cosmetics, in her proper role as Lady Desmond Ryder.

Seventeen

Desmond and Susan did not escape the crowd around the opera house without one last encounter with Annabelle.

Just as Desmond was putting Susan into his carriage, an out-of-breath footman came running up with a folded paper in his hand. "For you, m'lord," he told Desmond. "Most urgent. The lady is waiting for an answer."

With a feeling of premonition, Desmond unfolded the paper. It was a note from Annabelle, imploring him to call upon her that evening. She gave no specific reason for this request apart from a need to speak to him urgently.

A faint smile curved Desmond's lips. Annabelle was running true to form once again. Ruefully, he reflected if he had only been able to maintain an attitude of disinterest from the beginning of their acquaintance, he would probably have been spared much torment. But his experience had taught him something, both about women and himself, and on the whole he was not inclined to regret it.

This line of thought brought him naturally to Susan. He glanced toward the carriage. She was looking out the window, regarding him, the footman, and the paper in his hand with obvious curiosity. Desmond smiled at her, then turned to the footman. "I am afraid it is quite impossible for me to fulfill Miss Windibank's request," he said. "Unfortunately I have made other plans for this evening. Please give her my apologies, along with my best regards."

The footman bowed and hurried off, and Desmond turned back to Susan. He felt as though a burden had just slipped from his shoulders. He had refused a request of Annabelle's and done it without a shred of regret. It gave him a wonderful sense of freedom. One of the things that had concerned him most about falling in love with Susan was the idea he might be considered in some wise tied to Annabelle in spite of the fact she had refused his proposal of marriage.

Now he had renounced those ties once and for all. The idea gave Desmond a great deal of satisfaction. He disliked it that relations between him and Susan had been muddied by his attachment to Annabelle. The idea of a making a clean break with her now was the next best thing to never having been involved with her in the first place. But it seemed the break was not to be so clean as he had thought. Traffic in front of the opera house was heavy, and it was some time before Desmond's carriage was able to pull away from the curb. It had just done so when there was a flurry of footsteps behind them and a frantic rapping at the door of the carriage.

"What the—" began Desmond. Then his heart sank, for through the window he saw Annabelle's lovely face, bewitchingly framed in the hood of a blue velvet opera cloak.

"The *deuce,*" said Desmond furiously. *"Hell."* Raising the trapdoor in the roof, he called for the coachman to stop the carriage. "I'll be back in a moment," he told Susan, who was regarding both him and Annabelle with wide eyes. Giving her an apologetic smile, he opened the door and swung down.

On seeing him, Annabelle's face lit up in one of her dazzling smiles. "My lord, I am so glad I was able to catch you," she said, pushing back her hood and extending a gloved hand to him. "I simply had to speak to you a moment—I *had* to."

Desmond did not take the proffered hand. "What did you need to speak to me about?" he asked.

Annabelle pouted, glancing up at him through her lashes. "That is not a very warm greeting," she said. "You did not used to be so short with me, my lord."

"No," agreed Desmond baldly.

Annabelle looked annoyed, but managed another smile. "Indeed, you are very short, my lord," she said. "I would have thought you would have been more glad to see me."

Desmond said nothing to this. After a moment, Annabelle went on, in a grieved tone. "My lord, what has happened? Are you angry with me?"

"Not in the least," said Desmond. "But you'll have to excuse me, Miss Windibank. I cannot stand here talking to you, pleasant as that might be. As I told your footman just now, I have other plans for this evening. Did he not convey my message?"

"Yes," said Annabelle, her expression a nicely blended mixture of sorrow and disappointment. "He gave me your message. But I simply could not believe you would deal with me so harshly, my lord. As I said, I badly need to speak with you."

"What about?" said Desmond.

Annabelle drew an exasperated sigh. "I cannot tell you *here,*" she said. "Cannot you come and see me this evening, my lord? I cannot believe your other engagement is as pressing as *that.*" She threw a look at Susan that conveyed clearly her estimate of that young lady's character.

Desmond gave followed her gaze and smiled. "I'm afraid it is," he said. "If your business is pressing, you'd better tell it to me now, Miss Windibank. Otherwise, I'd recommend you consult someone else about it—Mr. Stevens, for instance."

Annabelle drew herself up to her full height. "Very well," she said. "I shall do that. And I hope you enjoy your *engagement,* my lord." With these words, she pulled up her hood again and flounced away.

Grinning, Desmond opened the carriage door and swung himself back inside. Susan, from the opposite banquette, looked at him questioningly. On an impulse, he came over to sit beside her. "Susan, I have been a fool," he told her.

"Have you?" said Susan.

Deliberately Desmond took her hand in his. "I hope you don't mind my calling you Susan," he said. "I know we've only been acquainted a week or so, but I feel as though I have known you much longer."

"You may call me Susan," assented Susan. She had been on fire with jealousy while his conversation with the blonde lady had been going on, but their evidently contentious parting had partly reassured her. Desmond's manner now accomplished the rest of the cure. She did not know exactly what he was leading up to, but she felt sure it boded no ill for herself.

"Susan, then," said Desmond, and smiled at her. "As I say, I have been a fool, but my eyes are open now."

"Are they?" said Susan.

"Indeed they are," said Desmond. He was looking down at her in a manner that brought a tinge of real color to her cheeks beneath the rouge. All at once, Susan decided she had had enough of circumlocution. She wanted to know the truth, and the easiest way to learn it was to ask.

"That lady," she said, "the one you were talking to just now. I had noticed her when we were in the park last week."

"Had you?" said Desmond. "I don't recall seeing her that day." With a smile, he added, "I was too busy looking at you, I suppose."

Susan chose to ignore this statement for the time being. "I wondered then who she could be," she continued. "I couldn't help noticing her because she was so very beautiful."

"Yes, she is beautiful," said Desmond. "But you are just as beautiful yourself."

Susan looked at him narrowly. Amazingly, he appeared to be in earnest. She wrote it off to the wig and cosmetics, however. "Well, I am sure I am much obliged to you for the compliment," she said. "But, Desmond, who is she?"

"Her name," said Desmond, "is Annabelle Windibank. She is a very lovely girl, as you have already noticed. At one time I was disposed to admire her very much."

"Yes?" prompted Susan, as he paused.

"Yes, to my shame I was," said Desmond. "Since then, however, my eyes have been opened, as I say. Opened to real beauty." And he leaned down and kissed Susan on the lips.

This action surprised him as much as Susan. He had not meant to kiss her until he had made sure of her feelings and of his own. But it felt right to lay his lips on hers, and in the process he found that he had obtained all the surety he needed. With a soaring sense of uplift, he knew that he really loved her in a manner he had never supposed possible. And he felt with a lover's instinct that his feelings were at least in some degree reciprocated.

"Oh, Desmond," whispered Susan. Desmond put

his arms around her and drew her close against him in a fierce surge of love and possession. She made no objection, surrendering herself to his embrace and putting her own arms around him. Desmond felt a happiness hardly human in its sublimity. Neither of them said a word more, and he held her thus all the way home.

At the steps of his own house, he had to release her. He did so reluctantly, wishing the interlude need never have ended. It had been heavenly to hold her and feel she was his, but now they were back to earth again, with earthly complications intruding left and right. It was necessary, for instance, to act with formal propriety as he helped her from the carriage and into the house. Once inside the house, the charade of formality had to go on, for Reese was there, hovering about in the background and keeping his usual unobtrusive watch in order to anticipate his master's needs. He could hardly know that on this occasion what his master needed most was privacy.

Desmond was both amused and exasperated. Here he was, a grown man of thirty years, and yet he was feeling as awkward as any schoolboy. He supposed he might dismiss Reese in order to talk to Susan privately, but a moment's reflection showed him this course was unwise. It was very late. He was already in an exalted and reckless state, and there was no saying what might happen if he got Susan to himself once more. He looked down at her wistfully as he helped her off with her shawl. "It's very late," he said. "I suppose I had better be wishing you a good night."

"Must you?" said Susan, sounding a little wistful herself.

"Yes, I think so," said Desmond, making no effort to conceal the regret in his voice. "But, Susan—

what we were talking of before. I would like to talk about it again with you sometime. May I?"

"Yes, to be sure," said Susan. Giving him her hand, she said formally, "Good night, my lord."

"Good night, Susan," said Desmond. Taking her hand in his, he bent over and kissed it.

Susan, in her room that night, thought a great deal about that kiss, and even more about the other kiss that had preceded it. She had the oddest sense she had imagined the whole thing. Surely dreams could not come true in such a convenient fashion. She simply could not believe Lord Desmond had really called her beautiful, kissed her, and implied in so many words he cared for her. *It's true,* she told herself. *It* is *true.* But try though she might to convince herself, the sensation of unreality remained.

As she lay in bed, waiting for sleep to come, she lived through the course of the evening, culminating in the moment when Desmond had laid his lips on hers.

"Oh," whispered Susan, as overpowered by the recollection as by the reality. "Oh, I do love him. I *do.*"

There seemed no longer any point in denying it. For days she had been fighting the attraction that had drawn her toward this man whose affairs had become so curiously entangled with her own. She had not dared hope he was attracted to her in return, at least not in any sincere and durable way. But now it seemed he was. Undoubtedly his intentions were honorable. His character was as well known to her as if she had been acquainted with him for years, and the idea he could have said the things he had said this evening for some base or dishonorable purpose was laughable.

Besides, Susan told herself wryly, *if he had been intent on seduction, he would not have sent me off to bed alone with only a kiss on the hand.* She shivered a little, considering what would have happened if Desmond had *not* sent her off to bed alone. Could she have resisted him? A hysterical laugh rose to Susan's lips. "I wouldn't even have wanted to," she said aloud.

Fortunately for her, Desmond had been content merely to kiss her and bid her good night. She could not doubt his intentions were honorable. That was a wonderful thing, for she could not imagine a greater happiness than to be married to him. But when she tried to revel in her happiness, she was plagued by an uneasy sensation there was a fly in the ointment somewhere.

Growing exasperated at length, Susan mentally shook out the folds of her happiness and began to examine it breadth by breadth to see wherein the flaw lay.

Was it the fact that Desmond was a member of the nobility? Considering this issue, Susan had to admit it did trouble her. She did not like to think that Desmond, by marrying her, would be lowering himself in the eyes of the world. But she reminded herself that one party in a marriage was almost certain to outrank the other socially, for matches between true equals must be necessarily rare.

Besides, Susan reminded herself with an inward smile, she was already a self-declared revolutionary who cared nothing for the opinion of the world. If she were to refuse to marry Desmond on these grounds, he would certainly point out the inconsistencies of her attitude. Naturally, she still wished she were the party *giving* distinction rather than the one *taking* it, but since she was not, she felt it would be ungenerous not to be true to her principles as well as her heart.

Having settled that rank was not an objection to her marrying Desmond, Susan went on to consider the next issue. Was she unhappy Desmond had once admired Miss Windibank? Susan had to admit to herself she did envy Miss Windibank's lovely face and figure. Likewise, she could summon up a faint jealousy when she imagined Desmond paying court to her. But neither of these emotions was very pronounced, for Desmond had said he thought her, Susan, lovelier than Miss Windibank, and he had proved it by his behavior, too.

This effectively removed any cause of real jealousy, for Susan did not doubt he meant exactly what he said. Desmond did not lie. He really believed she was worthy of his admiration and love. But when Susan considered this seemingly gratifying idea, she discovered therein lay the sting.

Desmond had said she was lovelier than Miss Windibank. But did he not really mean *Chloe de Havilland* was lovelier than Miss Windibank? It was ridiculous to suppose that she, red-haired, freckle-faced Susan Doyle, could compare in any way with Miss Windibank's dazzling blonde beauty. With the dark wig to cover her hair, and powder and paint hiding her freckles, she might be judged tolerably handsome, but in her natural state she was nowhere in the running. No one could think so, least of all a man of taste and discrimination like Desmond.

It followed, therefore, that when Desmond had called her beautiful, he had meant she was beautiful in the guise of Chloe de Havilland. And that meant what he admired—what he loved—was not the real Susan Doyle at all. It was a well-known fact that men valued beauty above all other qualities in a woman. Susan had seen it for herself, even in the limited society of Barnhart. Several times she had witnessed seemingly sensible men losing their heads for girls who had nothing apart from their faces and figures to recommend them. Was Desmond's love of this sort?

Susan very much feared it was. The thought sent her spiraling into depression. She would not, she thought, have minded so much if the beauty he esteemed was really her own. But it was not her own. It was an illusion, a combination of false hair and powder and paint.

Well, many women wear false hair, Susan reminded herself. *Aunt Sarah used wear a false front now and then, and Miss Glick in the village had those hideous side curls she pinned on for special occasions. And many women use powder and paint, too. Why, I wouldn't be surprised if Miss Windibank herself didn't use it. Her complexion is really too pink and white to be natural.*

But somehow these arguments did not comfort Susan. The plain fact was that she was an idealist—a foolish idealist, she told herself ruefully. She might want Desmond's love more than anything else on earth, but she did not want to win it through a trick. Other women might resort to deception and think there was nothing wrong in it, but she, Susan Doyle, could not do that. A fundamental honesty in her shrank as much from acting a lie as from speaking one.

But I haven't really been acting a lie, Susan assured her conscience. *Desmond knows I am wearing a wig and paint. I wasn't wearing them when I first met him, and he has seen me without them several times since.* Her conscience immediately pointed out that for the last three or four days she had been wigged and painted from morn to night. Knowing he admired her as a brunette, she had purposely appeared as a brunette before him, and this was the result.

Well, what am I to do about it? Susan demanded of herself. In facing this question she first realized her awful dilemma. Fundamentally honest she might be, but if it came to a choice between keeping Desmond's love and losing it, she wanted to keep it at any price. Yet if keeping it meant she must always be acting a charade, then she could never be really happy in its possession. Either way, misery loomed.

I must do the right thing, Susan told herself unhappily. *I must!* In this case, there could be no doubt what the right thing was. She must eschew disguise hereafter and show Desmond her real self. If this meant his feelings would cool toward her, then so be it. Love that was based on a false premise was not true love in any case. Susan assured herself she wanted no love that was not true, but she could not help thinking that life without Desmond, now she had come to know him, would be almost unimaginably bleak.

But I don't want him if he doesn't want me, Susan told herself. *I must let him get used to seeing the real me again and find out whether he still cares for me. If he does, well and good. If he doesn't, at least I will keep my self-respect.* There was, as she reminded herself, no need to actually despair until she had put Desmond's feelings to the test and found them wanting. All the same, however, Susan could not look forward to embarking on such a crucial test with anything but trepidation.

Eighteen

Desmond had gone to bed in a state verging upon exaltation. But when he awoke the next morning and began reflecting on his actions of the night before, his mood soon became much more sober.

It was not that he regretted kissing Susan. He had never regretted anything less, taking it in all. But when taken in connection with his long-term hopes and dreams, he saw it had been little less than madness. He had known Susan only slightly more than a week. She was living under his roof, with him acting the part of her protector. And during much of this time he had been, if not formally engaged to another lady, at least known to be courting her. Was it not madness to kiss Susan under such circumstances? Desmond thought it was. He could only bless heaven that Susan had not seemed to resent his presumption.

It would have been better to have waited, he told himself. *Her aunt will soon be returning to London and taking charge of her. I could perfectly well have waited until then to tell her how I feel. As it is, I've practically compelled her to accept me by giving her no chance to do anything else.* Much as he wanted to marry Susan, he wanted even more for her to be happy. It would not do to rush into a business that had such serious and long-lasting consequences for them both.

She is so young, he told himself. It gave him a

twinge of conscience to think just how young Susan was. Not even twenty-one yet, and her acquaintance with the world was very slight. It had been unforgivable of him to hurry her under such circumstances. He ought to have given her time to look around and decide what she wanted out of life, time to decide what would really make her happy.

Of course, in that case she might have decided her best chance of happiness lay in marrying some other man. Although Desmond thought the words half humorously, there was nothing humorous about the fierce rush of jealousy he felt when he imagined Susan with some other man. He smiled ruefully at his own inconsistency. *At any rate, I'm committed now,* he told himself. *Having gone so far as to kiss her, I would be a positive cad if I did not now declare both my feelings and intentions.*

Secretly, he could not help feeling rather glad this was the case. He was very eager to settle matters between him and Susan, and it was a relief to think he need not wait for days, perhaps weeks, to do it. But still he was nagged by a conviction his conduct had not been quite honorable.

To his surprise, Susan did not appear at breakfast that morning. This was an almost unprecedented occurrence, for she nearly always rose early, even when they had been out late the night before. He had often teased her about possessing the resilience of youth.

Now, as he drank his coffee and ate his ham and eggs, he found himself dwelling on this theme with morbid intensity. *She is only twenty,* he told himself. *Only twenty.* Still, he reminded himself once again that the die was cast. He would be obliged to make her an offer now simply to redeem his conduct of the night before.

It would be only the second time he had offered marriage to a woman. Desmond found himself nervous at the prospect, even more nervous than he had felt when he had proposed to Annabelle. But the reservations he felt now were different from the ones he had felt then. When he had proposed to Annabelle, he had been troubled by inner doubts, but they had all had to do with himself. He had feared lest his family and friends might be right in thinking he would be unhappy with her, but he had never thought to worry whether Annabelle herself would be happy. The only uncertainty he had felt concerning her was whether she would accept his offer or not.

Looking back, he could see now how shallow and self-centered had been his so-called love. Annabelle might be a mercenary coquette, but he had been little better himself. He told himself wryly there could have been no more fitting punishment for him than to have gotten his wish of marrying her. Fortunately, he had been spared that fate, but he would always have to remember his folly. Given the way he felt about Susan, this seemed punishment enough. He loved her and wanted desperately to give her nothing but the best all through life, and because of his past folly, he would have to begin by offering her a heart that had already been offered to another woman in circumstances of which he was now deeply ashamed.

The idea made Desmond feel simultaneously depressed and nervous. After breakfast, he fidgeted about the house, waiting for Susan to appear. Every minute seemed an hour, and he kept looking at the clock, cursing the slow progress of its hands. When eleven o'clock arrived and Susan had not yet appeared, he ventured to go to the door of her room and lay his ear against it. *Surely she must be awake by now,* he told himself. But he could hear no sound within the room. Another hour crept by with leaden feet, still unaccompanied by any sound of activity within Susan's room. Finally, Desmond felt he must do something or go mad.

I'll go for a walk, he decided. *Perhaps I'll go to White's and take a look-in. That will pass an hour or so, and surely Susan will be awake by the time I get back.*

This idea cheered him considerably. Having instructed Reese to tell Susan where he had gone and when he would return, he got his hat and coat and let himself out of the house.

Fresh air and exercise did a great deal to restore his equanimity. By the time he reached White's famous club with its bow-windowed façade, he was able to laugh at his earlier state of nerves. *What's an hour or two in a lifetime?* he told himself. *She's bound to come out of her room sometime. And then I can see her and talk to her and let her know how I feel. It ought not to be too hard. She's the easiest girl in the world to talk to. Besides, she must already know how I feel about her, after last night.*

The thought of last night put him in such a good mood that he was smiling as he entered White's. Several of his acquaintances commented on his good humor. "You look as though you'd just won a fortune at the tables, Desmond," remarked Sir Stanford, who was playing at whist with some friends in the card room. "I wish you'd give me some of your luck, for my own is sadly wanting."

Desmond, grinning, disclaimed any luck at cards.

"Ah, it must be a case of the other thing, then," remarked one of the cardplayers slyly. "You know the old adage 'Unlucky at cards, lucky at love.' "

Desmond denied this, but with such a self-conscious smile that a barrage of raillery immediately descended on his head. "Look at him! Grinning like a cat that's got into the cream pot. Don't tell *me* the little blind god hasn't been obliging with his arrows," cried one gentleman.

"Aye, there's a lady in the case, sure enough," agreed another.

"And I could hazard a guess who she is, too," added a third, grinning broadly. "Saw you with a dashed pretty girl at the opera last night, Des."

Desmond preserved a discreet silence, but once again his smile was sufficient indictment. "Look at him smile! Appears as though he's finding brunettes more satisfactory than blondes," crowed the third gentleman triumphantly.

"Not at all," said Desmond coolly. "Both are well enough in their way, but I prefer redheads."

This elicited much laughter from his audience, who declared he was a rare one and a good fellow and a number of other flattering appellations. Sir Stanford, meanwhile, was surveying him curiously. "So you prefer redheads, eh?" he said in a low voice. "Does this mean poor Miss de Havilland has gotten her congé?"

"Not at all," said Desmond. "As a matter of fact, I am taking her to Vauxhall tonight."

"Then what's all this about your preferring redheads? Going to make her wear a red wig for the masquerade, are you?"

Desmond laughed. "I might, at that," he said. And not another word would he say, although Sir Stanford did his best to coax him into telling more about his suddenly developed taste for red hair.

On the walk home from White's, Desmond found himself regretting a little his high spirits. He really ought not to have made that comment about red hair, for if all went as he hoped he would soon be engaged to Susan, and it was poor taste to make one's betrothed the subject of clubroom ribaldry. Likewise, he had let Sir Stanford assume Chloe de Havilland was his mistress without making any attempt to deny it. He supposed it was because he still felt a little uneasy about Susan's imposture, and it seemed safer to let Sir Stanford's assumptions stand rather than deny them and make him start questioning anew who Susan was and in exactly what relation she stood to him. After all, Desmond reasoned, the matter could scarcely cause misunderstandings between him and Susan, for she, better than anyone else, knew Chloe de Havilland was not his mistress. But still he could not quite like it.

The deed was done, however, and Desmond resolved to worry no more about it. Instead he began thinking about another issue. His conversation with Sir Stanford had reminded him he had not yet hired costumes for the masquerade that night. Eager as he was to get home, he thought he had better attend to this detail first.

So he flagged down a passing hackney and ordered the cabman to take him to a Bond Street costumier. There were all manner of fancy dress costumes at this establishment, but he knew from experience the crowd at Vauxhall would be a rough one, and he thought it better he and Susan should not attract too much attention. Accordingly, he engaged a black domino for himself and, with a smile, a rose-colored one for Susan. Knowing how she loved pink, it seemed the obvious choice, and he never doubted it would please her.

Susan, meanwhile, was also shopping for costumes, scarcely half a mile away.

She had awakened early that morning with her thoughts in a turmoil. The memory of Desmond's kiss was still with her as powerfully as ever, and she wanted nothing more than to surrender to all that kiss had promised. But a new day had dawned, and she reminded herself she had vowed the night before to sail no longer under false colors. She was Susan Doyle, not Chloe de Havilland, and it was essential that Desmond realize this before he went any further down the path he evidently meant to go.

Yet when she told herself she should go to the parlor for breakfast with her own honest face and hair, she found she could not do it. Just the thought of seeing Desmond after what had happened last night would have made it hard to face him. The idea of doing it while stripped of her disguise and the confidence it gave her was impossible.

Susan argued with herself, pleaded with herself, and scolded herself to no avail. *Not now,* she told herself. *Not this morning. Later today, perhaps, after I have washed my hair. It looks a fright right now.*

Having pacified herself with this excuse, Susan continued to lie in bed listening to the sounds of the household awakening around her. She heard Desmond's step when he first rose from bed, and the sound of his steps crossing the hall a little later. Later still, she heard his steps pause outside her own door. With a quick beating heart, she wondered if he meant to come in. He had come into her room once before, on the previous day. What if he should do so now? What would she say to him?

But after he had stood at her door for what seemed an eternity, she heard his steps retreating to the parlor again. They returned a couple of times during the next hour, but at no time did Desmond knock or make any attempt to come in. Not long after the third such visitation, Susan heard the front door open and shut. Flying to the window, she saw Desmond's hatted and coated figure striding purposefully down the street.

"He's gone," said Susan aloud.

There seemed no reason now why she should not get up. She did so, but made no move to order hot water to wash her hair. Instead, after putting on her shoes, stockings, and white dress, Susan went to the glass and stood looking at herself for a long time.

It seemed to her she had never seen her flaws so clearly. Her hair shone like a copper saucepan, and each individual freckle seemed to stand out against her skin with painful clarity. Susan shut her eyes. "I can't do it," she said aloud. "I can't." Tears welled up in her eyes, but she snatched up a handkerchief and wiped them away. She then sat down at her dressing table, put on her wig, and began deliberately to apply the cosmetic mask of Chloe de Havilland.

When she was done, she left her room and went down the hall to the parlor. "My Lord Desmond has stepped out for an hour or two, miss," Reese informed her, as she sat down at the table. "But he said he would be back by early afternoon at the latest."

Susan considered this information as she drank a cup of tea and ate what she could of bacon and eggs. Her nerves were so on edge that she knew there could be no relaxing with a book or newspaper until Desmond returned. She would be a bundle of nerves right up till the minute he appeared.

Casting about in her mind for something to do, she recalled the masquerade that evening. She and Desmond had not yet arranged for their costumes, although Desmond had mentioned on an earlier occasion they could hire dominoes for the occasion. As far as she knew, however, he had not yet done so. Susan rang the bell, and when Reese appeared, she asked, "Reese, do you know if Lord Desmond has already arranged for our costumes for tonight?"

Reese considered, then shook his head with decision. "No, I am sure he has not, miss. For tonight, you say? Dear, dear, I wonder if the matter has slipped his mind."

"I believe it must have done," said Susan. Diffidently she added, "I think perhaps I had better attend to the matter myself. He spoke of our wearing dominoes, and there should be no great difficulty about choosing those. Will you please call the carriage for me in a half hour's time?"

"Yes, certainly, miss," said Reese. Clearing his throat, he added, "I will be glad also to accompany you to the costumier's, miss. There might be some detail in which I could be of assistance."

He spoke firmly but respectfully, mindful of Desmond's orders that he should not allow Susan to go out alone. Susan knew nothing of those orders, but she was glad to have Reese's company. It would have been better to have Desmond's, of course, but she tried not to dwell on this thought.

As soon as the carriage arrived in response to Reese's summons, they sallied out together to a costumier's. Susan was dazzled and enchanted by the choices offered at this establishment. She might have appeared in any character from a milkmaid to a musketeer, but though some of the fancy-dress costumes were lovely, she was glad she and Desmond had settled on dominoes. *It makes the choice much easier,* she told herself. This reminded her of how she had agonized over which flavor of ice to order at the pastry cook's her first day in London, and how Desmond had settled her dilemma by buying her one of each. *How wonderful he is,* she reflected silently. *What other man in the world would be so indulgent of my foolishness?*

The thought brought a wistful smile to her lips. It lingered there as she made her selection of the different dominoes offered by the costumier. She chose black for Desmond at Reese's advice, but hesitated a little over her own. Part of her wanted very much to choose a pink domino, but that meant she would have to wear her wig to Vauxhall. She could hardly wear pink as a redhead, she assured herself. But wearing her wig meant she would have to break her vow and appear again before Desmond in the guise of Chloe de Havilland. She could not convince herself such a guise was necessary on this occasion, for if she was masked and robed in an all-encompassing domino that would be all the disguise she would need.

In the end, she selected a white domino, telling herself this was a safe choice in either case. She could wear it equally well as a brunette or a redhead, and it would go nicely with any of her gowns. *But I believe I'll go as a redhead,* she told herself, as she and Reese rattled home in the carriage afterwards. *Yes, assuredly I shall go as a redhead. It's best I should be honest from now on.*

And then she reached Desmond's house and entered the parlor to find the pink domino spread temptingly over the back of the sofa.

Nineteen

Susan was staring at that rose-pink domino when Desmond's voice came from behind her. "Do you like it?"

Turning around, she saw Desmond standing in the doorway to the room. "Do you like it?" he said again, coming a step nearer and smiling down at her.

Susan opened her mouth, then closed it again. "Like it?" she repeated hoarsely. "Oh, yes. Is it for tonight?"

"Yes, for the masquerade. I just recalled today I hadn't attended to the matter of our costumes. So I went out and hired a couple of dominos." With satisfaction, he looked at the pink domino. "I thought pink was a safe bet, knowing it is your favorite color."

"Yes," said Susan in a hollow voice. "Pink is certainly my favorite color." She looked past Desmond to Reese, who was standing in the hall just beyond. "It was very kind of you to get me this domino, my lord," she said, raising her voice and fixing Reese with an imploring eye. "I would rather wear this pink one than any other."

Reese understood. He gave a slight nod, picked up the package containing the black and white dominoes, and disappeared from view.

Desmond, meanwhile, was telling her how he had

missed her at breakfast that morning. "I had hoped to get a word with you early," he said. "I wanted to explain about last night." He hesitated, then went on in a rush. "Susan, I know I ought not to have kissed you last night, but I couldn't help myself. It's all I can do to keep from doing it again right now."

He was looking down at her with a mixture of love and longing that was impossible to mistake. Susan, however, knew it *was* a mistake. The pink domino proved it. It was Chloe de Havilland he loved and longed for, not Susan Doyle. She turned her face away, feeling suddenly unable to hear any more. "No," she whispered. "Please, no, my lord."

Desmond misunderstood the words and the gesture. "I won't! I confess to the temptation, but I have myself well in hand, I think. But, Susan, I must talk to you. You mustn't think I meant anything dishonorable or disrespectful last night."

"I know you didn't," said Susan desperately. "I know exactly what you meant by it."

"Do you?" said Desmond. He looked deeply into her eyes.

Susan returned the look as long as she could, then looked away. "Yes, I do," she said. "But oh, my lord, would you mind if we spoke of it another time? At present I am feeling not quite the thing. I would rather discuss it later."

Again she turned her face away, but not before Desmond saw she was on the verge of tears. "What's wrong?" he demanded. "Has something happened? Susan, it's nothing I have done, is it?"

"No," lied Susan valiantly. "Nothing you have done." Forcing a smile, she said, "I have the headache, I think. Just let me lie down for a while, and by tonight I should be able to talk all you like."

Her smile reassured Desmond, though not entirely. He still wondered if she had misinterpreted his actions the night before. She said she had understood them, but did she really understand that he loved her and wanted to marry her? *Well, if she doesn't, I'll make her understand tonight,* Desmond told himself.

He was disappointed not to be able to do it now, but Susan had spoken of their going out tonight as a settled thing, so it was evident she was not offended with him.

I will make her understand everything tonight, Desmond assured himself, and tried to content himself with this prospect.

Nevertheless, the afternoon that stretched before him seemed uncommonly long and dull. Desmond put in the hours as best he could, but he was glad when dinner was announced and Susan appeared, wearing her flowered silk dress. To his disappointment, however, she was also wearing her wig. He had hoped that since they were both to be wearing masks and dominoes, she might dispense with any additional disguise. "Do you mean to wear that tonight?" he asked, gesturing toward her head delicately.

"Wear what?" said Susan, turning to look at him.

"Your—er—wig, of course," said Desmond.

"Yes, of course," said Susan. Desmond took warning at her voice, which was short to the point of being snappish. Evidently she was still not in her usual spirits. He decided he had better wait a while longer to broach the subject of his feelings for her. Accordingly, he kept the conversation light both during dinner and during the long drive that brought them to the land-gate of Vauxhall Gardens.

The famous gardens were looking their best that night, with a full moon adding its luster to the thousands of twinkling lanterns hung from trees and shrubs. "Oh," said Susan, drawing in a long breath. She looked from the bandstand to the crowds of gaily costumed passersby, laughing, talking, and consuming ham, chicken, and rack-punch in the supper boxes. "How delightful! It is all perfectly lovely."

Desmond agreed it was, but to himself he thought there was nothing lovelier in the whole of Vauxhall than Susan's face upturned to the glow of moon and lanternlight. He stole frequent glances at her as they strolled about the garden's walks, inspecting an illuminated cascade, a Gothic temple, and a spurious hermit in a pasteboard hermitage. Desmond suggested renting a supper box so Susan could sample the garden's famous ham, but Susan said she was not hungry. "I would rather walk around," she said. "Can we go that way, my lord?" She pointed down one of the walks. "There appears to be an unusual crowd gathered down that way."

Desmond agreed that they could certainly go that way, and they strolled together down the tree-lined walk. The sound of music came distantly from the bandstand, and the moon glowed silver overhead. The crowd proved to be gathered around a fortune-teller who was telling the fortunes of a blushing young lady to the accompaniment of laughter and raillery from her companions. Susan and Desmond watched for a few minutes, but Susan soon declared she had had enough of it. "If only there weren't so many people," she said, looking with disfavor at a rustic who had trodden upon her foot. "I wish we could get away from the crowd for a while."

"Then let us take the Dark Walk," said Desmond, leading her toward another path branching off from their present one. "It tends to be more private than the others."

He did not add that the Dark Walk was notorious for attracting courting couples. *With luck, I can do a little courting of my own,* Desmond thought.

He was growing more and more anxious to speak to Susan about the matter that lay nearest his heart. It seemed to him the time was nearly ripe. She had relaxed a good deal since they had come to the gardens and seemed much her usual merry self.

He looked down at her again as they walked along the shadowy path. Once more he wished she might have dispensed with wig and cosmetics, but the matter no longer loomed large in his estimation. Wig or no wig, she was Susan, and he cared for her just the same.

The Dark Walk was living up to its reputation that night. Soft laughter came from either hand as Desmond and Susan strolled along it, and as they rounded a clump of trees, they came on a couple unashamedly locked in a passionate embrace. Susan gave a slight gasp, and Desmond felt her grip on his arm tighten. He laid his other hand over hers where it lay on his arm and gave it a reassuring squeeze.

Presently they came to a bench standing by itself in a leafy arbor. Desmond recognized it as an ideal spot for his purposes. Susan made no objection to being led to the bench or in sitting down upon it, but he felt a tension in her figure that had not been there before. He was silent a moment, considering how best to begin. Susan, too, was silent. The only sound was the music from the bandstand and the splash of water in a distant fountain.

Finally Desmond decided the direct approach was best. "Susan, you know I love you, don't you?" he said.

Susan said nothing. Her face turned toward him in the darkness, and he could see her eyes, wide and questioning, looking back at him. "I love you," he repeated, taking her hand in his and pressing it. "I know it may seem rather sudden and premature, but I didn't want you to misunderstand."

"No?" said Susan.

"No," he said firmly. "I thought it better you should know how I feel. Of course I understand this must be a surprise. We've only known each other a short while, and I wouldn't expect you to return my feelings yet. Indeed, it's possible you never may. But I hope—oh, how I hope that I can convince you to care for me in time."

Susan gave a shaky laugh. "What makes you think I do not care for you now?" she asked.

Although Desmond had hoped she did care for him, to hear it confirmed was like catching a glimpse of heaven. "Do you?" he said. He caught her hand in a tighter grasp and leaned forward with breathless urgency. "Susan, do you?"

"Yes," whispered Susan.

Desmond waited to hear no more. He caught her tight against him, and Susan lifted her face to his in what was so palpably an invitation to be kissed that Desmond did not hesitate. He kissed her long and hard, and she kissed him back with a passion that delighted him. "Oh, Susan," he whispered.

"Desmond," she whispered back, burying her face against his chest.

As far as Desmond was concerned, the whole matter was settled then and there. Susan loved him, and there was nothing more in life to wish for. He was so happy he was perfectly unconscious both of the passage of time and the gradual encroachment of other courting couples into the wood around them. It was not until he felt Susan shiver that he woke up to the fact that it was growing late, and that two couples were romping about in a flagrantly half-dressed state only a few rods away.

"I think it's time we were going," he told Susan in a low voice. "These masquerades do tend to get out of hand as the night wears on."

Susan, with a blushing glance at the half-dressed couples, agreed they had better be leaving. They hurried along the paths, more crowded with revelers than ever, and out by the land-gate. During the carriage ride home, Susan was very quiet. She let Desmond hold her hand, however, and he was as perfectly happy as before.

He was almost sorry to reach home, as it meant they must be separated for the space of the night. In the parlor he stood looking down at her. Susan looked back at him steadily. In the next room, Reese was busy shutting windows and extinguishing lights.

"Susan, I hardly know how to say what this evening has meant to me," he said in a low voice. "I wish more than anything in the world that it need not end. Of course there's tomorrow, and the day after that, and if you are with me, those are bound to be wonderful days, too. But I will always remember tonight."

"So will I," said Susan in a low voice. She was still regarding him in that steady, concentrated way. Now she took a step forward and put her hands on his shoulders, tilting her face up to him. As before, Desmond recognized it as an invitation to be kissed.

Once again he had no objection to accepting that particular invitation, though this time he was made a little uncomfortable by the sound of Reese in the next room. "My dear, you make it very hard for me to let you go," he told her, pressing her close against him. "I wish—how I wish—we were married already."

Susan went very still in his arms. "Married?" she repeated.

"Yes, married," said Desmond, wondering why she sounded so strange. "You don't think I would have kissed you and told you I loved you if I did not mean to marry you!" Putting his hand beneath Susan's chin, he tilted it so she was forced to look at him. "Surely you did not think me such a shocking loose screw as that?"

Her eyes held his briefly, then dropped. "No, I did not think it," she said. "But I don't think—I am not at all sure I wish to be married, my lord."

Desmond looked at her, unable to believe he had heard her aright. "Not wish to be married?" he repeated. "But I thought you said—Susan, don't you care for me after all? I was afraid I had been too precipitate. If only I had waited—"

"I do love you," said Susan. "I do!" Her voice was passionate, and Desmond could not doubt she meant exactly what she said. But still he found it hard to believe what her words, in combination with her actions, must mean.

"You love me—but you won't marry me?" he said slowly.

"Why need we marry if we love each other?" whispered Susan. And she pressed her body against his in a way that made her meaning perfectly clear.

Desmond felt as though the world were spinning around him. At that moment, he wanted nothing so much as to make love to Susan. And it was very evident that Susan was willing to be made love to. But there was something wrong somewhere—he *knew* there was something wrong. Perhaps it was the legacy of some Puritan ancestor or the lingering effects of a conventional upbringing, even some contradictory signal emanating from Susan herself. Whatever the case, he simply could not abandon himself to the moment and make love to Susan without benefit of marriage. He knew he could not, and with a terrible effort he thrust her away from him even as she sought to insinuate herself more closely within his arms. "No," he said.

Susan stared at him, her eyes wide.

"It isn't right," he said, trying to explain his conduct to himself as much to her. "I want to *marry* you, Susan, not just make love to you."

Susan continued to stare at him. "I don't think you really want to do either," she said. Turning, she ran from the parlor.

Twenty

Desmond's first impulse was to follow her. It was difficult to resist that impulse—as difficult to resist as the impulse to make love to her had been a moment before. But he managed to resist it all the same and by use of the same rationale.

If he followed Susan to her room, he might be able to make her understand how much he loved and wanted to marry her, but it was equally possible he might be seduced into making love to her.

That might lead to results even more disastrous than their present misunderstanding. Better he should wait for some less emotionally charged time and place in order to make his explanation.

At the moment, there seemed nothing to do but go to bed. Desmond went to bed, therefore, but not to sleep. For hours he lay awake, thinking over the evening's events. Susan loved him, but would not marry him. She was willing to make love to him, but not to be his wife. How to reconcile two such seemingly irreconcilable ideas?

Desmond was acquainted with the concept of Free Love, of course. His own opinion was that it sounded well on paper, but was likely to run up against difficulties when practiced in real life. Still, he could see how Susan, in her revolt against conventionality, might think it a viable option to matrimony.

In his heart of hearts, however, he could not help wondering if Susan's reluctance to marry him might be rooted less in revolutionary principle than in a simple lack of feeling. Perhaps she doubted the sincerity of her love for him and hesitated to take a step so irrevocable as marriage. Perhaps even—horrible thought—she wished to avoid committing herself in case some more desirable *parti* came along.

Just like Annabelle, Desmond told himself. For a moment, he felt convinced that all women were fickle and mercenary wretches.

Then he caught himself with a feeling of self-reproach. Susan was *not* like Annabelle. She had proved that a dozen times and in a dozen different ways. It might be that she was fickle, but was that not understandable given the circumstances? She was only twenty, she had lived very retired most of her life, and he was probably the only man besides her cousin whom she had ever known intimately.

Even before tonight, he had had doubts about the wisdom of marrying her when she was so little acquainted with the world. Now, with sudden clarity, Desmond saw it would be not merely unwise but immoral. Of course she would not want to commit herself. He remembered how she had spoken in the store that day when he had told her that she would find it easier to make up her mind if she had only one choice. *But that would not be making up my mind at all, my lord. That would only be accepting what I was compelled to take.*

The plain fact was that Susan did not know her choices at the present moment. And she would not know them until she had lived a little time in society. It need not be London society; any society would do where she might meet other eligible men and could gain some perspective on who and what would ultimately offer her the best chance of happiness. In order to make this evaluation without bias, it was essential that she not be tied to him, Desmond, in any way. She must feel herself perfectly free to choose, even if her choice turned out to be someone other than him.

Desmond, lying in the dark, saw all this as clearly as though it had been written in characters of fire on the ceiling of his bedchamber. He blessed heaven he had been able to resist the temptation to make love to Susan that evening. What complications might not that have added to the situation! But as matters stood now, his course was perfectly clear and straightforward.

Not easy, but clear and straightforward, Desmond told himself wryly. Paradoxical as it seemed, it was necessary that he and Susan should part if they were to determine whether they were meant to be together. At present, propinquity rather than true love might have inspired Susan's feelings for him. *And perhaps mine for her,* Desmond told himself in a moment of honesty. Certain as he was that his own feelings had roots in more enduring soil, he could see it would not hurt to try them by a period of separation, since separation was necessary anyway.

The only question was how separation was to be achieved. He could not simply turn Susan out of the house, and as yet there had been no word from her aunt. *It's been more than a week since I sent Theodosia Doyle that express,* Desmond told himself. *Why doesn't she come?*

She came the next morning.

Desmond was first alerted to Mrs. Doyle's arrival by the sounds of altercation in the hall outside his bedchamber. He sat up in bed, listening. Reese could be heard speaking in agitated tones very different from his usual emotionless diction. "Indeed, ma'am, if you will only wait in the parlor I will be happy to call his lordship. He is not yet risen from his bed. You must not, ma'am—indeed, you must not—"

"I must and will talk to Lord Desmond this minute," declared a resolute feminine voice. An instant later the door of Desmond's room flew open, and Theodosia Doyle sailed into the room.

Mrs. Doyle was a large, dark-haired woman with a normally mild and gentle demeanor. On the present occasion, however, she appeared flushed and furious. She swept Desmond's room in a glance, then turned her gaze piercingly to Desmond's face. "Where is she?" she demanded. "Where is my niece?"

Desmond, in his nightshirt, felt distinctly at a disadvantage, but he summoned up his savoir faire and did the best he could under the circumstances. "Good morning, Mrs. Doyle," he said politely. "May I say how happy I am to see you?"

Mrs. Doyle brushed these civilities aside with visible contempt. "Where is my niece?" she repeated. "I demand you bring her to me at once. Good God, I was never so shocked in my life as when I received your letter. I would not have thought it of you, my lord. I do not know you well, but you have the reputation of being an honorable man."

"I *am* an honorable man," said Desmond indignantly. "Your niece is perfectly safe and well, ma'am."

"And you can say that, after she has been living under your roof for more than a week?"

"Yes, I can," said Desmond with spirit. "I have taken the utmost pains to preserve her reputation."

"By keeping her in your house—a *bachelor's* residence?" Mrs. Doyle's voice was scathing.

"It was either that or let her seek her fortunes in a boarding house," retorted Desmond. "Perhaps you are not well acquainted with your niece, ma'am. Having taken the decision to leave her other aunt's home, she was resolved to be perfectly independent. I tried to show her how utterly impossible it was that she should lodge by herself, but the best I could do was to convince her to stay here, paying me a small rent for the use of my guest bedchamber. I thought if she were living in my home, I could at least keep an eye on her. I am sorry if you do not like my solution, ma'am, but really I fail to see what else I could have done under the circumstances."

This speech had given Mrs. Doyle pause. "I see," she said in a milder voice. "I did not realize that was the way of it, my lord. If what you say is true, then it seems I am much obliged to you. But, oh, could you not at least have arranged for some decent older woman to stay with Susan while she was here? You and I may know she acted as she did in innocence, but the world will judge her much more harshly."

"The world need never know anything about the matter," said Desmond patiently. "No one but myself and my servants are acquainted with the fact she has been staying here. And I would speak for my staff's discretion as readily as my own."

Mrs. Doyle still looked troubled, though the shadow on her brow had lifted somewhat. "Is that so indeed, my lord? I hope it is, for my niece's sake. When I got your letter, I was horrified. I was staying in Vienna at the time and set off for home as soon as I could. I have been travelling for three days straight, and we had a miserable passage from Calais. What with one thing and another, I have been very much tried."

Desmond said sympathetically that he was sure she had been. "I hated to call you back from your journey, ma'am, but it did not seem to me any time should be lost. Susan—Miss Doyle—absolutely refuses to return to Barnhart. And though I suppose I might have taken her there by force, I must say I had reservations about returning her to her other aunt's care after what Susan told me. It seems to me she has been grossly imposed upon."

"Indeed, yes," said Mrs. Doyle. Her eyes kindled once more, but Desmond was relieved to see her anger was not directed at him. "I always thought Sarah Hawkins was a fool, but I never suspected she was a villain. To think of her trying to pitchfork Susan into marrying that ape of a son of hers! She knew well enough such a scheme would never have succeeded if *I* had been about."

"I thought that might have been the way of it," said Desmond. "From the way Susan described it, it sounded as though there was definite coercion involved. Mrs. Hawkins has a deal to answer for."

"Yes, indeed. I am shocked to think she would attempt such a scheme. But I can easily see how it would have been a temptation. Susan is a considerable heiress, you know, and I have no doubt Sarah would have liked very well to have secured her fortune for her son if it could have been managed."

"I suspected there was a financial incentive somewhere," said Desmond. He tried to keep his voice level, but his spirits had sunk to hear Susan was an heiress. As an heiress, she might marry almost any man she chose, or even choose not to marry at all if it suited her best. Of course he wanted Susan to be able to choose—in theory, at least. But in practice, the thought of her choosing some other man hurt horribly.

Mrs. Doyle threw him a quizzical look. "Indeed, there *is* an incentive, my lord. Sarah Hawkins knew well enough that I mean to bring Susan out next spring. I have no doubt she tried to hurry this marriage along in order to circumvent my plans."

These words caught Desmond's attention. "So you do mean to bring Susan out?" he asked. "She mentioned that you had spoken of doing so at one time, but seemed to think you had given up the plan."

"No, I have not given it up. I merely thought it would be better to wait. Of course girls as young as sixteen and seventeen are frequently presented, but I myself think that is far too young. I was married at sixteen myself, and though my marriage was a very happy one, still I would not advise any girl to do as I did." Mrs. Doyle's eyes were frank as she looked at Desmond. "To my mind, twenty-one is a much more reasonable age to make one's bows. And since Susan is such an heiress, she is bound to be a success no matter when she is presented. She will be much less apt to be seduced by a plausible rogue if she is twenty-one rather than sixteen or seventeen."

Desmond could not help wincing a little at these words, though he knew they had no application to him. He had carefully refrained from seducing Susan, and his desire to marry her had nothing to do with her fortune, he assured himself. But Mrs. Doyle's words confirmed his own feeling in the matter. Susan would need both time and experience before she would be ready to embark on such a momentous step as marriage. "I think you are very sensible, ma'am," he said. "Still, rather than waiting until next spring, you might want to consider presenting Susan this spring, or at least during the little Season this fall."

"Indeed?" said Mrs. Doyle, looking at him narrowly. "And why would you say that, my lord?"

"Because your niece has been following a rather independent course since coming to London," said Desmond, trying not to flush under her scrutiny. "I doubt you will succeed in getting her to go back into the schoolroom now she has had a taste of freedom. Indeed, she has—er—been leading a fairly active social life since coming to London. Not in a guise anyone is likely to recognize," he added hastily, seeing Mrs. Doyle's look of horror. "And not in the same circles she will be frequenting after she is presented. I took care at least to prevent that, though I could not prevent her from going into public altogether."

He explained to Mrs. Doyle about Susan's career as Chloe de Havilland. Mrs. Doyle could not help smiling at his account, although it was obvious she was horrified as well. "I thought you said you had taken pains to safeguard my niece's reputation," she said reproachfully. "To take her to the opera and Drury Lane and Vauxhall does not seem much like discretion to *me.*"

"Perhaps not," said Desmond. "But she had declared her intention of going to such places alone if I did not accompany her. On the whole, I thought accompanying her by far the lesser of the two evils."

"But in such public places as that, people must have seen her with you. And they will be thinking she is—oh, you know what they will be thinking!"

"Yes," admitted Desmond. "I do regret that very much, ma'am. But as I said before, it seemed to me the lesser of the two evils that people should think her my mistress rather than letting her go alone among the scaff and raff of London. Besides, she was disguised so well that I doubt you would have recognized her yourself if you had met her."

"You say so," said Mrs. Doyle skeptically. "But I hope you will forgive me if I take leave to doubt it, my lord. It seems to me that if she has been going out as much as you say, someone will be bound to recognize her. And that leaves her in a most unfortunate position, to put it no stronger."

Desmond drew a deep breath. "I don't think I have compromised your niece's reputation," he said. "But if I have, then I am quite prepared to marry her."

"That won't be necessary, my lord!"

These words, spoken from the bedroom doorway, made both Desmond and Mrs. Doyle look around. Susan stood in the doorway, her copper curls aglow, but her eyes cold as ice. Desmond, in his nightshirt, was more than ever conscious of being at a disadvantage. "Susan!" he said.

Susan gave him and his nightshirt a scornful glance, then deliberately turned to address her aunt. "Hullo, Aunt Theo," she said. "You needn't bully poor Lord Desmond into marrying me. My reputation is, I assure you, quite unscathed."

"Well, my dear, I am sure I hope you are right," said Mrs. Doyle, looking uncertainly from her to Desmond. "But you seem to have been behaving in a sadly harum-scarum fashion. I think you ought to be very grateful to his lordship for offering you the protection of his name."

"I am *very* grateful to his lordship," said Susan, speaking in a clear, deliberate voice. "No one knows better than his lordship just how grateful I have cause to be to him. But I feel as though I have trespassed upon his hospitality long enough. If you can wait just a few minutes, Auntie, I will pack my things, and then we can relieve his lordship of the burden of my presence."

Mrs. Doyle agreed they ought to lose no time in removing her from Desmond's home. They both left his room, Susan to pack and Mrs. Doyle to send away her carriage. "It will be better if we take a hackney to my house, though it's not really the thing for ladies to ride in them," she told Susan as they went out of the room together. "However, it's better my servants shouldn't know where you have been staying this while."

As soon as both ladies had left the room, Desmond sprang from his bed and began making a frantic toilette. He burst out of his room just in time to catch Susan as she was leaving with her bundle of belongings. "There you are, my lord," she said, turning to regard him coolly. "I had told Reese to give you my thanks once again, but now I may render them in person."

"Susan," said Desmond in an imperative voice. Susan's eyes flickered, then dropped, but she went on as coolly as before.

"About my jewels," she said. "Aunt Theo says she will gladly reimburse you for what you have spent on my behalf. She will drive over to fetch them tomorrow—"

"There's no need for that. I'll fetch them right now," said Desmond, and did so. Having put the box in her hands, he stood hesitating a moment. He knew he should say something more, but it was awkward with Mrs. Doyle looking on. Still, he could not let Susan leave without making some attempt to set matters straight. "Susan, you must know you have been no burden to me at all," he said. "You *must* know it. It has been a pleasure having you here."

Susan looked at him steadily. Her expression was skeptical, but once more he thought he detected a flicker of doubt in her eyes. "You have not trespassed on my hospitality in the least," he went on, smiling at her reproachfully. "So please don't talk about gratitude. I don't want your gratitude. I want—"

Here Desmond stopped short. He had been on the verge of making another declaration, despite the presence of Mrs. Doyle. But it was not her presence that restrained him. It was his own conscience, which reminded him he must not place the slightest fetter on Susan's freedom. "May I call upon you?" he said abruptly. "I would like to think we may continue friends, even if you are no longer staying under my roof."

Susan regarded him a moment longer with an inscrutable expression. Finally she nodded. "Certainly, if you like," she said. She then turned and hurried down the steps to the waiting hackney.

Twenty-one

The weeks that followed were difficult ones for Desmond.

He thought he had endured torture during the four months he had been enamoured of Annabelle. Now he realized he had not known what torture was. When he had longed for Annabelle, it was really an idea he had been longing for—a glorified image no more real than a dream.

With Susan, what he longed for was not a dream, but rather a warm and tangible reality. And the passing of that reality from his life had left an unimaginable void.

It was not that he never saw Susan. He saw a great deal of her—too much, it seemed to him sometimes. Mrs. Doyle had heeded his advice and arranged to have her presented that spring along with the other debutantes. As Desmond had anticipated, she had made an instant success. A pretty young heiress with engaging manners left nothing to be desired as far as the bucks of the *ton* were concerned. She was mobbed with suitors wherever she went, and Desmond could hardly get near her even on those occasions when he made the effort to do so. He did not make the effort very often because he had found, early on, that Susan seemed not to welcome his company. She was perfectly polite when they met, but there was a reserve in her manner that chilled Desmond to the bone.

His only source of hope was that she was not yet engaged to anyone else. Her name was linked now and then with one gentleman or another, but so far all these alliances had been fleeting. Desmond continued to hope he might yet have a chance of winning her for himself, though he could not imagine how he was to win her when Susan continued to hold him at arm's length. All he could do was continue to call on her, send her the occasional bouquet, and solicit a dance from her now and then. He hoped that by showing her his feelings were enduring, he might one day inspire a return of the love he had once thought he possessed but seemed now to have lost forever.

Unfortunately, despite his unrelenting efforts, he had not accomplished this business by the Season's end. Mrs. Doyle was preparing to go to Brighton for the summer and taking Susan along with her. Desmond called on them before they left, and found Susan full of enthusiasm for the trip.

"I have never seen Brighton before," she said. "Everyone tells me it is a delightful place. Do you summer there yourself, my lord?"

"No, I usually summer at my estate in Hampshire," said Desmond. It occurred to him Susan's question might have been not a straightforward inquiry but a hint. Was she implying he, too, ought to come to Brighton? Desmond was ready to go to Brighton or anywhere else at the drop of a hat if Susan wanted him there. "Perhaps I *could* go to Brighton this summer," he said, looking at her closely. "I have not reserved any lodgings, but I daresay I could find a place to stay if I made inquiries."

"I daresay," was all Susan said in reply. Desmond waited to see if she would say anything more to encourage him to come to Brighton, but she did not, and he concluded he had been mistaken about her words being a hint. It was evidently a matter of disinterest to her whether he went to Brighton or not.

In the end he did go, although he was able to secure lodgings for only a couple of weeks in July. He managed to see Susan several times during this period, but these visits were unsatisfactory. She was always surrounded by a crowd of admirers and too busy to do more than exchange a few words with him.

On the last day of his stay, he overheard a couple of dowagers tranquilly discussing the probability of Miss Susan Doyle's marrying Sir Cedric Grantham, who had met her at one of the local assemblies and become wholly smitten with her.

"I understand it is all but settled," one of the dowagers told the other. "Miss Doyle has done pretty well for herself. Of course she is an attractive little thing—*if* you don't mind red hair—but I do think Cedric might have looked higher for a bride. However, they say she has a considerable fortune, and that no doubt allows him to regard her red hair with complaisance."

This speech made Desmond see redder than Susan's hair. He was tempted to confront the dowager and tell her any man fortunate enough to win Susan had achieved the highest prize going. He refrained, however, and after the dowagers had gone, his anger was succeeded by a fit of melancholy. If Susan were indeed engaged to Sir Cedric Grantham, then all hope was lost. He was so depressed that, in the end, he decided against calling on her in person to take his leave, as he had planned. He contented himself by writing her a note informing her of his departure, then shook the dust of Brighton from his feet.

The rest of the summer he spent at his estate in Hampshire, nursing a wounded heart and fatalistically scanning the newspapers each day for the announcement of Susan's engagement.

To his surprise, day succeeded day, and no announcement appeared. By the time September had come around and the only word in the paper concerning Susan was a notice to the effect that Mrs. Andrew Doyle and her niece were returning to London for the Little Season, Desmond allowed a faint hope to creep back into his heart. Along with this hope, he felt a desire to know the truth, even if it were a truth he found painful. So he resigned his estate into the hands of his bailiff, bade Reese pack his bags, and returned to London in time for the beginning of the Little Season.

One of the opening events of the Season was a rout given by Lady Grantham, mother of that Sir Cedric whose name Desmond had heard linked with Susan's. Desmond was determined to go because he felt sure Susan would be there, given the alleged relations between her and the heir of the house of Grantham. Fortunately, he received a card from the Granthams, saving him from the solecism of appearing without one—a solecism he was quite prepared to commit.

Still, he was in no very good mood as he knocked for admittance that evening upon the double doors of the Granthams' town house. Having been admitted by a supercilious butler and passed from landing to landing by a succession of equally supercilious footmen, he was at length admitted to the ballroom where Lady Grantham was receiving her guests with smiling hospitality.

After greeting his hostess, Desmond stood looking around him. The ballroom was very crowded, but the lady he was looking for was a distinctive figure, and it was not long before he spied her familiar head of fiery curls amidst the crowd on the dance floor. His heart leaped at the sight of her, but sank again when he saw her partner was Sir Cedric. It seemed a confirmation of his worst fears. Just then he felt a touch on his sleeve. Turning, he found himself face to face with Annabelle Windibank.

Annabelle was smiling up at him with the smile he had once found so impossible to resist. Desmond found he was easily able to resist it now. Its allure struck him as a singularly contrived business, and, thanks to the knowledge he had gained from Susan, he was able to perceive she owed a good deal of the beauty of her eyes and almost the whole of the beauty of her complexion to artificial means. Even her celebrated figure appeared to owe something to art as well as nature. Could this be the woman he had once worshipped as a goddess? Desmond looked her over with a feeling of bemusement. Annabelle bridled under his gaze, tossing her head and lowering her eyes in a show of modesty. "Good evening, my lord," she said. "It's been an age since I've seen you."

"I've just got back to town," said Desmond. He spoke absently, for he had caught sight of Susan and Sir Cedric coming off the floor. "Please excuse me, Miss Windibank," he said. "There's someone I must speak to." He hurried off in Susan's direction, leaving Annabelle to make what she could of his brusque departure.

Susan, out on the floor, was perfectly aware of his approach.

She had been aware of him from the moment he entered the room. Out of the corner of her eye she had watched as he greeted Lady Grantham and was joined a moment later by Miss Windibank. At the sight of Miss Windibank's tall, statuesque figure, Susan felt a surge of jealous hatred. In the last few months she had heard a good deal about Desmond's devotion to Miss Windibank. Most people seemed to feel he was going to marry her, though they shook their heads over the notion of his falling prey to such a shallow coquette.

To Susan, this news had come as a terrible shock. She had known there had been passages between Desmond and Annabelle—Desmond had alluded to them that night at the opera—but she had gathered they were ended and that he regretted them. Now, however, she began to wonder if she had understood him correctly. Perhaps she had misunderstood—or perhaps he had been purposely misleading her. She did not like to believe it of him, but the opinion that he was smitten with Annabelle had such widespread credence it seemed almost easier to believe it rather than the wishes of her own heart. In truth, her heart had sustained so many dreadful shocks since the night Desmond had first kissed her that she did not know what to believe.

She had supposed, that evening at the opera, that Desmond loved her—or at least that he loved what he perceived her to be. Of course he was mistaken, being rather in love with the glamour of Chloe de Havilland, but she did not doubt the nature of the feeling itself. Later that night, after parting from Desmond, she had sworn she would eschew disguise and appear thereafter in her own red hair and freckled skin.

But when it had come to the point, she had found she could not do it. She simply could not take the chance of losing him. She had been angry with herself, and angry with him, too, for forcing her into a false position.

It had been hard not to snap at him when he had asked if she would be wearing her wig to the masquerade that night. But she had worn the wig nevertheless. And she had known in her heart she would continue to wear it, so long as it seemed the best means of securing his love to her.

Yet when he had spoken of marriage just before

they had parted for the night, she had experienced a revulsion of feeling. How could she marry him when she knew he did not really love her? She had always prided herself on being an honest girl, and to marry a man under such circumstances seemed not merely dishonest but wicked. Yet she loved him so dreadfully that the idea of renouncing him altogether was out of the question. And so, in desperation, she had offered herself without benefit of marriage, feeling this was the best compromise between what her heart was feeling and what her mind was telling her was right and true.

And he had turned her down.

If there were any experience more humiliating than that, Susan did not want to know what it was. Her cheeks still burned when she recalled the way Desmond had thrust her away from him. Shame and embarrassment had overwhelmed her, and she had turned and run from the room, feeling she could never look him in the face again.

Yet at the same time, she wanted desperately for him to follow. In her heart, she thought she understood why he had rejected her. His sense of honor might well prevent him from taking what she had freely offered. But had it been necessary to reject it so brusquely? Susan did not think it was.

And so when Desmond did not come, she concluded it was because he simply did not want her. Perhaps he had suddenly seen beyond the wig and paint and realized she was not the girl he had fallen in love with. Perhaps he had some other, unfathomable reason for his rejection. She only knew her heart was broken, and that she felt more humiliated than she had ever felt before in her life.

Until the following morning, that is.

When she had heard Desmond tell her aunt, *I*

don't think I have compromised your niece's reputation. But if I have, then I am quite prepared to marry her.

At that moment, all the pieces had seemed to fall into place. Desmond did not want to marry her at all. He was only offering for her because he thought he had compromised her reputation. This horrible idea took possession of Susan's mind, driving out every other consideration. Grimly she resolved Desmond must not be allowed to think she would accept an offer made solely out of pity. So she had swept into the room, rejecting his offer with icy contempt and making it clear she had no further use for him now her aunt had arrived.

On the whole, Susan thought she had carried off the situation well. Even during her parting with Desmond, she had kept her composure and not allowed his protestations of how much he would miss her get under her skin. Susan knew how much those protestations were to be believed, she assured herself.

Unfortunately, this knowledge did not prevent her from missing him. She had not been gone from his house twenty-four hours before she found herself aching for his presence, and during the weeks that had followed the ache had settled into her heart in what threatened to become a chronic condition.

Susan had fought against it conscientiously. She had done her best to fall in love with other men—with any man other than Lord Desmond Ryder. Yet Desmond simply would not allow himself to be supplanted. He was always turning up just when she congratulated herself that she was beginning to recover from his spell. He did not court her in a steady and straightforward fashion, like one of her real suitors. It was as though he knew she was trying to forget him and had set himself maliciously to appear in her life just often enough to prevent her from doing it.

Susan spent a great deal of time wondering morbidly what Desmond's motive for this could be. She was quite sure now he did not love her and never had. Even if he had experienced a passing fancy for Chloe de Havilland, that must have ended when she threw off her wig and paint and began appearing in her true character. Besides, there was Annabelle Windibank. Susan had seen Annabelle a number of times since being presented, and each time she had been forced to admit Annabelle really was beautiful—a touch vulgar in her manners, perhaps, but undeniably beautiful. Susan felt gloomily certain her own good looks were modest in comparison.

To be sure, since being presented by her aunt, Susan had come in contact with quite a number of gentlemen who had signified her caliber of good looks was more than acceptable to them. Some of them, of course, were merely fortune hunters, but there were others whose sincerity was beyond doubt—Sir Cedric Grantham, for instance. And yet, try as she might, Susan could not care for these gentleman beyond mere friendship. She reflected bitterly it appeared to be her destiny not to love the men who esteemed her for herself, but rather to sigh after one who did not.

These thoughts were in her head as she watched Desmond chat with Annabelle. She drew a deep sigh, which caused Sir Cedric to inquire anxiously if something was amiss. "Nothing, thank you," said Susan, forcing a smile to her lips. "I am merely a bit fatigued. I think perhaps I will sit this next dance out."

Sir Cedric was at once all solicitude. He insisted on returning her to her aunt and fetching her a glass of punch. Susan wondered why she found his solicitude so annoying. She had never minded when Desmond had indulged her whims.

Once more she recalled that afternoon in the pastry cook's when he had bought her three different flavors of ices. The remembrance brought such a searing sense of loss that Susan immediately sought to blot it from her mind. It did not help that Desmond was at that moment making his way in her direction. Susan determinedly averted her eyes, but she was not surprised when she heard his voice a moment later addressing her aunt. "Good evening, Mrs. Doyle. I have come to pay my respects to you and Susan."

Reluctantly, Susan raised her eyes to his face. As always, she felt a jolt of recognition—a recognition that went past her mind all the way to her heart and soul. "Good evening, Lord Desmond," she said formally.

Desmond bowed. Susan wondered gloomily whether he meant to ask her to dance. If he did, she told herself, she would excuse herself. There was no need to subject her feelings to such an ordeal. Yet when Desmond followed up his bow by inviting her to stand up with him for the next set, her refusal was hardly a definite one.

"I don't think—I am rather fatigued after dancing with Sir Cedric," she faltered.

A shadow crossed Desmond's brow at these words. "I understand," he said. He was silent a moment, and Susan had the oddest sense he was hesitating on the brink of some decision. "I understand," he repeated. "But if you cannot dance with me, perhaps you would accompany me to the refreshment room and let me get you some supper? I have not seen you in weeks, and I would welcome the chance to renew our acquaintance."

Susan knew she ought to say no, if only to spare the feelings of Sir Cedric, who had just arrived at her side with a glass of punch. But instead she said weakly, "Well—perhaps for a few minutes, my lord." Turning to Sir Cedric, she thanked him for the punch, but explained that she had decided to allow Lord Desmond to take her to the supper room to fetch something more substantial.

Sir Cedric, as she had expected, was injured by this speech. "But you must know I would have been glad to fetch you anything you like, Miss Doyle," he protested. "I offered to fetch you cakes or sandwiches, but you said all you wanted was punch."

Susan was displeased by these reproaches, which she feared might make Desmond imagine she had changed her mind on his behalf. She said stiffly she had suddenly found she was hungry. "But aren't you going to at least drink the punch I brought you?" persisted Sir Cedric. Susan seized the glass, drained it in a draught, and handed it back to him. "I'll be back," she said shortly. Desmond gave her his arm, and together they made their way to the refreshment room.

There were a number of people in this room, eating sandwiches, lobster patties, chantilly, ices, and cakes. "What may I get you?" Desmond asked, picking up a plate and looking at her inquiringly.

"Nothing," said Susan. "I don't think I'm hungry after all." She found herself on the verge of tears for no good reason. Desmond was looking at her closely, and she blinked rapidly, hoping to forestall the deluge. "It's so hot in here," she said. "And so crowded. If only I could get away from all these people—"

"That's easily done," said Desmond. Taking her arm again, he steered her through the crowd to the card room next door. There were fewer people in this room, but Desmond did not pause there. Instead, he led Susan into the adjoining room, which proved to be the Grantham's library.

No one was in the library. Desmond glanced around, then walked over to the window, drew back the curtains, and flung wide the casements. A strong breeze swept into the room, rustling the papers on the table and swirling Susan's hair around her face. She shut her eyes, willing herself back to composure.

"Better?" inquired Desmond.

Susan nodded. After a moment she opened her eyes.

Desmond had returned to her side and was looking down at her. "It's such a pleasure to be alone with you again," he said. "It's been nearly five months since I've had a chance to be alone with you. Four months, three weeks, and a day, to be exact."

Susan was so astonished by this speech she could not reply. Desmond went on looking down at her, his expression searching. "Of course, it's not surprising you've been in such high demand," he said. "I expected no less when your aunt presented you. Is it true you and Sir Cedric are engaged to be married?"

This question, spoken in a jealous tone, further astonished Susan. She quite literally could not find words to speak. Desmond misinterpreted her silence. "Forgive me," he said with a bitter smile. "I know it's none of my business. I had heard the rumors, and I wondered, that's all." Turning his back on her, he stood looking out the open window.

Susan, staring at his back, found herself suddenly ablaze with anger. How dare he act as though it were a matter of concern to him whether she were engaged to Sir Cedric? For five months—or rather for four months, three weeks, and a day—he had been content to fob her off with the occasional call and the odd bouquet or box of confection. And all the while he was, no doubt, assiduously courting Miss

Windibank and was perhaps even now engaged to marry her.

"Why, I understand you are engaged yourself, my lord," she said in a tightly controlled voice. "Miss Windibank is certainly a very lovely girl, though I had imagined from things you once said that you preferred brunettes to blondes."

Susan was appalled as soon as these words were out of her mouth. What had possessed her to say such a thing? She must have sounded like a jealous cat.

Desmond spun around, looking astonished. "What's that?" he said. "You thought I was engaged to Annabelle Windibank?"

"Everybody thinks so," said Susan defensively. "I have heard it from a dozen people that you were engaged, or about to become engaged, to her."

"But it's not true," said Desmond. "I explained all that to you the night we went to the opera."

Unconsciously he had drawn nearer as he spoke. Looking into his eyes, Susan felt a faint lifting of her spirits. "You said you were disposed to admire her very much at one time," she reminded him.

"Yes, and I also said that since then my eyes had been opened to real beauty. And I meant it. I meant everything I said that night. You ought to know I'm no kind of liar." Desmond continued to look down at her. "And I don't believe I said anything, either then or later, about preferring brunettes to blondes."

"Didn't you?" said Susan. "Ah, well, it's no matter." She turned away and began to study a volume of Livy lying open on the table.

"No, I most certainly did not say anything of the kind," said Desmond. "If I had said it, it would have been an untruth. I think both blondes and brunettes are all very well in their way, but it is red hair I like best of all."

These words made Susan lift her eyes from Livy in a hurry. "Red hair?" she repeatedly stupidly. "You like red hair?"

"Perhaps that is too general a statement," said Desmond. "I should say rather that I like *your* red hair. Or perhaps—"

He stopped. Susan looked at him, and was filled with a sudden confidence. "Or perhaps?" she prompted.

Desmond's eyes held hers steadily. "Perhaps it would be more accurate to say that I love it," he said. "As I love everything about you."

"But I don't understand," complained Susan. The complaint was a mild one in its way. Having just heard Desmond loved her, she could not feel too terribly aggrieved, but she found herself repeating helplessly, "I don't understand. I thought you—that you—"

"That I what?" said Desmond.

Susan swallowed and said in a small voice, "That you loved Chloe de Havilland."

"Chloe de Havilland?" repeated Desmond blankly. "You thought I loved Chloe de Havilland?"

"Yes," said Susan in a smaller voice still.

"Now it's I who don't understand," said Desmond. "I thought Chloe de Havilland didn't really exist. Or rather, I thought she was you—an aspect of you—"

"An improved me," said Susan grimly. "You liked me better in that wig, with paint and powder on my face, than you liked me as I really am. Didn't you?"

"No," said Desmond. It was only the one word, but it was spoken in a way that admitted no misunderstanding.

After a moment, Desmond began to speak again in a quiet, reflective voice. "I liked Chloe de Havilland very well," he said. "She was entertaining in her way, and attractive, too. But only because her way was also your way. Because it's you I love—it's *you,* Susan. I confess I prefer you as God made you, but if you want to wear a dark wig, or a blonde one, or shave your hair altogether, I'll love you just the same."

This was a very satisfactory speech, as Susan was obliged to admit. But another doubt had surfaced in the meantime, and she could not help giving voice to it. "Why did you not tell me this before?" she asked with a quaver in her voice. "All this time—all these months—four months, three weeks, and a day"—she managed a shaky laugh—"you never said a word about loving me."

"But I told you before!" said Desmond. "I told you that night at Vauxhall."

"Yes," agreed Susan. She drew a deep breath. "But then you pushed me away from you that night and never said another word about it."

Desmond looked thunderstruck. "But surely you didn't think—my dear, you must have known why I had to do that! I couldn't have taken advantage of you in that way."

"You acted as though you didn't even *want* to take advantage of me," said Susan with ascerbity in her voice.

Desmond looked at her and smiled. "Did I not?" he said, and something in the way he spoke was sufficient to lay all Susan's doubts to rest.

"Well, then," she said, after a moment's pause. "Why did you not say something to me the next morning—the next morning when my aunt came to fetch me? You let me go without saying a word about love. And since then, too, you have never said a word about it. You acted as though you didn't care if I married Sir Cedric or anybody else!"

"God knows *that's* not true," said Desmond fervently. "I have suffered agonies of jealousy at the thought of your marrying Sir Cedric. But I thought you ought to have a chance to see what other men offered before you were tied down to me. You said once that if your choices were limited to one, you were not choosing at all but only accepting what you were compelled to take. I could not bear to think you might accept me only because you had no other choice."

"Desmond," said Susan, "you are an idiot! I was talking about combs when I said that, not men."

"Perhaps I am an idiot," said Desmond humbly. "But I meant it for the best, Susan. And say what you will, I can't regret that I gave you a chance to look around. You were so young—you *are* so young."

Susan smiled. "I am not so young now," she said. "You know I had my birthday in June, Desmond. I am twenty-one now, and twenty-one is plenty old enough to know one's own mind."

"I hope so," said Desmond. "Because having given you four months and three weeks and a day to consider the matter, I am not inclined to let you consider any longer. If you love me and you'll have me, I'll marry you tomorrow—or at least at the earliest moment it can conveniently be arranged."

Susan gave a deep sigh of satisfaction. She reflected that four months, three weeks, and a day were not too long to wait to receive a proposal like that one. "Well, Desmond, I think I must say yes," she said. "Assuming you don't insist I wear a wig to the wedding!"

"Never a wig," said Desmond fervently. "I don't care if you never wear a wig again. In fact, if you like, we can solemnize the compact by burning the beastly thing."

Susan said reprovingly that that would be very silly and wasteful. "Hair smells dreadfully when it burns, Desmond. And, you know, I might want to wear that wig again sometime. For a masquerade, perhaps. Or perhaps for other occasions as well." Her eyes sparkled as she looked up at him. "Who knows? I may even want to revive Chloe de Havilland from time to time. She enjoyed a great deal of freedom, that girl, and since I am become a respectable woman again, I might need an outlet for my less respectable urges. Yes, I quite think I could enjoy playing Chloe on occasion, especially since it would give me an opportunity to wear all those pink dresses, which will otherwise be quite wasted!"

"It's just as you like, my dear," said Desmond. "But I assure you that as far as I'm concerned you can wear pink every day without troubling with a wig. You look delightful in pink—as delightful as in anything else."

Susan laughed. "Now I know you must love me," she said. Desmond began to move toward her, no doubt with the intention of demonstrating the truth of this statement. Before he reached her, however, an interruption occurred. The library door opened, and Annabelle Windibank walked into the room.

"There you are, Desmond," she cried, her face lighting up at the sight of him. "I wondered where you had gone. Oh, and it's Miss Doyle, isn't it?" Her smile dimmed a little at the sight of Susan, but the next moment she was smiling as confidently as ever. "I wonder if you wouldn't mind excusing us, Miss Doyle," she said, addressing Susan in a patronizing voice. "I would like a word—just a word—with Lord Desmond in private. You must know he and I are *very old friends.*"

Susan opened her mouth, but before she could speak, Desmond intervened. "There's no need for Miss Doyle to leave," he said. "Anything you can say to me, Miss Windibank, you can certainly say to her. You must know she has just done me the honor of consenting to become my wife."

Annabelle went stock still at these words, the smile frozen on her face. "Your wife?" she gasped.

"You don't mean you and Miss Doyle are to be *married?*"

"That's just what I do mean," said Desmond, drawing Susan's arm within his own. "You may be the first to wish us happy."

Annabelle neglected to follow this suggestion, however. She went on regarding Desmond and Susan with narrowed eyes. "But is not all this very sudden?" she asked. "Why, I did not even know the two of you were acquainted, let alone that you intended to marry!"

"We've been acquainted for a long time," said Desmond. His eyes danced as he looked down at Susan. "In fact, there are people who would probably say it's high time we *were* getting married, considering the degree of acquaintance between us!"

Susan could not help emitting a gurgle of laughter at this speech. Annabelle's eyes narrowed further. "Indeed," she said. "But I wonder if Miss Doyle knows it was me you wished to marry not so long ago?"

Susan gave her a sunny smile. "Indeed I do know," she said. "*Everyone* knows that, Miss Windibank."

"And you don't mind taking my leavings?" Annabelle's voice was spiteful.

Susan looked up at Desmond and smiled. "Sometimes," she said, "the leavings are the best part."

"Indeed! Well, I wonder how you will like sharing those leavings with Lord Desmond's mistress? You know he has a mistress, don't you, Miss Doyle? I've seen her with him myself—a most handsome girl, and wearing the diamonds he bought for her. She goes by the name of Chloe de Havilland, I believe. How will you like sharing your husband with Miss de Havilland?"

Annabelle paused triumphantly, imagining she had just delivered a most telling blow. She was thus considerably shocked when both Desmond and Susan burst out laughing. "I will not mind at all," said Susan, between gasps of laughter. "Indeed, Miss Windibank, I am well acquainted with Miss de Havilland, and I think her a delightful girl. If my husband chooses to continue his relationship with her after our marriage, it will be with my full knowledge and consent."

"Well, I never!" Annabelle's eyes were near to popping as she surveyed the two of them. "I think you are both *disgusting.* Disgusting and immoral! Why, you deserve each other, upon my word." And with this pious remark, she turned and left the room.

It was some time before Desmond and Susan were sober enough to speak. "Did you hear that? We deserve each other," said Desmond, wiping tears of laughter from his eyes. "Miss Windibank little knows how right she is."

"Truer words were never spoken," agreed Susan. She gave another gasp of laughter. "So Miss Windibank thinks you gave Chloe de Havilland diamonds? I can see I must have my diamond necklace reset if I intend to wear it again as Lady Desmond." She smiled up at Desmond. "It's just credible that I would share *you* with Miss de Havilland, but no one would ever believe two women would share a diamond necklace!"

Desmond said recklessly he would buy her another necklace, or any number of them if she wanted them. Susan, in a reproving voice, said there was no need to be extravagant. "I would not want people to think I am marrying you for mercenary reasons, especially your family. Oh, Desmond, I must confess I am a little afraid at the thought of meeting them. I hope they do not think I have taken advantage of you. And I hope your brother does not ever recognize me as Chloe de Havilland!"

"He might," admitted Desmond. "Merrivale is an uncommonly astute fellow. But really, when I think of it, there's no reason why I could not tell him the truth of the matter. I think I would like to do so, for he would appreciate the humor of it."

Susan said dubiously she supposed it would be all right. "I only hope he does not think me a sad romp," she sighed.

"He will think you rather a godsend," prophesied Desmond. "And I believe you really are one, Susan. Only think what would have happened if you had not run out in the road that day as I was driving by! It was providence that you did, without question. Or perhaps I should say rather it was destiny." Inwardly Desmond smiled at the thought. Once he had thought destiny had intended him to suffer with another woman. Now he knew he was meant to be happy with this one.

"Destiny," repeated Susan reflectively. "Yes, I think it must have been, Desmond. I think we were destined to be together."

"We were," said Desmond. And responding to what was, unquestionably, the prompting of destiny, he took her in his arms and kissed her.